PRAISE FOR

FOR REAL

"A breath-of-fresh-air look at the ups and downs of sisterhood. Both heartwarming and funny, *For Real* left me wishing I had a sister of my own."
—Trish Doller,
author of *Where the Stars Still Shine*

"[Cherry] creates a wildly diverse cast of characters, writing with both ease and emotional intelligence. A comic romp with considerable wisdom on the side."   —*Kirkus Reviews*

"Funny and lighthearted, this novel nevertheless delivers truth in tender ways and is paced at lightning speed, making it a strong choice for reluctant readers."   —*Booklist*

"Fresh, fun, and packed with adventure." —*VOYA*

"A sweet and funny story of sisters bonding."
—*Publishers Weekly*

ALSO BY ALISON CHERRY

Look Both Ways

Red

FOR REAL

Alison Cherry

EMBER

Text copyright © 2014 by Alison Cherry
Cover photographs copyright © 2014 by Verity Smith/Image Brief;
digital imaging by Brian Sheridan

All rights reserved. Published in the United States by Ember, an imprint of Random House Children's Books, a division of Penguin Random House LLC, New York. Originally published in hardcover in the United States by Delacorte Press, an imprint of Random House Children's Books, New York, in 2014.

Ember and the E colophon are registered trademarks of Penguin Random House LLC.

randomhouseteens.com

Educators and librarians, for a variety of teaching tools, visit us at
RHTeachersLibrarians.com

The Library of Congress has cataloged the hardcover edition of this work as follows:
Cherry, Alison.
For real / Alison Cherry. — First edition.
pages cm
Summary: When shy, intelligent, eighteen-year-old Claire convinces her beautiful, popular sister Miranda to team up and compete against Miranda's cheating ex-boyfriend on a reality television show, Claire is the one to capture a fellow contestant's attention.
ISBN 978-0-385-74295-5 (hc : alk. paper) — ISBN 978-0-307-97992-6 (ebook)
[1. Reality television programs—Fiction. 2. Sisters—Fiction. 3. Adventure and adventurers—Fiction. 4. Voyages and travels—Fiction. 5. Dating (Social customs)—Fiction.] I. Title.
PZ7.C41987For 2014
[Fic]—dc23
2013026009

ISBN 978-0-385-74296-2 (trade paperback)

Printed in the United States of America
10 9 8 7 6 5 4 3 2 1
First Ember Edition 2016

In memory of my dad,

who taught me to embrace the absurd things in life

1

On the tiny screen of my phone, I watch Jayden Montoya grill grubs over a campfire. It's hard to hear much of anything over the noise of the party inside, and I can barely make out the sizzling, popping sounds the grubs make as they sear on the car door he's using as a hibachi. As Jayden reaches in with a pair of eyelash curlers to select a snack, the firelight ripples over his chiseled abs and biceps. So far, he's spent the whole episode wearing only a pair of low-slung shorts. The show's producers have probably forbidden him more clothing to drive up ratings. Not that I mind—Jayden isn't exactly the smartest one on the island, but he's by far the best eye candy. I wish I were watching this on a real television. I fear I'm missing nuances of his six-pack.

The camera zooms in on Jayden's tanned, stubbled face as he pops the grub into his mouth and chews, and I'm impressed that he doesn't even flinch. Then again, he's been eating them all season, so he's probably used to it by now. I've heard they taste like chicken with an undertone of almonds, if you can get over the texture.

As Jayden goes for a second grub, someone reaches over

my shoulder and snatches my phone out of my hand. I spin around to find my sister, Miranda, standing on the step behind me, the porch light glowing through her wavy blond hair like a halo. "There you are," she says. "I've been looking all over for you. What are you doing?"

I give her my best nonchalant shrug. "Just getting some air."

Miranda stares down at my phone with a combination of horror and fascination. "Ew, Claire, is he eating *bugs*? What *is* this?"

"The finale of *MacGyver Survivor*. It's that show where people have to survive on an island by making tools and shelter and stuff out of things like Xerox machines and garlic presses and bowling pins and—"

One of her eyebrows goes up—I've always wished I could do that. "You're watching reality TV *now*? Don't you want to celebrate my graduation?"

"Of course I do. I'm just . . . taking a break." I had intended for the break to last until Miranda was ready to leave, but she doesn't need to know that.

My sister sighs. "Come back inside," she says more gently, sitting down next to me on the steps. "Everyone's dancing. You'll have fun, I promise."

Maybe that's Miranda's definition of fun, but it's the farthest thing from mine, and she knows it. The very thought of dancing in a crowd of strangers makes me want to vomit—I can't even bring myself to waltz with my dad at family weddings. "I'm perfectly fine," I say. "Go enjoy the party."

"You shouldn't be out here alone. I can't keep an eye on you this way."

"I don't need a babysitter. It's not like anyone's going to attack me. I've been out here half an hour, and nobody's even *talked* to me."

"If you came in, you could meet some new people." The edge of pity in her voice makes me cringe. She's probably remembering the time before she started college, when I was so painfully shy that she was basically my only friend. It's been a really long time since that was the case, but in my sister's world, my small, tightly knit group isn't nearly enough. To her, you're doing something wrong unless *everyone* wants to hang out with you.

"Miranda, I suck at parties," I say. "I don't know why you even brought me."

She drops my phone back into my lap. "I brought you 'cause I wanted to hang out with you, silly. And what else were you going to do tonight, sit in the hotel with Mom and Dad?"

When I don't answer, Miranda nudges my shoulder with hers and puts on her best pleading face, her big blue eyes widening to cartoon-character proportions. It's the look she always used to give me when she'd eaten all her Halloween candy and wanted me to share mine. "Come on, Clairie, please? I barely even got to see you this weekend with all the commencement stuff."

It's true, I've hardly seen Miranda since my parents and I arrived in Vermont. To be honest, I haven't seen much of her since she left for Middlebury four years ago. Except for a few days here and there, she's spent all her school vacations backpacking with friends and boyfriends and her summers teaching English in exotic locations. I was hoping for a few hours alone with her this weekend, but as usual, there hasn't been time.

"Plus, Samir and I leave for Brooklyn tomorrow, and you guys haven't hung out at all," Miranda continues. "How can I move in with a guy who doesn't have the Little Sister Stamp of Approval?"

I can't tell whether she actually wants my opinion of Samir or not, so I try to be diplomatic. "I talked to him for a minute when we got here," I say. "He seems really . . . charismatic." When I spotted him in the kitchen half an hour ago, my sister's boyfriend was swirling his four-dollar box wine around in an actual wineglass and talking about how "print is no longer a viable form of storytelling in this modern age." He seemed to be delivering most of his monologue to his own reflection in the kitchen window. As I slipped out the back door, I heard a girl telling her friend that Samir had his genius-level IQ tattooed on his arm.

Miranda doesn't notice the distaste in my voice. "He's brilliant onstage. Did I tell you he's the only person in the whole theater program who had more than one agent come see him in *Angels in America*?"

I know I should keep my opinion to myself—it's not like *I* have to date the guy. But Miranda has a history of choosing boyfriends who aren't nearly good enough for her, and it sucks to see her doing it again. "I heard him talking earlier about how print is dead," I blurt out. "Has he not noticed that you're a creative writing major? Isn't your own boyfriend supposed to support you?"

4

My sister smiles and shrugs. "It's fine, it's not personal. He just really believes in what he does. And hey, you guys will have tons to talk about—he just found out that he and his brother got picked to do some race-around-the-world reality show on LifeLine. You watch all those race shows, right? Maybe you could give him some pointers on eating bugs or something." She stands up and holds out her hand to me, and the porch light glints off the silver rings she's wearing on every finger. "Come inside with me and talk to him, okay? Just for a little while? It would mean a lot to me."

I know from experience that Miranda won't give up without a fight. And if I go inside with her, she'll probably do most of the talking, anyway. My sister's been picking up conversational slack for me since we were little kids, and it's a pattern we still fall into when we're together. All I'll have to do now is smile, nod, and try not to say anything stupid. Hanging out with Miranda, her pretentious boyfriend, and a swarm of drunk, dancing college grads isn't exactly ideal, but it's still better than not hanging out with her at all.

"Fine," I say. "I'm coming."

I glance at my phone one last time—the three finalists on *MacGyver Survivor* are having a fish-gutting contest—and drop it into my bag. Miranda pulls me up, and I brush the splinters from the porch steps off the butt of my jeans.

The party has gotten significantly louder and more crowded since I escaped to the back steps. I hang on to Miranda's shoulder as we work our way into the packed living room and snake through a sea of grinding bodies and beer breath and hands wielding red plastic cups. One of those generic pop songs about falling in love in the summer is blasting on the stereo, and my sister manages to sway her hips in time with the beat while she's walking—I had no idea that level of coordination was even possible. As she exchanges greetings with every single person we pass, squeezing outstretched hands and kissing cheeks, I let my hair fall over my face and do my best to remain invisible. It works, and nobody makes eye contact with me or asks who I am.

My sister stops in the middle of the room and cranes her neck to see over all the people pressing together and spinning apart. "Samir was in here earlier, but I don't see him now," she calls over her shoulder. I can barely hear her over the thumping bass. "I'm going to see if he's in his room, okay? It'll only take a second. Stay right here so I'll know where to find you." I can't believe she's about to leave me alone after dragging me in here, but I nod, and she heads for the stairs.

I quickly discover how ridiculously uncomfortable it feels to stand still in the middle of a mass of dancing strangers. Everyone else seems to be moving together like a single sweaty, pulsating organism, but I keep getting bumped around pinball-style by stray hips and butts. For one insane moment, I try to streamline the process by dancing along with them, but as soon as I start thinking about it, I'm paralyzed with awkwardness. I watch a skinny girl to my left undulate against a tall, shirtless guy—she doesn't seem to be having any trouble, even in her four-inch heels. How is it that everyone but me inherently knows how to dance? Am I missing part of a chromosome?

The skinny girl notices me staring as I clumsily shift

from side to side, and she shoots me a *what are you gaping at?* look. It's clearly time to abandon ship, regardless of Miranda's instructions. Being short has its advantages, and I manage to squeeze into a long corridor crowded with girls in filmy dresses waiting for the bathroom. Then I see the comforting flicker of a television beckoning from the room at the end of the hall, and my knotted muscles start to relax as I make my way toward it.

On the screen, a peroxide blonde is flinging men's clothes out the window of a McMansion while shouting a steady stream of bleeped expletives. I recognize her as Chastiti, one of the four trophy wives from *Sugar Daddies.* In front of the TV, two guys and a girl are sprawled on a ratty orange sofa that's leaking stuffing the consistency of cotton candy. The whole room has an acrid smell, and I spot a bong shaped like a pair of boobs on the coffee table—classy. Nobody has heard me come in, and I stand very still in the darkness, trying to keep it that way.

"This show is so stupid," says the guy on the left. "Who watches this crap?"

"*You're* watching it, dumbass." The guy on the right chucks his plastic cup at his friend's head, and a fine rain of beer spatters the carpet.

"Yeah, but, I mean, do people watch it for real? Like, every week?"

"Somebody must, or it wouldn't still be on," the girl says. "This is, like, the third season."

"It's the fourth," I hear another voice say, and it takes a minute before I realize with abject horror that it's mine. *Well*

7

done, brain, with your endless store of TV trivia and inability to let an error stand uncorrected. So much for invisibility.

All three people on the sofa turn and stare at me blearily, and a heavy silence stretches out for five seconds, then ten. It quickly becomes unbearable, and I start babbling to fill the space. "I think a lot of people watch this kind of show 'cause they want to feel better about themselves," I say. "It's really cathartic to see other people making horrible choices, you know? And it's always nice to see someone who has the shoes you want, or the house you want, or the boyfriend you want, or whatever, but who still objectively sucks as a human being, so you can be like, 'Sure, she's prettier and richer than I am, but I'm still superior.'"

All three of them continue to stare; the guy on the right's mouth is hanging open a little. "Hi," I finish lamely. Thank God the room is dark enough that nobody can see me blushing the color of a raw steak.

"Do you *like* this show?" the guy on the left asks, completely missing the point. His eyebrows almost touch in the middle, like two caterpillars making out.

"No, I—I want to work in television. Some reality shows are actually good. Not this one, obviously." On the screen, Chastiti screams, "If you ever *bleeeep bleeeep* me over again, I will cut your *bleeeep bleeeep* off; don't you think I won't!"

Nobody says anything for a minute. Then one of the guys on the couch asks, "Who *are* you?"

"I'm Claire."

"You don't go here, do you? You're, like, twelve."

I draw myself up to my full, unimpressive height. "I'm

8

eighteen. And no, I don't go here." I don't tell them I'm only a senior in high school—it's embarrassing to be a year older than most of my class, but I was still too shy to speak to strangers the year I should have started preschool. "I'm Miranda's sister," I offer instead.

"Miranda *Henderson*?"

"Yeah."

"You're her *sister*? Seriously?"

I feel my cheeks grow hotter, if that's even possible. I know what these people are thinking—I've seen that same expression reflected back at me all my life. How could this girl, this short, dark-haired, socially challenged girl with the glasses, be related to gorgeous, willowy, outgoing Miranda? I watch them search me for some sign of my sister's grace, her unique sense of style, her warm, breezy way of putting everyone she meets at ease. They don't find it. I got all the awkward genes in the family. And all the spouting-media-theory-at-total-strangers genes, apparently.

"Seriously," I say. For some reason, it comes out sounding like an apology.

As if to prove that we actually are related, Miranda comes barreling into the room just at that moment and grabs my hand so tightly it's painful. This is not the happy, bubbly Miranda of ten minutes ago; she's wild-eyed and breathing hard, and the glow of the television reveals tearstains on her cheeks. I've never seen my sister lose control like this in public. Something must be very wrong.

"Come on," she says, her voice choked with anger. "We have to leave. *Right now*."

"Mira, what happened? Are you okay?"

Miranda drags me out of the room without answering. We rush down the hall and past the bathroom line, and a chorus of whispers swirls in our wake. I clutch my *Doctor Who* tote bag to my side to avoid whacking people as we stampede through the living room. "What's going on? Why are we—"

My sister stops just short of the front door. Samir is standing directly in her warpath, and he isn't wearing a shirt. The girl in the kitchen was telling the truth—there's a large *CXLVI* inked onto his right bicep. I have no idea if an IQ of 146 really makes you a genius, but even if it does, tattooing it on your body definitely bumps you back down a notch.

"Get the hell out of my way," Miranda orders in a tone that could cut steel. Her cheeks are bright pink, the way they always get when she's furious.

He doesn't move. "Come on, Miranda, stop being so melodramatic. She's just a friend. We were saying good-bye."

"Most people say good-bye to their friends with their *pants on,* Samir!" Miranda shouts. "And if you don't move out of my way, I will *show* you melodramatic!"

My face goes hot as I realize what's happening. I wish I could storm up to Samir and punch him right in the face, but even if I were brave enough, there's no way I could escape from Miranda's viselike grip. The room has gone quiet, and everyone is staring at the three of us. Someone has even turned down the music.

"It didn't mean anything," Samir says, rolling his eyes.

"God, grow up already. You know I love you, so why are you being so possessive? I'm moving *in* with you!"

"Not anymore, you're not." Miranda shoves past him and out the front door, hauling me along behind her. She's squeezing my fingers so hard they're going numb.

Samir follows us out onto the porch, but slowly, as if my sister isn't really worth pursuing. "Miranda, come back inside. Let's talk about this like adults." He sounds more like an irritated babysitter than a repentant boyfriend.

We're already halfway across the lawn when Miranda whips around. "I am *done* talking to you, Samir, about this and everything else. I hope you and your *friend* have a super-awesome, happy little life together!" She lets go of me and takes off down the block, and I jog to catch up.

Samir stays where he is, his arms crossed over his bare chest. "You're gonna regret this, you know," he calls after Miranda. "Wait till you're stuck in some sad corporate cubicle, looking at pictures of me walking the red carpet with a supermodel on each arm. You're gonna think, 'That could have been me, if I'd just gotten over myself before it was too late.'"

Miranda doesn't respond, but by the time we reach the car, tears are streaming down her face. When I put my hand tentatively on her back, it only makes her cry harder. I want to say something comforting, but I'm at a total loss—nobody has ever soothed me after a breakup, since I've never had anyone to break up *with*. What finally comes out of my mouth is an extremely unhelpful "What the *hell*?"

"I know," she sobs. "I went upstairs to find him, and he

was in bed with . . . with that stupid bitch, Janine . . . and I can't . . . and he didn't even . . ." Now she's crying too hard to speak in coherent sentences. When I glance back toward the house, Samir's still on the porch, leaning jauntily against the doorjamb and watching us.

Come on, Claire, I tell myself sternly. *Your sister's falling to pieces right in front of you. You have to do something.* "We need to get you out of here," I say.

"I don't think I can drive." My sister swipes furiously at her eyes, obviously enraged to be showing any weakness. Her mascara smears across her cheeks like zombie makeup.

"I'll drive. Where are your keys?"

Miranda hesitates, like she's not sure I should be driving her beloved car. But her desire to leave wins out, and she hands over the keys. I unlock the door, and she slumps in the passenger seat like a marionette with cut strings.

I'm not certain which way to go, but I head in the general direction of the hotel where my parents and I are staying. After a few minutes of riding in silence, Miranda takes a deep, shaky breath. "I almost moved in with him," she says quietly. "I really thought I was going to end up with him. How could I have been that stupid? You saw right through him, and you only met him for, like, six seconds."

I feel awful for her, but I can't help being slightly pleased that she's given me credit for being right—that isn't exactly a frequent occurrence. "You weren't stupid," I say. "You loved him. There's no way you could have known that he'd, um, do *that.*"

"The worst part is that I'm pretty sure he's done this before, to other girls, but I thought—I mean, he told me that he—I don't know, I just thought I was different or something." She swallows hard, and two more tears trail down her cheeks. "God, he sucks *so much.*"

"I'm so sorry, Mira," I say. "I wish there were something I could do." She sniffles in reply.

When we stop at the next light, my sister seems to become aware of our surroundings for the first time. "Where are you taking me?" she asks.

"I was heading back to the hotel. Is that okay? There's an extra bed in my room . . . maybe we could get some ice cream and watch a terrible movie or something? It might help take your mind off things."

She gives me a weak smile. "Thanks, Clairie, but I'm just going to go home."

"Do you want me to stay with you in your apartment tonight? Maybe you shouldn't be alone right now."

"No, I mean *home* home. Back to Braeburn."

"You want to drive to the Catskills now? It's eleven-thirty."

"So?"

"What about all your stuff?"

"It's packed. I can load up the car and be on the road in an hour. There's no traffic, so I should make it home by four." Miranda sits up a little straighter, and before I know it, she has total control of the situation again. "I'll drop you at the hotel on the way, okay? Can you tell Mom and Dad what happened?"

I wish she'd give me a chance to take care of her a little; Miranda's so self-sufficient that I never get a chance to do anything for her. But I guess she doesn't really need me now, either. "Do you want company?" I ask in a last-ditch effort to be helpful. "I could come with you."

I'm sure she's going to tell me no, but instead she says, "Really?"

"Sure. I can help you load the car, too."

"That would be great, Clairie. Thanks. I assumed you wouldn't want to. I know you like to stick to the plan."

"I don't care about the plan," I say. "I want to help. I'm totally here for you."

"Thanks. Turn right at the light, okay?"

It isn't exactly the evening I imagined, but in a terrible, warped way, it's actually better. I obviously wish Miranda's whole life hadn't crumbled, but part of me is glad I don't have to share her with a hundred other people tonight. Instead, I get hours of one-on-one time to bond with her, plus whatever time she spends in Braeburn making new plans for the future. My sister wants me with her as she starts to heal, and the image of me hiding out on the back steps with my phone won't be the one that lingers in her mind until the next time we're together.

I have another chance to prove myself, and it starts right now.

* * *

I call my dad as soon as we're on the road and tell him Miranda and I are headed back to Braeburn. He's disappointed that we'll have to cancel our family brunch at the

Mangy Moose in the morning, but I explain what happened at the party, giving as few embarrassing details as possible. He asks to speak with Miranda, but I can see she's not in the mood, so I tell him she's driving and promise to text him when we get home.

Unfortunately, Miranda doesn't seem to be in the mood to talk to me, either. She's in her own world, and as we get farther away from Middlebury, I watch her withdraw into herself more and more. Within twenty minutes, I'm bored out of my mind and wondering why I'm even here. I try to turn on the radio, but my sister switches it off immediately. "I don't want to form associations," she says. "I'm going to hate whatever songs I hear right now for the rest of my life. That asshole doesn't get to ruin any music for me." For a second I consider pulling out my phone and watching the rest of *MacGyver Survivor,* but Miranda would probably toss me out on the side of the road if I did that. So I settle for texting my best friend, Natalie, to tell her I'm on my way home, then silently watch the road signs tick off endless identical miles of highway.

But after an hour, my desire to reach out to my sister becomes unbearable, and I can't stay quiet any longer. In one of my less eloquent moments, I blurt out, "I don't want to, like, force you or anything. But do you want to talk about it? 'Cause I can listen. I mean, if you want."

Miranda heaves a soul-deep sigh. "There's nothing to talk about. He lied to me, he cheated on me, all my plans are ruined, and my life sucks. End of story." Her voice is totally flat, and it scares me. My sister has always had a certain wild spark to her, and I can't find even the slightest trace of it now.

"You could go to Brooklyn without him," I say.

"I don't have anywhere to live. Samir and I were going to stay at his uncle's while he was in India for the year. He said he'd let us live there rent-free in exchange for dog-sitting. I'm still waiting to hear back about a bunch of publishing internships and stuff, and I can't pay rent until I have a job."

"Oh." I didn't know about the internships or the dog-sitting, and it makes me wonder how many other things Miranda hasn't told me. "Maybe Mom and Dad could help you out at the beginning? You could find a roommate on Craigslist or something, right? I could help you look. I could help you look for apartments, too, if you want. And you could always get a job as a barista at—"

Miranda squeezes the bridge of her nose, like this conversation is giving her a headache. "Can we not talk about this?" she says. "I know you're trying to help, but I can't even think about it right now."

"Sure. Sorry. I was— Sorry." I scramble for something else to say, something that will prove to Miranda that being with me is preferable to being alone right now. Finally, out of desperation, I say, "Want to play the Limerick Game?"

I have no idea where that came from. We haven't played the Limerick Game in years. But when we were younger, we used to play it all the time to entertain ourselves on long car trips. One of us would name a person, and the other would have one minute to come up with a limerick about that person. But as I'm cursing my stupidity—of course my distraught sister doesn't want to play the Limerick Game—I'm surprised to see the corner of Miranda's mouth hitch into a semi-smile.

"Wow. I haven't thought about *that* in forever." She shrugs. "All right. It's better than thinking about my stupid life. You want to go first?"

I smile, thrilled this is working. "Sure."

"Okay. Do Mr. Trevor. Your sixty seconds start . . . now."

Mr. Trevor is the ancient PE teacher at our high school. I suffered through his class sophomore year, and Miranda had him twice. He wears fluorescent tracksuits and is always blowing this horrible, shrieky whistle—he no longer has the lung capacity to yell all day, since he's spent forty years chain-smoking behind the gym.

"And . . . go!" Miranda commands one minute later. I dramatically clear my throat.

"There once was a man named Ron Trevor,
Who swore he'd teach high school forever.
You'd think he'd aspire
To someday retire,
But if you asked when, he'd say, 'Never!'"

Miranda laughs. "Well done. Give me one."

"Okay, do Joss Whedon."

My sister's eyebrows furrow. "Who?"

"Really? You don't know who that is?"

She shrugs. "An actor?"

"*Buffy*? *Firefly*? *Angel*? *The Avengers*?"

17

"What, he was in those?"

I have to forcibly restrain myself from smacking my forehead. "No, Mira, he *wrote* them. He's really, really famous."

"God, sorry! Not everyone has watched every episode of every TV show ever. Just give me someone else, okay? Someone real?"

"Screenwriters are real!"

"Someone we *know,* Claire!"

Considering how popular Miranda has always been, you'd think she'd care at least a little bit about pop culture. I'm about to make a comment to that effect, but I remind myself that my sister deserves to be let off the hook tonight. "Fine. Do Barack Obama. You know who *that* is, right?"

She rolls her eyes. After I time out a minute, she recites:

"There once was a guy named Obama,

Who met the esteemed Dalai Lama.

They talked about Zen

And the purpose of men,

Then traded bad jokes 'bout yo mama."

We fly through the dark, tossing limericks back and forth for nearly an hour, and I watch my sister's tight shoulders start to relax. The rhymes become increasingly ridiculous as we get tired, and every time Miranda laughs, I feel a warm glow of satisfaction deep in the center of my chest. Finally, around two in the morning, she announces, "I want to do one for Samir."

"All right," I say. Maybe she'll open up and talk to me about the breakup if I don't make a big deal out of this. "Your sixty seconds start . . . now."

When her time is up, Miranda recites in a steady voice:

"There once was a jerk named Samir.

If he drowned in the ocean, I'd cheer.

He hopped in the sack

With that ho Janine Black,

And I hope someone poisons his beer."

I smile. "Nice. Excellent poetic use of 'ho.'"

Miranda's quiet for a minute, and then she says, "Hey, thanks for coming with me tonight."

"Of course," I say. "I'm always here if you need me. But I know you're going to be fine. You're so strong, you'll be back on your feet in no time."

"I hope you're right," she says.

"I am. Trust me. You always bounce back so fast. Plus, the worst part's over. Things are going to start getting better now. All we need is the right revenge."

I mean it as a jokey, offhand comment; I'm just trying to get Miranda to smile again. But as the oncoming headlights sweep over my sister's face, I see the spark in her eyes reignite.

"What exactly did you have in mind?" she asks.

2

We brainstorm revenge ideas the rest of the way home. Should we put raw seafood under the hood of Samir's car? Photoshop pictures of him in women's underwear and send them to all the major casting agencies? Hire someone with an STD to seduce him? But none of those ideas seems quite right, and we still haven't come up with a winning plan by the time we pull into our driveway at four o'clock.

I get into bed with complicated, heist-style scenarios swirling through my head, and I vow to stay awake until I come up with a dazzling plan to surprise Miranda with in the morning. But tonight has worn me out, and against my will, I fall asleep almost immediately.

The chime of a new text wakes me from a dream about rappelling through the skylight of the Louvre and stealing an Impressionist painting of Samir's face. It doesn't seem like it could possibly be morning already, but sunlight is streaming through my curtains. I grope around for my glasses so I can read the message.

NATALIE: Everything ok? Why are you back early?

ME: Long story. Miranda's here too.

NATALIE: ?!?!? Must hear everything! Coming over.

ME: If you expect coherent sentences, bring coffee and muffins.

All my other friends have already left town for their jobs at camps and theater festivals—our town's so tiny that there's nothing to do here over the summer. It's going to be deadly boring next week when Natalie starts her internship at Paparazzi Press, a small publishing house in New York City. She and I had originally planned to spend the summer in the city together, and I'd applied for production assistant positions at pretty much every major TV network. But it turned out that even the fetch-and-carry jobs were supercompetitive, and everyone turned me down. So instead of delivering coffee to famous directors and producers, I'll be spending the summer behind the counter at Jojo's Joe, serving the extremely nonfamous population of Braeburn.

Natalie arrives fifteen minutes later with three takeout cups and a paper bag full of muffins. This morning she has on shiny, bubble-gum-pink combat boots, tights printed with skulls, and a black tulle skirt that was probably born to be a petticoat. Her glossy black hair is up in a ponytail, revealing long earrings made of pink feathers. Nat has lived in Braeburn all her life, but her fashion sense belongs to a much larger city. Her parents, who both grew up in conservative

21

Vietnamese families, are completely mystified by the way she dresses.

"Double cappuccino, banana nut," she says by way of a greeting, shoving a cup and the bag into my hands. "I got cranberry pecan for Miranda."

"Perfect, thanks. That's her favorite."

Natalie flops down on the green leather couch in my living room, and a small cloud of cat hair poofs up from the cushions and settles back down on her tights. She grabs the remote and deftly flips through channels as only an expert television watcher can until she finds a marathon of *Speed Breed.* Like me, she thinks better with some ambient noise.

"Ooh, is this the episode where Amber seduces the tattooed plumber?" I ask.

Natalie considers the TV carefully. "It could be the one where Jakarta does twelve pregnancy tests in a row—"

"—and then smashes the mirror on the medicine cabinet when they all come back negative!"

"Yesss! I *love* this one." She takes a long sip of her coffee, then grabs the soft yellow pillow my grandma crocheted and nestles into it. Since Nat and I met three years ago, she's spent so many hours snuggling with that pillow that I think of it as hers. When she's settled, she says, "So what happened? Tell me everything."

I repeat the story of Samir, and Natalie reacts with appropriate gasps and exclamations. "What a douche," she says when I'm finished. "But I guess it's good she found out *before* they were living together, right? Is she moving home?"

"For a little while, I guess, until she figures things out. She didn't want to talk about it last night."

"God. What are we going to do about Samir?"

This is one of my favorite things about Natalie. It's never "What are *you* going to do about your problem?" It's "What are *we* going to do?" "We came up with some revenge ideas last night," I say. "But it was really late, and I think they were pretty stupid. Just pranks, mostly."

"No, it can't be a prank. Miranda lost someone she loved, so we have to find something Samir loves and take it away. What does he care about?"

"Besides himself? I have no idea. I met the guy for three seconds, and that was three seconds too long. You should have seen him gazing at his own reflection in the window. It was nauseating. And I literally saw him sign a cocktail napkin, tuck it in some girl's bra, and tell her it would be worth a ton someday."

"Okay, so he's an egotistical fame whore. We can work with that." Natalie chews meditatively on her coffee stirrer. "Miranda has a finished novel, right? Would it piss him off if she got published before he accomplished anything big? If she got famous first?"

"Yeah, absolutely. But she's been trying to sell that book for a year already. She's gotten enough rejections to decoupage her entire kitchen table."

"What's the book about?"

I stuff some muffin into my mouth as I try to remember exactly how I've heard Miranda describe it. "It's a 'lyrical exploration of love, loss, and coming of age in a 1930s West Virginia coal-mining town.'"

Natalie bursts out laughing. "Ooh, nice one. That's funny. But seriously, what's it about?" Then she sees the expression on my face, and her smile collapses. "Oh. You're not— *Oh*."

"But you can help her, right? You have publishing connections now."

She snorts. "An unpaid internship is not 'connections.'"

"Fine, so we'll get her famous some other way. She's good at lots of stuff, right? Help me out here. How do people get famous really fast?"

We gaze idly at the TV as we think. On the screen, twenty-four-year-old Jakarta dumps an armful of pregnancy tests onto the drugstore checkout counter. The mountainous woman behind the register looks totally unfazed as she slides them over the scanner one by one, painfully slowly. A voiceover informs us that if Jakarta wins the $200,000 prize for getting pregnant first, she's going to open a combined dog and human salon called Primp My Pooch, where pets and their owners can be groomed to match.

"If I needed instant fame," Natalie says slowly, "I'd do that." She nods toward the television.

"What, buy a bunch of pregnancy tests?"

"Go on a reality show. Those people are household names, and they don't even have any skills."

It's brilliant—I can't believe I didn't think of it first. And aside from the fact that my sister's not exactly a fan of reality TV, she's perfect for the screen. She's beautiful, she's personable, and she's good at almost everything. Plus, she has some nice messy emotional baggage, which is like peanut butter in a mousetrap for producers.

"Natalie Phan, you are a genius," I say.

"I know." Nat reaches around and gives herself a pat on the back.

"No, you don't even *know* how perfect that is. Last night, Miranda told me that Samir's going to be on LifeLine's new race-around-the-world show. He'd go crazy if Miranda got on some other show and stayed in the game longer than he did."

"Oh my God, *yes*. I love this." Natalie grabs her phone. "Let's see who's casting right now."

"Miranda will never go for it, though. She thinks reality TV is, like, the entertainment equivalent of eating Twinkies."

Nat looks puzzled. "Twinkies are delicious."

"And this is why you're my friend. But Miranda's more of a crème brûlée girl."

"Let's just look, okay?" Her eyebrows scrunch together as she scrolls. "Okay, she's not a lesbian looking for love. She's not a single man who wants to lose fifty pounds. She's not a trained bounty hunter, as far as I know. Ooh, how about *Catwalk,* the definitive pet fashion show? I've seen her make amazing Halloween costumes for Chester and Otto."

"I'm not sure dressing up the cats on national television is the best way to prove she's cooler than Samir."

"Valid point." Natalie's quiet for a minute. "How about *Hive Mind*? 'Contestants live together in a house and compete in cooperative challenges against groups of social animals, including meerkats and hyenas.'"

I wrinkle my nose. "I don't really think that's her style."

"A bunch of these are team shows, like *Jack of All Trades* and *Oregon Trailblazers.* How about—" Her eyes suddenly widen. "Oh my God, Claire. Look."

She passes her phone over. The text on the screen reads,

Ruby Harris Casting, in association with LifeLine TV, is holding emergency casting calls in New York City and Los Angeles this Saturday, June 8. We are seeking two last-minute replacement teams for *Around the World,* a new race-around-the-globe show to air during prime time. If you're unmarried, between the ages of 18 and 35, and want to challenge yourself physically and mentally while competing for a million dollars, we want to see you there!

My jaw nearly hits the floor. "You've *got* to be kidding me."

"This has to be it, right? The show Samir's on?"

"I don't know what it's called, but she said 'some race-around-the-world show on LifeLine.' There can't possibly be two of them."

"It's a sign," Nat says. "The universe is trying to tell us that she has to audition for this show."

"It's perfect. But how are we going to convince Miranda to do it?"

"Convince me to do what?" My sister is standing at the bottom of the stairs in a Middlebury tank top and rumpled sushi-print pajama bottoms. There are dark circles under her eyes, but even after a night of tossing and turning, her hair looks artfully messy, like a stylist arranged each piece.

I jump up. "Hey! You're awake! How do you feel today?" I wonder if I'll be able to feel a shift between us this morning, now that we've spent all that time bonding over revenge and she's seen how good I am at being her friend, not just her little sister. "Natalie got you a muffin."

Her face brightens the tiniest bit. "Yeah? What kind?"

"Cranberry pecan."

"Awesome." She takes the bag and sits down next to me. "Thanks, Nat."

"You're welcome. Hey, Claire told me about Samir. That totally blows."

All three of us jump as a piercing shriek and the sound of shattering glass come from the television. "*What* are you guys watching?" Miranda asks. She stares as slivers of mirror rain down on the used pregnancy tests around Jakarta's bare feet.

"*Speed Breed*," Natalie says, her mouth full of muffin.

"Seriously? You guys watch *Speed Breed*?"

It occurs to me that this isn't the optimal show to have on while we try to convince my sister to become a reality TV star. I grab the remote and scroll through the cable guide until I find an old episode of *Obstacle Kitchen*. "I know, it's dumb. But not all reality shows are like that—lots of them are about talent and intelligence and problem solving. See, look at this one. These people are gourmet chefs *and* athletes. Pretty impressive, right?"

Miranda watches two men in chef's whites and Spandex shorts leap over a series of hurdles between two rows of stainless steel prep tables. Each of them clutches a large bag of onions to his chest. When they reach the cutting boards at the far end of the room, they grab enormous knives and start dicing at superhuman speed.

"I don't get this at all, but if you guys enjoy it, more power to you," my sister says, obviously confused about why I'm lecturing her on the merits of reality TV. "So, what were you going to try to get me to do?"

I take a deep breath. Now that I actually have to broach this subject with Miranda, it doesn't seem quite as awesome as it did a few minutes ago. Natalie gives me an encouraging nod. "Well, we were thinking about ways to get revenge on Samir," I start.

Miranda snorts. "I still like the lobster-in-the-engine plan."

"We don't think it should just be a prank, though. It needs to be something—" I stop when I see Miranda's eyebrow shoot up. "What?"

"You're being serious right now, aren't you."

"Well, yeah. Why wouldn't I be?"

"Claire, we were just kidding around about all that," she says. "Things don't really work that way. Crappy stuff happens, and you wallow a little, and you drink wine and take a lot of naps, and after a while it starts to hurt less. People don't actually get revenge on each other. That only happens in movies."

And just like that, I know last night hasn't changed anything at all between us. To Miranda, that wasn't real bonding time—it was only a game. She was just humoring her baby sister. I feel like I'm playing Chutes and Ladders, and after climbing all the way to the top of the board, I've slid back down to the bottom with no warning.

"But we came up with something really good," I say. "You could actually use this."

"It's pretty epic," Natalie says, and I love her for backing me up.

Miranda sighs. "Go ahead, let's hear."

I'm even more nervous to present our idea now, but I forge ahead. "Okay, so, you know that race-around-the-world show Samir's going to be on? We just saw online that they're holding emergency auditions for two more teams—someone probably failed a drug test at the last minute or something. How awesome would it be if *you* went on the show and totally kicked his ass?"

Miranda looks at me like I've just suggested she amputate her own arm without anesthesia. "You want *me* to audition for *reality television*?"

"I know it's not something you'd normally do. But come on, don't you want to take him down in front of the whole world? *Everyone* would remember that. Every single time he went to an audition, he'd be 'that guy who got his butt handed to him by his ex-girlfriend on TV.' Nobody would ever respect him again."

A complicated expression flits over Miranda's face. "I'm not really in any state to go on TV right now. I don't want millions of people seeing what a mess I am."

"You don't seem like a mess at all," I say. "You *never* seem like a mess."

"And you have so much travel experience," Natalie chimes in. "You'd have no trouble navigating your way around. I bet you could beat Samir without even trying. Plus, there's a million-dollar prize."

Miranda still looks skeptical. "I am good at traveling. But how would I even get on a show like that? Don't they only take super-crazy, over-the-top people?"

Natalie puts on her patient face. "Why do you think producers like those people?"

I raise my hand high in the air. "Ooh, ooh, I know this one."

Natalie points at me. "Yes, Claire?"

"Because producers love drama."

"Exactly. And what's more dramatic than a girl trying to take down her cheating ex on national television?"

"Nothing," I say. Natalie leans over and high-fives me.

Miranda absentmindedly breaks her muffin into pieces. "It's not actually a terrible idea. But if I *am* going to audition—and I'm not saying I will—I'll need a teammate, right? I guess I could ask Aubrey . . . she managed to talk the conductor out of kicking us off the Eurostar that time we bought the wrong tickets. Or maybe Vivian would go with me? She's pretty badass. . . ."

As Miranda lists her Middlebury friends, my mind starts wandering. I see myself behind the counter of Jojo's Joe, lonely and friendless, fighting with the perpetually broken espresso machine. And then I imagine myself bonding with my sister—*really* bonding this time—as we race around the world together, getting revenge on the person who hurt her.

If there's one thing I know inside and out, it's reality television. I could teach Miranda how to handle the constant presence of the cameramen, how to avoid being manipulated by the producers, how to craft a good sound bite. For once, I'd actually be the leader. Even if we didn't make it very far on the race, this might show my sister what a competent person I've become.

Before I can change my mind, I say, "What about me?"

"What *about* you?"

"I'll audition with you."

My sister's eyes widen with surprise. "Seriously? *You* want to audition?"

"I mean, I think I could be helpful. I know a ton about reality TV."

"Producers love sister teams," Natalie adds. "Especially ones like you two, 'cause you're so different from each other. And oh! I could go to New York with you for your audition, since my internship starts a few days later, and we could all stay with my aunt Layla and do New Yorky things! It would be awesome."

Miranda doesn't look remotely convinced. "Are you sure you can handle that, Clairie? You can barely even speak in front of strangers."

Her comment feels like a slap in the face. Maybe that was true when I was eight, but I can't believe Miranda still sees me that way. Yeah, I'm still shy at parties, but that doesn't mean I spend my entire life timid and tongue-tied. I'm sure I could survive a few minutes of answering a casting director's questions, especially if my sister were right next to me. The race itself would be scarier—on this kind of show, pausing even long enough to psych yourself up for something can get you eliminated. But I can tell it's going to take something drastic to show my sister I'm not a child, and who knows when I'll have an opportunity like this again?

"I could do it," I say. My voice comes out a little sharper than I intend.

"I'm not trying to be mean or anything," Miranda says. "You know I think you're awesome just as you are. But I don't want to get all the way to New York City and have you freak out and change your mind at the last second."

Maybe she's not *trying* to be mean, but that still stings. "I don't back out of things at the last second."

"Well, sometimes you do. Remember when you were on the bus to sleepaway camp and you made it stop again halfway down the block so you could get off? Or the time you were an eggplant in that school play about nutrition and you refused to go onstage?"

"I was eleven when the camp thing happened, and I was *six* in that school play!"

"But it's not like those were the only times, Clairie. I mean, I took you to a party yesterday and you hid outside the whole night, just like you always do. And that's fine, that's the kind of person you are. But maybe it means you're not cut out for this kind of thing. If we actually got on TV, I wouldn't be able to take care of you. I barely have the energy to take care of myself right now."

Part of me wants to yell, *No one's asking you to take care of me!* But I swallow my frustration, since losing it will only make me seem even more childish. Telling my sister I've grown up isn't going to do anything, anyway. I have to make her *see* it.

"I'll definitely be nervous," I say. "But I'm not going to let you down. It'll be a stretch for us both, right? I don't know anything about performing, and you don't know anything about television. We'll help each other."

Miranda takes Natalie's phone and reads the casting notice. "You're really serious about this?"

"Absolutely. I'm willing to give it a shot if you are." I try to look confident as I hold out my hand to her. "What do you think? Want to destroy the douche bag together?"

My sister still doesn't look convinced. But after a long pause, she reaches out her hand and gives mine a firm shake. "Okay," she says. "If you think you can do it, we'll give it a try."

I grin at her. "You won't regret this," I say.

I can only hope I won't, either.

3

Two days later, Miranda and I are at the W Hotel in New York City, joining an enormous line of people waiting to audition for *Around the World*.

The W is sleek and austere, all white marble and polished wood and minimalist flower arrangements. It's the kind of place that makes you want to whisper, even in the middle of the day. The décor is the exact opposite of my internal state—I'm insanely nervous, and my stomach feels like it's on a spinning teacup ride. But I'm supposed to be in charge today, so I hold my head high and try to look strong and confident for Miranda.

My sister hasn't said much this morning, and I worry she's still annoyed about last night. Natalie's aunt Layla wanted to take us out to a drag bar, but I convinced Miranda we needed to prepare for our audition instead. My sister had never even seen a race show before, so I was excited to teach her how much strategy they involve. But she was restless and unfocused the whole evening, fidgeting and complaining that she felt like she was back in a theory class. When Natalie and Layla finally came home at one in the morning, giggling about their six-foot-four waitress named Uvula, Miranda barely said a word before she shuffled off to bed. I haven't mentioned it to her—I know how upset she is right now, and I don't want to make things worse. But it still sucks that I finally had a chance to shine and she wasn't even paying attention.

"You okay?" I ask now as we get in line behind a team of ponytailed girls.

"I'm fine," she says automatically.

I'm about to reach out and touch her shoulder, tell her that I'm here for her and that she's going to do great, but she turns away and says, "Save my spot while I run to the bathroom."

As she walks away, two guys get in line right behind us. One of them is wearing a gray knit hat despite the fact that it's about ninety degrees, his brown hair sticking out the front in a way that looks both messy and artful. He starts playing a game on his phone while his teammate, an Asian guy who towers over him by six inches, opens a copy of *War and Peace*. After a few seconds, Hat Guy nudges Tall Guy. "Hey, was it a weasel or a mink that bit that kid's finger off on *Paws of Fury* last season?"

Tall Guy sighs. "Do I look like the kind of person who watches *Paws of Fury*?"

"Are you kidding? That show is *awesome*. I totally remember that episode, too . . . some idiot thought he was buying his kid a ferret, and the thing went crazy. What was it, though? Crap, I'm gonna lose this round."

I usually avoid talking to strangers in lines, especially when I know I'll have to keep standing next to them for ages.

But just like at Miranda's graduation party, I find I can't help myself. Trivia is my downfall.

"It was an ermine," I say.

Hat Guy glances up at me, surprised. His eyes are a bright, startling shade of blue. Now that I'm looking at him more closely, I notice that his T-shirt has a picture of zombies and says GOT BRAINS? He looks back down at his phone and taps the screen, and there's a cheerful pinging sound. "Nice!" he says. And then those piercing eyes return to me. "You're good."

His gaze is really intense, and I feel my face heating up. "One of my many useless talents," I say.

"It's not useless at all. A bunch of friends and I are training for the Pop Culture Olympics—there's a huge prize if you win. So far I kind of suck at it, though." He shows me the trivia game on his phone, which is asking if he wants to start a new round. "There's a two-person setting. You want to play?"

"Okay." Competitive trivia is sure to take my mind off the audition. But when I move closer to him so we can both see the screen, some sort of spicy boy smell hits me and my brain threatens to stop functioning altogether. "I'm Claire, by the way," I manage.

"Pleasure to meet you, Claire." He says it in this warm way that makes it sound like more than a formality. "I'm Will Divine."

"*Will Divine?* That's your actual name?" I realize how rude that sounds a second too late.

In response, he digs a worn leather wallet out of his back pocket and presents me with a Pennsylvania driver's license. It is indeed his real name. I glance at his birthday and see

36

that he's twenty-one. His hair is shorter in the picture, and I like it better how it is now.

"I know it's ridiculous, but it's actually easier to get on a reality show if you have a weird name," he says. "So I guess it's good for something."

"But on your SATs and medical records and stuff, it says, 'Divine, Will.'" In my nervous state, this strikes me as the funniest thing I've ever heard, and I start giggling like a maniac. Horrified, I clap my hand over my mouth. "Oh my God, I'm so sorry. You must hear that all the time. I'm sure it's really annoying."

"Don't worry about it," he says. I search his face for signs of irritation, but instead he smiles at me, revealing a dimple in his right cheek. I have an unaccountable urge to reach out and touch it. What is *wrong* with me?

"This is Lou, by the way," Will says, gesturing at his partner. Tall Guy looks up for half a second and gives me a flat-handed wave.

"Hey," I say, but he goes right back to his book.

Will holds up the phone. "Shall we?"

He wasn't kidding—for someone who's training for the Pop Culture Olympics, Will is shockingly bad at pop culture trivia. By the time Miranda returns from the bathroom, I've answered nine questions correctly, and he's only gotten three. When the round ends, I look up to find my sister staring at us, shocked and confused to see me interacting with a cute stranger.

"This is Will Divine," I say, and by some stroke of luck, I manage not to laugh. "This is my sister, Miranda."

Will's reaction to my sister is exactly the same as every guy's: he takes a minute to appreciate her gorgeous face, and then his eyes dip down, just for a second, to check out her cleavage. "Pleasure to meet you, Miranda," he finally says in exactly the same way he said it to me. Suddenly I don't feel quite so special.

Miranda catches the boob sneak peek, and her face hardens. She gives him a cursory "Hi," then starts digging around in her bag. "Claire, I have an extra magazine in here. Do you want it?" she asks, like I'm not obviously doing something already.

I know she's just trying to be nice by offering me an escape, but I don't need to be rescued right now. "No thanks, we're in the middle of a game."

"Oh, okay," she says, but she still looks unsure that I know what I'm doing. "It's here if you change your mind." She opens a battered novel and turns away.

"What're you reading?" Will asks.

"A book." Her eyes warn him not to press any further.

"Ooookay then." He holds his hands up in surrender and turns to me with a *what's her problem?* look on his face. I shrug and roll my eyes, trying to show him that I have a better attitude than she does, even if I'm not as aesthetically pleasing.

"So, you want to play another round?" he asks.

I've had basically no practice with flirting, but I feel like I need to do something to prove I'm as girly as Miranda. So I channel every dating show I've ever seen and try to make my voice sound coy. "Sure, if you want to get your ass kicked again." I'm surprised by how good it sounds, but I still feel my cheeks turning pink, which probably cancels out any mild sexiness I've managed. Miranda glances up sharply, but I avoid her eyes.

Will grins at me. "I'm just getting warmed up. You haven't seen what I can do yet."

I shrug in a way I hope looks nonchalant. "Fine. Show me."

I obliterate Will five more times before he finally surrenders and puts the phone away. By now, we're almost at the front of the registration line. "Do you live in the city?" he asks. "You should join our Pop Culture Olympics team. You'd steamroll everyone."

You have to be twenty-one to do the Pop Culture Olympics, but I don't want Will to know how much younger than him I am, so I say, "We're from upstate, actually. We just came down to do some auditions."

He nods, and I flatter myself by thinking he might look a little disappointed. But then he turns his attention back to my sister. "Is this your first time at an open call?"

"Mm-hmm," she says without looking up from her book.

"Have you been to one of these before?" I ask.

"I've probably done twenty of them. They're really good practice."

"For what?"

"Trying out characters, seeing how believable I can make them. I'm an actor. I mean, I'm in school for it. At NYU."

"Of *course* you are," Miranda mutters under her breath.

"This is the only show I really want to be on, though," Will continues. "I was so pissed we didn't get to audition the first time around—they only interviewed the first two hundred teams, and we were number 204. We got there five hours early, but it turned out people had camped out in the parking lot overnight. The line's a lot shorter this time, 'cause this audition is so last-minute."

"Wow. Well, I guess it all worked out, right?"

"It certainly did." Will looks back over at Miranda. "Hey, are you okay? You look nervous. You're gonna be fine, I promise."

"I *am* fine," she snaps. Her phone starts buzzing in her bag. "I have to take this," she says. "Save my spot."

As soon as she's out of earshot, Will leans toward me. "What's her deal? Is she always like that?"

I glance at Miranda to make sure she's not paying attention to us. "Sorry," I whisper back. "She's usually really friendly, but she had an awful breakup a couple days ago— she caught the guy cheating the day before they were supposed to move in together. So I guess she's just bitter toward all guys right now. Her ex was also an actor, so I'm sure that's not helping, either. Don't take it personally."

"Wow," he says. "That sucks."

"Yeah. That's why we're here, actually—her ex is on the show, and we want to take him down."

Will's eyes widen. "Seriously? He's on *this* show?"

"Yup."

He gives a low whistle. "Oh man. You guys have got this audition in the bag."

"Not necessarily. I'm sure there are tons of really interesting people here."

"No, I mean . . . trust me. You're going to do really well today."

"Thanks." I know it makes no sense, since I don't even know him, but Will's confidence in us makes me less nervous. We *do* have an interesting story to tell.

I don't know where the time has gone, but somehow we're at the front of the line. Miranda rejoins us as an extremely bored-looking man in a lavender shirt pushes a clipboard toward us across the registration table. "Print and sign your names here," he says, reciting the words as if he's said them so many times that they no longer have any meaning.

When we've signed in, he hands us applications, both of which say "NYC: Applicant 87" in the corner. "Please proceed to the Great Room, fill these out, sign the waiver in the back, and listen for your number to be called. If you fail to present yourselves, the production assistants will move on to the next number and you will move to the back of the line. You will have approximately three minutes with the casting team. Be prepared to wait between two and three hours." As soon as he's done with these instructions, his eyes slide off us. We're dismissed.

Miranda takes her application and heads toward the holding room, but I hang back. It only takes a minute to sign in, and maybe if I wait for Will, he'll come sit with us inside. If I play this right, I could have hours more with him.

"Come *on*, Claire," my sister calls.

I motion that she should give me a minute. "See you inside?" I ask Will.

He looks up and smiles, then drops his voice so I have to step closer to hear him. "I'm pretty sure your sister wants to kick me in the teeth, so it's probably better if I stay out of your way. Break a leg in there, though."

"You too," I say, trying not to show how disappointed I am.

"Hey, listen. If you change your mind about the Pop Culture Olympics, give me a call. I'd love to have you on our team." Instead of jotting down his number on a scrap of paper or something, Will grabs my hand and starts writing on the inside of my wrist with the pen from the sign-in table. It's a weirdly intimate place to be touched by someone you just met, and it sends a little shiver through me. His gray hat is inches from my face as he bends over my arm, and I smell hair products and heat.

"Okay," I breathe.

"Hey," lavender-shirt guy barks. "Are you registering or not?"

Will shoots me one more gorgeous smile before he turns away. "See you," he says.

I certainly hope so.

I follow my sister into the enormous holding room. The walls are lined with gold pillars, and the ceiling is covered in rows of plaster flowers, each of which cradles a lightbulb in its center. At the far end of the room is a door marked PRIVATE, which must be where the auditions are being held. People are sprawled all over the carpet in groups, chatting and laughing and snacking. It seems like everyone's dressed to stand out—there's a guy in a purple suit and a fedora, a girl in a tutu, and another girl in a floor-length velvet cape with a dragon on the back. In the middle of a removable dance floor left over from an event, a guy in a yellow Spandex bodysuit is doing a slow, robotic dance while another guy beat-boxes to accompany him. I would hardly go so far as to say that these are "my people," but it is kind of refreshing to be in a place where originality counts for more than shampoo-commercial beauty.

Miranda picks her way through the tangle of auditioners and finds an empty spot along the wall, and I sit down next to her. When I point out the girl in the cape, I expect her to laugh, but she just gives me a tiny smile and starts filling out her application. "What's wrong?" I ask. "Are you mad at me?"

She looks back up. "No, of course not. Why would I be mad at you?"

"You're acting kind of weird. Are you nervous? It's going to be—"

She cuts me off. "I'm fine, seriously. It's just . . . this week has been so ridiculously crappy, and all I want to do right now is hang out in my pajamas and eat chocolate and read, and instead I'm at an audition, where I have to act all happy and shiny and put-together. And it's not like I want to leave, 'cause I *really* don't want that ass-hat to win a million dollars. But I wish all of this could've happened in a couple weeks, when I felt more like a human and less like a ball of angst, you know? And that guy in line wasn't helping. I didn't like how he was looking at us."

Not every guy who looks at you wants to screw you over, I

want to tell her. *Not every guy is like Samir.* But I can't help being a little bit pleased that Miranda thinks Will was looking at me the same way he was looking at her.

"I thought he was really nice," I say.

"His name is *Will Divine.* It's ridiculous."

"His *name* isn't his fault. He didn't make it up. I saw his driver's license."

Miranda sighs. "Whatever. It doesn't matter. He's just some random stranger."

"Don't think about anyone else here," I say. "Focus on us. Yeah, you've had the worst week ever, but we have an awesome story to tell the casting people, and we're going to rock this audition. And you don't look like a ball of angst. So don't worry, okay?"

"I'm not *worried.*"

"Think of what Samir's face is going to look like when he gets eliminated because of us," I say, and she finally smiles.

We settle in to wait. I try to look engrossed in filling out my application, but really I'm scanning the crowd for Will. I finally spot him with a group of girls across the ballroom, his hand resting casually on one of their arms as he talks. I tell myself she could be a friend, but that doesn't make me feel any better. If Miranda hadn't acted so standoffish, that could have been me. That could have been my arm.

As if he can feel me looking, Will turns in my direction, raises an eyebrow, and shoots me a smile. I feel a tingle in my wrist, where his number is inscribed on my skin.

I smile back and make myself a promise: no matter what my sister thinks, I am not finished with Will Divine.

AROUND THE WORLD

What is your greatest fear?

MIRANDA: *Never becoming a successful writer*

ME: Cockroaches

Name three (3) things you love.

MIRANDA: *Books, traveling, and my friends/family*

ME: Trivia, television, and my sister

Name three (3) things you hate.

MIRANDA: *Cheating, my ex-boyfriend, and the other woman*

ME: Genocide, dancing in public, and cockroaches

What are you best at?

MIRANDA: *Writing*

ME: Pop culture trivia

What are you worst at?

MIRANDA: *Pop culture trivia*

ME: Schmoozing with strangers

Name three (3) adjectives that best describe you.

MIRANDA: *Creative, adventurous, outgoing*

ME: Intelligent, logical, motivated

Name three (3) adjectives that best describe your partner.

MIRANDA: *Shy, smart, loyal*

ME: Charismatic, strong, talented

Describe your relationship with your partner.

MIRANDA: *Excellent*

ME: Excellent

Name something that drives you crazy about your partner.

MIRANDA: *She acts like I'm an idiot for not knowing anything about pop culture.*

ME: She knows *nothing* about pop culture. It's embarrassing.

Is there anything you will not do under any circumstances? Please explain.

MIRANDA: *Eat bugs. Get pregnant. Undergo plastic surgery. None of that requires an explanation, I hope.*

ME: Anything that involves cockroaches. Because they are disgusting.

Why do you want to be on this show (besides the million-dollar prize)?

MIRANDA: *I spent the last year dating a self-involved, cheating asshole who wants to be famous. He's on your show. I'm here to keep him from succeeding.*

ME: I'm here to support my sister. Letting her loose in the world of reality TV on her own would be like tossing a baby into a swimming pool without water wings.

4

Three hours later, someone finally calls our number, and Miranda and I struggle to our feet. The production assistant who takes our applications has so much product in his hair that his head is probably a fire hazard, and I have a strong urge to poke at the sculpted curl on his forehead to see if it snaps off. On one side of the private room are a couple of empty folding chairs, and facing them is a small camera flanked by two casting directors. The woman is wearing a leopard-print blouse and shoes, and her arm is tattooed with a formation of flying birds. The guy has one of those incredibly annoying pencil-thin beards. Seriously, just have a beard or don't.

"Hi," says the woman. "I'm Charlotte, and this is Jim. We're in charge of *Around the World* casting for the North-east region." They each extend a hand, and I wonder if this is some kind of test—which hand am I supposed to shake first? My Internet research on auditions said to go straight for the highest-ranked person, but I can't tell which one that is. While I'm debating what to do, Miranda gives the woman's hand a firm shake, then approaches the man. I follow her lead, and then I'm immediately furious with myself. *I'm supposed to be the one leading today.*

"It's so nice to meet you," Miranda says, her voice totally calm and confident, like she's done this a hundred times. "I'm Miranda Henderson."

"And I'm Claire," I say. "Henderson. I mean, obviously. 'Cause we're sisters." I sound so stupid that I want to slap myself in the face.

Charlotte looks less than thrilled by us. "Great. Why don't you have a seat, and we'll get started."

We sit, and I stare into the steady red light of the camera. Oh God, it's been on this entire time, which means my awkward introduction has been immortalized for posterity. I smile into the lens, as if that'll somehow undo the damage.

Charlotte flips through our applications. "Miranda and Claire," she says. "Why don't you tell us a little bit about why you want to be on our show."

For a second, Miranda doesn't say anything, and before I know it, I'm babbling. "Well, Miranda just graduated from Middlebury, up in Vermont, and the other night we were at this graduation party, and her boyfriend—who was a total fame whore, by the way—well, Miranda couldn't find him, and . . ."

It's like I'm having an out-of-body experience—half of me is spewing verbal garbage, and the other half is hovering six feet in the air, dying of embarrassment. Last night, I'd made a huge deal to Miranda about keeping our answers succinct in order to make the most of our time with the casting directors. And here I am, not even a minute into our audition, making their eyes glaze over.

Fortunately, Miranda cuts me off. "We're here for revenge," she says. Short and sweet; a perfect little sound bite. Maybe she was listening to my instructions after all.

The producers perk right back up. "Revenge?" Charlotte says, making a note on her legal pad. "Revenge on whom, exactly?"

"My cheating ex-boyfriend. Three days ago, I found him in bed with another girl right before we were supposed to move in together."

"Ouch," Jim says appreciatively.

Charlotte looks confused. "Sorry, I'm not sure I understand. How will being on *Around the World* allow you to get revenge on your ex-boyfriend?"

"Well, here's the thing," I say. I'm starting to calm down a little, and I want to give this talking thing another shot. "We're pretty sure you know Miranda's ex-boyfriend."

"His name is Samir Singh," she cuts in before I can screw up the punch line. "He's a contestant on your show."

Charlotte's and Jim's eyes widen simultaneously, like it's a choreographed dance. They look at each other behind the camera and exchange a series of barely discernible nods. "Get Keith in here," Charlotte calls to the production assistant. "He's going to want to see this." The PA nods his shellacked head and leaves the room.

When he's gone, Jim says, "How do you know about Samir's participation in the race? If he broke the nondisclosure agreement, that's a serious violation."

For a second, I'm afraid this might be enough to get Samir kicked off the show—that would be pretty good revenge in and of itself, but nobody would get to *see* us humiliate him. Fortunately, Miranda just shrugs. "He never explicitly told me anything, but I knew he was auditioning, and now he's suddenly going to be gone for a month. It doesn't take a genius to put two and two together."

This seems to satisfy Jim. "And why did you choose Claire to be your partner for the race?"

I'm about to say, "The whole thing was my idea, actually," but Miranda chimes in first. "Claire's completely obsessed with reality TV. You wouldn't believe how much time she spends watching it, and she remembers everything she sees—she has an amazing mind for trivia. She may not be your typical charismatic contestant, but I think it'll be good to have a partner with that kind of encyclopedic knowledge."

That isn't how I expected her to spin things, and I feel a stab of disappointment. Of course my store of TV trivia will come in handy, but I had hoped Miranda wanted me on the race with her because of who I am, not what I know.

Before I can respond, the PA comes back with a bearded man in a gray suit who's carrying a cell phone in each hand. "Hold on, okay?" he says into one of them. Then, to Charlotte and Jim: "Make it quick. I've got a location scout on hold."

"Keith," Charlotte says, "I'd like you to meet Miranda Henderson, Samir Singh's ex-girlfriend." She doesn't introduce me, which seems unfair.

Keith looks Miranda up and down, like she's a show pony

he's thinking about buying, then turns and addresses Charlotte like we're not even here. "*Our* Samir Singh?"

"That's right."

"*Ex*-girlfriend? Not girlfriend?"

"Yes, ex-girlfriend."

"Recent breakup?"

"Three days ago."

"Amicable?"

"No."

"I hate Samir," Miranda pipes up. "I swear, I'll do anything to keep him from winning a million dollars." It's exactly the right thing to say. I shoot her a smile that says *you're doing great,* but she doesn't seem to notice.

Keith nods slowly. "Love it," he says to Charlotte. "Good find." Then he puts one of the phones back to his ear and leaves the room. "Where is the damn permit?" I hear him bark as the door shuts behind him. "The goats are non-negotiable."

"Keith Childs, one of our producers," Charlotte explains.

"He's a little ray of sunshine," Jim adds, totally deadpan, and I giggle before I can help myself.

"So, Miranda and Claire, you've got a compelling reason for being here," Charlotte says. "We obviously like your story. But we need to know if you're serious about the race in addition to the revenge. It's pretty challenging, both physically and mentally. Are you up for the adventure?"

"Definitely," Miranda says. "I have tons of travel experience, and I've dealt with some pretty crazy stuff abroad. And Claire . . . well, she tends to play things a little safer, but I'm prepared to help her through and teach her everything I know."

I feel my face going hot. For a minute, I struggle to think up a response other than *I'm the only reason you're even here. Why are you treating me like I'm five?* But I can't fight with my sister in front of Charlotte and Jim—we have to present a united front or they might think we're problematic.

I finally find my voice again. "Fortunately, it, um, works both ways," I say. "I've watched a lot of shows like *Culture Shock* and *Supersonic Safari,* so I'm the one who understands how the strategy of a race works. I have a lot to teach Miranda, too." *For example, don't throw your partner under the bus in front of the casting team.*

"Well, good," Jim says. "You're both bringing unique strengths to the table. That's important."

"That's all we have time for right now, but we'd love to have you fill out some more extensive paperwork," Charlotte says. "Can you stick around for a little while?"

"Absolutely," I say. "We'd love to."

"It was really good to meet you," Miranda says. "We hope to see more of you soon."

"Likewise." Jim shakes our hands, and I pray mine doesn't feel too sweaty. "Follow Brandon, and he'll get you sorted out."

As we follow the flammable PA through the Great Room, Miranda grabs my arm. "That was awesome!" she whispers. "I can't believe this is actually working! They loved us!"

There are a lot of things I'd like to say to her, like *I'm sorry, did you say* us*? Because you're acting like you're the* *only one here who matters.* Supporting Miranda through this will be harder than I expected if this is how she's going to act the whole time. But I don't want to bring her down when she seems so happy and determined. So I remind myself that we're on the same side, that we're one step closer to reaching the goal we both want. Once we're on the race, she'll see how much I have to offer.

"You did great," I say.

"It wasn't as hard as I thought it would be," Miranda replies.

I try not to wish she had returned the compliment instead.

* * *

After dinner, Natalie and I sprawl on the couch in her aunt's guest room and turn on a marathon of *Derby Doctors,* a show about ER physicians on roller skates. When I reach across her for the Cheez-Its, she grabs my arm and inspects the inside of my wrist. "Is that a phone number?" she asks. "Whose is it?"

I'd entered Will's number into my phone and scrubbed the pen off the best I could in the hotel bathroom, but I should have known nothing would escape Nat. "Just this boy I met at the audition today." Even saying it to my best friend makes a blush threaten to creep up my neck.

Natalie's eyes widen with delight. "You didn't say anything about *boys* earlier! Why are you holding out on me? Tell me *everything.*"

I shrug. "It's really not that big a deal."

"Yes it is! We've only been out of Braeburn two days and you're already picking up guys! I knew you had it in you."

The blush wins. "I didn't pick him up!"

"Oh, so he picked *you* up? That's even better!"

"Nobody picked anybody up! We were standing in line in front of him, and he was playing this trivia game on his phone, and he asked if I wanted to play. That's all."

"And you kicked his ass, right?"

I smile. "Five times."

"That's my girl. So what's his name? When are you going out?"

"His name is Will Divine. He was cool, but it was really nothing. I'll probably never even see him again."

"How'd he do today? Maybe he'll be at the next round of auditions."

"No idea."

Natalie rolls her eyes. "Well, text him and ask, woman! Why do you think he gave you his number?"

I swallow hard. "You really think I should?"

"You better, or I will."

Nat lunges for my phone, but I manage to grab it first—there's no way I'm letting her get involved in this. She'd probably send Will something like, *Hey, hot stuff, wanna come over and play strip trivia? No matter who loses, we both win.* Instead, I settle on:

ME: Hey, this is Claire from the audition. How'd you guys
    do today?

54

The moment I hit send, my heart starts pounding like it's trying to escape from my chest. But five minutes later, he still hasn't responded. "I don't think he wants to talk to me," I say. "He probably has a girlfriend."

But then my phone chimes.

WILL DIVINE: Hey! Good, I think. They made us fill out a bunch of paperwork. You?

Natalie squeals, and I shush her—I don't want Miranda running in here and finding me all fluttery and ridiculous over a boy I barely know. "What do I do, what do I do?" I hiss.

"Act happy, but not *too* excited. And keep it simple. You don't want to overwhelm him with your awesomeness this early in the game."

I roll my eyes and type,

ME: Us too. ☺

Moments later, my phone chimes again.

WILL DIVINE: Told you. I knew you had it in the bag.

Nat puts her hand over her heart and fake-swoons. "He *believed* in you, right from the very moment he saw you," she says. "How *divine.*"

"Oh my God, shut up." I giggle and shove her with my shoulder. "What now? Do I write back?"

"Type, 'You were right,'" Nat says. "That way you're say-ing, 'You're so smart' and 'Why, yes, I *am* awesome' at the same time."

"You're really good at this."

"I know," Nat says. Modesty has never been one of her strong points.

I type it, and a minute later, Will writes back.

WILL DIVINE: Always am.
ME: Mm-hmm . . . except when it comes to pop culture trivia . . . ☺
WILL DIVINE: Ooooh, burn. Just wait. I'm gonna take you down next time.

"Next time!" Natalie bounces up and down on the sofa. "He thinks there's going to be a next time! He's totally flirt-ing with you!"

I spend a good five minutes typing and deleting things before I finally send:

ME: I'd rather fight you for a million dollars.
WILL DIVINE: Fingers crossed for both of us . . .

When I start to respond, Nat stops me. "That's enough," she says. "Leave him wanting more."

She's probably right. I don't want to seem needy. So I put down the phone, turn back to the television, and hope that Will's sitting in his own apartment somewhere, sighing wist-fully and counting down the hours until he can see me again.

5

After our first audition, things happen surprisingly fast.

It only takes two days for Charlotte to call and say we've passed the network's background check and that we're moving on to the next round of auditions. Normally that would involve spending a week in Los Angeles, but everything is being fast-tracked since this is an emergency situation, so instead we'll spend one more day with the producers in New York. The next round will involve a psychological screening, a multiple-choice personality test, and a physical exam, as well as a more comprehensive interview with the casting and production team. Just hearing all those words makes me feel like I have a drunk hummingbird crashing around inside my rib cage, but I want Miranda to see how cool and collected I can be, so I try to swallow down my nerves.

On audition day, we arrive at the Westside Hotel at 6:45 a.m., large coffees in hand. I don't really need mine—my blood pressure is already sky-high from adrenaline and fear—but Miranda yawns hugely every few seconds and grips her cup like it's a life raft. She was out late partying with a couple of her Middlebury friends last night, and I'm worried she's going to be totally off her game today. I'm not sure I can do this if I can't rely on her for backup.

"You ready?" I ask as we approach the hotel entrance.

"Totally," she says. "As soon as I finish this coffee, I'll be set." But when she takes off her sunglasses to rub her eyes, she winces.

"I hope last night was worth it," I say. I probably sound like a bitter old lady who shoos kids off her lawn, but it's hard not to be a little cranky. Considering Miranda's the whole reason we're at these auditions, I shouldn't be the only one taking them seriously.

"Oh God, it was totally worth it," my sister says, missing the point entirely. "The Hangover Pandas played an amazing set, and the opening act was way better than I expected. They were called Threat Level Rainbow, and they had an electric violinist. We danced for, like, five hours. It was exactly what I needed to get my mind off everything. You should've come with us."

Miranda doesn't seem to realize that she didn't actually invite me along—she flew out of Layla's apartment last night with a breezy "Later!" leaving me in front of the TV like she always used to do in high school. But I just say, "Oh, great, dancing in a crowd of sweaty strangers. My favorite."

Miranda tips her head way back and drains her coffee. "I don't get it. How are you okay with being on national television, but you're scared of dancing?"

"I'm not *scared*," I snap. "I just don't like it. That's not the same thing. And it's not like we'll have to dance on the race.

We'll have to, like, ride in rickshaws and paddle kayaks and stack watermelons into pyramids. I don't mind doing those things."

We push through the glass doors and into the lobby. A long line of people—way more than I expected—leads up to a registration table, and nearly every team is wearing matching clothing. Oh God, did I miss something? Teams on race shows do tend to dress identically, but I had no idea people did it for auditions, too. Miranda's wearing a flowy, sky-blue top and chunky brass jewelry, and I'm in a T-shirt depicting a Triceratops in a ninja mask. It's like we're trying to broadcast how little our insides match.

Then I notice something else about the teams around us: it's not only the clothes that match, it's the people inside them. I grab my sister's arm. "Mira, am I going insane, or are we surrounded by identical twins?"

I see from my sister's face that it's not just me; the entire line is composed of about forty sets of twins. It's the most surreal thing I've ever seen. The two girls in front of us are talking quietly with their heads bent close together, and when Miranda taps one of them on the shoulder, they spin around in unison, like they could both feel it. They have long, glossy black hair and huge anime eyes, and the way they move like perfect mirror images of each other is extremely unsettling. As they wait for my sister to speak, each tucks a strand of hair behind her ear, perfectly synchronized. It's like they've spent hours rehearsing the gesture.

"Um, hey," my sister says. "Are you guys waiting to audition for *Around the World*?"

The twins laugh in harmony, letting out exactly the same number of "ha's." One of them says, "No, this is the line for—"

"—*Twin Cognito*," the other picks up. "There's another audition going on—"

"—over there, though." They point to our left.

Miranda looks incredibly creeped out. "Um, cool. Thanks."

Both twins flip their hair over their shoulders. "No problem," says one. "Hey, we really like your—"

"—bag. And where did you get those—"

"—shoes? They're *fabulous*." They don't even seem to notice I'm here.

Miranda stares back at them in disbelief, and I finally say, "Hey, we have to go. Thanks for your help." They smile, their heads tilting exactly the same number of degrees, then turn back around and resume their murmuring. They're probably speaking in secret twin language.

"That was insane," Miranda whispers as we head across the lobby. "What the hell is *Twin Cognito*?"

"It's this show where identical twins trade lives and try to trick everyone into thinking they're each other, and whoever fools people the longest wins. It's all filmed with hidden cameras. It doesn't usually last very long, but it's really funny when a criminal prosecutor has to teach kindergarten or something. Oh, and there was this one episode where one twin ended up getting pregnant by the other twin's husband."

Miranda shudders. "That is disgusting. Hey, do you see the other registration table?"

"No. Maybe we should ask at the front desk?"

"I'll do it. Be right back."

As Miranda walks away, someone calls my name, and I see Will Divine waving at me from across the lobby. Today he has on a Superman shirt with a button-down over it, the sleeves rolled up over his muscled forearms, and he's still wearing that gray knit hat. I'm so happy to see him here that my stomach does a little flip, and I break into a goofy grin as I wave back. Then I remember Charlotte's instruction not to communicate with any of the other teams, and I quickly lower my hand in case someone's watching. Instead, I pull out my phone and text him.

> ME: You trying to get me in trouble for fraternizing with the enemy? ☺
>
> WILL DIVINE: What can I say, I'm a rebel. How do you feel about bad boys?
>
> ME: Not good enough to risk my million dollars . . .
>
> WILL DIVINE: I'm sorry, YOUR million dollars? I believe you mean MY million dollars.

Miranda reappears by my side. "They said to walk straight back toward the coffee bar and there'd be a table on our left." My phone chimes again.

> WILL DIVINE: If you're as good at racing as you are at trivia, I have my work cut out for me. . . .

I bite my lip to keep from grinning, and Miranda looks at me curiously. "Who're you talking to?"

"Will Divine."

A crease appears between her eyebrows. "That guy from the last audition?"

"Yup."

"How did you get his number?"

"He gave it to me the other day." I tuck my phone back into my bag.

"Oh. Well, just be careful, okay?"

"Of what? We're texting. It's not like he's going to give me an STD through the phone."

Miranda rolls her eyes. "Whatever. Let's get more coffee, okay?" She goes ahead of me, and I manage to sneak a little wave at Will before I follow her.

Miranda stocks up on espresso, and then we find the right registration table, where five PAs are lounging around, chewing matching wads of green gum. When we give our names, one of them pulls out a clipboard and makes a couple check marks. I try to see how many other names are on the list, but she puts it away too fast. "Follow Ashleigh, okay?" she says, and a girl with blond pigtails hops up and bounds toward the elevators. She looks younger than me.

Ashleigh leads us to room 618, and by the time we get there, my palms are sweaty and my heart is performing a polka on fast-forward. "I'm really nervous," I whisper to my sister.

"It's going to be fine," she whispers back. "They loved us the other day." But she and I both know it was only her they loved—there was no *us* about it. I vow to do better this time. *You're the one with all the knowledge,* I remind myself. *It takes more than charisma to succeed in a race.*

62

Ashleigh knocks gently on the door before she swipes it open with a key card. "Which of you is Claire?" she asks. "You'll be in here with the producers first. Miranda, you have your psych eval first, so you can follow me to the eighth floor."

My whole body goes cold. "Wait a second," I say. "We're a team."

"Yeah, I know." Ashleigh snaps her gum.

"So aren't we auditioning together?"

"Not today. Good luck! Have fun in there!" She gives me a perky little smile, then shoves me through the doorway. I whirl around and meet my sister's eyes for a split second before the door swings closed between us. She suddenly looks wide awake.

On the opposite side of the room are six people in suits, seated in a row behind a boardroom table. One of them is Charlotte, and I'm relieved to see a familiar face. There's also a large camera on a tripod, manned by a guy with those weird plugs in his earlobes. Everyone is facing the Interrogation Area, where a single chair is flanked by white-hot lights. The pigtailed PA hasn't made a mistake. I really am supposed to be in here alone. What if Miranda was right and I can't handle it? She'll never forgive me if we get eliminated because I pass out on the floor. I squeeze my clammy hands into tight fists and order my body to keep breathing and stay upright.

Charlotte beams at me like we're best friends. "Claire! I'm so glad to see you. Let me introduce you to our casting team." She points at each person in turn and rattles off a rapid-fire stream of names, none of which I retain. There's a guy with a bushy Santa Claus beard, a platinum-blond woman who looks like she just downed a shot of lemon juice, a fidgety guy with a lot of piercings, a freckled woman with a sun-burned nose, and a woman who looks remarkably like Oprah. I move forward, shake each extended hand, and try not to look like someone has shot me between the eyes with a stun gun.

"It's nice to meet all of you," I say, and my voice comes out steadier than I expect.

"Have a seat, and let's get started," Charlotte says.

I perch on the edge of the chair and fold my hands in my lap, trying my best to look relaxed. It's easily ten degrees warmer under the lights, and a bead of sweat crawls down my spine. I'm not sure if it's from the heat or the fear.

"How are you this morning?" Santa asks.

On the verge of hyperventilating, thanks. Anyone have a spare paper bag I could breathe into for a while? "Um, fine, I guess," I say. "Surprised. I thought I'd be auditioning with my sister, since we're, you know, a team."

"We like to get a sense of what each individual person brings to the table," Charlotte says. "So, let's dive right in. We talked a lot about Miranda and Samir the other day, so we know why she's here. But we didn't get to talk much about you. Why are *you* here, Claire? Why do you personally want to be on *Around the World*?"

Thank goodness we're starting with something easy—this time, there's no one to take over for me if I start babbling like an incoherent fool. "Well, I'm here to support my sister," I say. "I was there the night Samir cheated on her, and it was a seriously ugly scene. I've never seen her fall apart like that. Honestly, from the second I met him, I thought Samir was a total douche bag—oh God, sorry, can I say that in here?"

Oprah smiles. "You can say anything you want. We've heard a lot worse than 'douche bag.'"

"Okay, well, um, that's what he is. Really smug and pompous and self-centered, you know? Like, he has his IQ tattooed on his arm, if you can believe that. I don't know what Miranda saw in him—he's not nearly good enough for her. I can't wait to help her take him down."

"Sounds like you really idolize your sister," Lemon Juice says.

That makes me seem like some sort of Miranda groupie. "I don't know if 'idolize' is the right word," I say carefully. "But I really admire her and respect her, if that's what you mean, and I love her more than just about anyone."

"Do you think she loves you back?" asks Sunburn.

"Well, yeah, of course. She's my sister."

"And do you think she respects you?" Charlotte asks. There's a weird look on her face. Is that . . . *pity*?

"Yes," I say. "I think she does."

"You don't sound so sure about that," Charlotte says. My voice sounded pretty confident to me, but now I start to doubt my conviction. Maybe she heard something I can't detect because I'm too nervous. "I'm sure your sister always means well, but she was pretty patronizing to you in your audition the other day, didn't you think? How did that make you feel?"

These questions are starting to make me uncomfortable. Are they trying to drive a wedge between Miranda and me on purpose? *The network loves drama,* I remind myself. *You don't have to do what they want. Stay in control.*

"I don't know what you're talking about," I say.

Now there's pity on *everyone's* faces. "We've all seen the tape, Claire," Charlotte says gently. "You don't have to pretend for us. Miranda basically said that you're reluctant to try new things and that you need to be sheltered and protected. I mean, it doesn't seem that way to *us*. You're an adult, too, and between the two of you, it sounds like you're the one who really understands the strategy of this race. But your sister obviously wasn't taking you seriously. Does that happen a lot?"

I swallow hard. Even if they are trying to manipulate me, Charlotte's validating everything I've been feeling over the last few days. I *am* the key person on this team, the one who got us here and did all the research and taught Miranda how to handle herself. And she's been breezing along and taking credit she doesn't deserve. If other people think that, too, maybe it's not just me being resentful. Maybe it's a fact.

"It's okay to talk about it," Oprah says in a soothing voice. "We're not going to tell Miranda, if that's what you're worried about."

I take a deep breath. "I *don't* need to be sheltered," I say. "And I do try new things. I was a super-shy, scared kid, and

Miranda still sees me that way sometimes, but that's not who I am anymore. It was my idea to audition for this show in the first place, not hers. She didn't even want to do it."

"I think it's a brilliant revenge strategy," Piercings chimes in. "Kudos to you for coming up with it. Why was she against it?"

"Miranda doesn't understand reality TV," I say. "I mean, she gets that it's entertaining, but she doesn't understand why it's actually important. When I talk about how I want to be a field producer or a story editor someday, she tries to be supportive, but I can tell she doesn't see what I see in it. To her, it's all just fluff."

"Tell us what you see, Claire," Charlotte prompts.

For most people, this wouldn't be a personal question— they like reality television because it's funny and takes their minds off their lives, like I told those stoners at the graduation party. But for me, it has always been more than that. This is something I've only ever discussed with Natalie, and I'm not sure I want to spill my guts to six strangers and a camera. But I guess this is what I signed up for when I agreed to audition.

"Reality TV is a great equalizer," I tell those six eager faces. "Pretty much everywhere else, in entertainment and in real life, the beautiful, charismatic people like my sister get special privileges. They don't have to try, and things just happen for them. But on reality shows, you have the same chance of succeeding even if you're awkward and average-looking, like me. As long as you're smart and creative and you have an interesting story to tell, nobody really cares if you suck at small talk or if you're wearing the wrong jeans, you know? Like, have you guys ever seen that show *GuilloTeen*?"

"Once or twice," Charlotte says. She looks really interested in everything I'm saying.

"There was this guy last season—Ray, I think? He was like a hundred pounds overweight, and he had this awful mullet, and he talked about comics constantly. If he went to my school, he'd be a total laughingstock. But he outsmarted everyone, and he won. And when they interviewed him afterward, he started crying, and he talked about how nobody had ever taken him seriously before because he wasn't suave and thin and hot. But the producers of that show gave him a chance when nobody else would. And now people all over the country know how awesome he is, and they know that people like him *can* be awesome. That's what reality TV is about for me."

"Wow," Santa says. He's nodding slowly, like I've given him a lot to think about. Oprah is scribbling notes in her pad, and Piercings looks like he's about two seconds from starting a slow clap. For the first time, I'm relieved that my sister's not in the room. I would never have been able to get all that out with her looking at me, not to mention talking over me.

"Those are very astute observations, Claire," Charlotte says. "You'll make a great producer someday. Thank you for sharing that with us. Now, let's switch topics for a few minutes. What can you tell us about your dating life?"

At first I think I must have heard her wrong. "I'm sorry, my . . . what?"

"Your love life," Sunburn says. "Do you have a boyfriend? Or a girlfriend?"

What does this have to do with racing around the world? Are they asking because of the Samir situation? "No," I say. "I like guys, but I don't have a boyfriend. Is that a problem?"

Sunburn laughs. "Of course not. Tell us about your last boyfriend. How long were you together?"

And just when I thought I had my feet under me, I'm totally out of control again. The casting team looked so impressed with me a minute ago, and I don't want to tell them that I've never even had a real date, unless you count the handful of times Doug Garfield and I cut study hall to make out in his car. "Um," I say, scrambling for a way to spin the truth. "I'm not really into serious relationships. I like to keep things casual, keep my options open, you know?"

"Are you telling us you're totally inexperienced with boys?" asks Sunburn.

"No, of course not," I say, like that's the most ridiculous thing I've ever heard.

"I get it," Piercings says. "You like to play the field. I respect that." Behind him, the cameraman waggles his eyebrows at me. *Ew.*

"And why do you find yourself shying away from commitment, Claire?" asks Charlotte. "Is it because you don't believe in love?"

I start laughing. "No. I believe in love."

"Even after what Samir did to your sister?"

"Sure. One guy being a moron can't destroy an entire concept."

"So if you believe in love, why don't you believe in relationships?"

"I *believe* in them. The right person just hasn't turned up yet." Horrifyingly, an image of Will Divine pops into my head, and I feel myself starting to blush. I push the thought away. "I go to a really small school—there are only, like, two hundred guys, and I've known a lot of them since I was three. When you've seen someone peeing in the sandbox and licking scented markers, it's pretty much impossible to date him, you know?" Everyone laughs, and I relax a little.

"Sounds rough," Santa says. "Did your sister have the same problem finding people to date in high school?"

"I guess not, no. She actually dated a fair number of people."

"How do you explain that?"

I shrug. "I don't know. Maybe I have higher standards than she does."

"Or maybe Miranda's more open-minded than you are?"

"You don't know the guys at my school. If you did, you'd understand why I'd rather not open my mind too much." Everyone laughs again, and a warm feeling blooms in my chest. I'm actually doing this—I'm sitting in front of a bunch of executives, without Miranda, and I'm totally holding my own. They think I'm funny, and in a *ha-ha* way, not a *what a freak* way.

"Tell me, Claire," Charlotte says. "If a situation were to arise on the show in which only you *or* Miranda could continue racing, would you help your sister and risk being eliminated, or would you save yourself?"

"What?" I say. "That would never happen—we're on the same team, so we'd be eliminated together, right?"

"Pretend it was a possibility. What would you do?"

I'm honestly not sure. The whole point of us being here is for Miranda to get revenge on Samir, so if he was still in the game, I guess I'd have to let Miranda keep racing, regardless of what I wanted. But what if she'd already gotten her revenge, and Samir wasn't a factor anymore? I have more to prove than she does. If I wanted to show the world I was a competent, fierce contender who deserved to be taken seriously, I couldn't afford to sacrifice myself for someone else. Sure, it might make me look generous, but it would also make me look weak. It's exactly what Miranda would expect me to do, and it would show her that I consider myself disposable. If I think of myself that way, how can I expect her to disagree?

In any case, Charlotte's question is purely hypothetical. I'll never really have to compete against my sister in the race. And I can tell what the producers want me to say.

I square my shoulders and look Charlotte right in the eye. "I'd let Miranda be eliminated," I say. "When it comes down to it, I'm not racing for her. I'm racing for myself."

* * *

Dear Claire and Miranda,

I'm delighted to inform you that you've been selected to compete on *Around the World,* LifeLine TV's highly anticipated new race-around-the-globe show! We think viewers are going to respond well to you and your story, and we're so glad you decided to audition. Welcome aboard!

Because your team is a last-minute addition to the show, you will have very little time to prepare for the race, and we apologize for the inconvenience. Attached are several waivers and confidentiality agreements, which you must sign and return to us via fax or email within *twenty-four hours.* Please include a copy of your valid United States passport. I have also attached a list of mandatory vaccinations required for international travel, which you must receive from an infectious disease specialist or travel clinic as soon as possible.

The race begins in Los Angeles on Wednesday, June 19—eight days from now—and the network will fly you into LAX on the 17th and pay for your hotel accommodations until you depart. Regardless of when you are eliminated from the race, you will not return home until July 12. You may not tell *anyone* where you are going, aside from your emergency contact. Doing so will be considered a breach of contract and is grounds for elimination.

Everything you bring on the race must fit inside one hiking backpack. Additional luggage will not be allowed. Keep in mind that airline size and weight restrictions vary by carrier, and remember to pack for diverse climates—LifeLine reserves the right to send you *anywhere* in the world! You will not be responsible for any specialty items, such as parkas, snow-shoes, or swimwear, but all other clothing must be your own. During the rest periods between legs of the race, you will be provided with sleeping accommodations, but you may choose to bring sleeping bags or bedrolls for napping at other times. You may not bring cell phones, GPS equipment, computers, or any other electronic communication devices on the race, nor may you bring any cash. Feel free to bring paper maps and guidebooks.

Good luck, and happy racing! We look forward to seeing you in Los Angeles.

All the best,
Charlotte Sweeney,
Ruby Harris Casting

(MESSAGE RECEIVED JUNE 11, 7:14 PM)

WILL DIVINE: WE MADE IT ONTO THE SHOW! You?

ME: You are not my emergency contact, so answering that question is a breach of contract and grounds for elimination. ☺

WILL DIVINE: OMG YOU MADE IT TOO!!!! Congratulations!

ME: I have no idea what you're talking about. (!!!!!!!!!!! You too!!!!!)

WILL DIVINE: See you in LA. Can't wait to fight you for my million dollars.

ME: I believe you mean MY million dollars.

WILL DIVINE: ☺

6

The California sun is bright as a spotlight when Miranda and I climb out of the network car and follow a production assistant toward the outfield of Angel Stadium. I hoist my new red hiking backpack onto my shoulders and am dismayed once again by its weight—I brought as little as I could, but the straps are already starting to cut into my shoulders.

Miranda pauses at the edge of the field, where four other teams are already gathered. They're not doing anything but milling around and shaking hands, but they're already being filmed from several angles by burly camera operators and sound people with audio mixers strapped around their waists. I squint and try to pick out Will and Lou, but they don't seem to be here yet. Samir and his brother aren't either, and I'm glad—I can't wait to see the look on his face when he arrives and spots us.

"Wow," my sister says. "We're actually here. We're really *doing* this."

"We are."

Miranda bumps my shoulder with hers. "Hey, Clairie? I

don't think I've actually said this yet, but thanks for coming here with me. I know this is hard for you, so it means a lot."

"It's going to be great," I say, willing my stomach to unclench from where it's coiled like a spring in the corner of my torso. "We're going to rock this race. Samir won't know what hit him."

"Go, Team Revenge," Miranda whispers fiercely. She grins and holds out her hand for one of those cheesy exploding fist-bumps. I start to feel a little calmer as I touch my fist to hers. This past week, I've finally felt like my sister and I are a true team—she's even the one who managed to convince my parents I'm responsible and mature enough to go on the race. During the day, we shopped for clothes and gear, and we spent our evenings poring over strategy websites and watching old race shows online. Every time one team sabotaged another, we took notes and discussed similar tactics we could use on Samir. My sister consulted me on everything and took my opinions seriously, and for the first time, it felt like we were equals reaching for the same goal. I pray this dynamic won't break down the second the stress of racing kicks in. I've seen lots of teams turn against each other when things get rough.

Our PA leads us onto the field, where she hands us over to a scruffy guy in a backward Angels cap. His name tag says CHUCK, and from the number of electronic gadgets on his belt, I gather he's in charge. He nods appreciatively at our matching T-shirts, which are bright red and say TEAM REVENGE in white letters. Natalie made them for us as a going-away gift—on shows like this, teams tend to nickname each other right away, so it's best to get there first. Nat also bought me lucky smiley-face underwear, and I'm wearing that, too. I need all the luck I can get.

"Miranda and Claire," Chuck says, checking our names off on his clipboard. "Welcome. Let's get you guys miked up, okay? You can put your packs over there."

There are a bunch of backpacks lying on their sides near second base, and we add ours to the pile. We barely have them off our shoulders before a sound guy appears beside me and tucks a small battery pack into the back pocket of my jeans. Then, before I have time to process what's happening, he has his hands up my shirt, threading a wire around my body and clipping a microphone the size of a pencil eraser to my bra. When I squirm, he rolls his eyes as if I've recoiled from a handshake. "This'll go a lot faster if you hold still," he says, totally deadpan, like he touches strangers' boobs every day. Which, come to think of it, he probably does.

Miranda is similarly violated—she handles it better than I did—and then we're released, so we wander toward the group of other racers on the lawn. Two guys who could easily be models are sprawled on the grass with their eyes closed, soaking up the sun, and a pair of girls in matching sorority T-shirts sits beside them, giggling at everything they say. The girls look eerily alike, despite the fact that one of them is blond and the other is African American. A team of guys with glasses and oversized superhero shirts are eyeing the girls warily, as if they've just remembered they forgot to get vaccinated for cooties. Off to the side is a pair of slightly older women, maybe thirty-five, in pink yoga pants. They look the friendliest, so Miranda and I approach them.

"Hi," my sister says, sticking out her hand. "I'm Miranda, and this is Claire."

It's kind of annoying that she still introduces me to strangers as if I can't speak for myself, like she used to when we were kids. "Nice to meet you," I say, just to prove I can talk.

Both women shake our hands enthusiastically, beaming at us with glossy, bubble-gum-pink mouths, and introduce themselves in thick Brooklyn accents. The one with the purpley-red hair is Jada, and the frosty blonde is Tawny. "What's that about?" Jada asks, pointing at the writing on Miranda's T-shirt.

My sister explains about Samir, and both women's eyes go wide. "Whoa," Jada breathes. "Which one is your ex? Is he one of the hot ones on the ground?"

"I wish," Miranda says, and Jada laughs. "No, he's not here yet."

"I heard those guys over there are strippers from Vegas," Tawny says. Anywhere else I'd question her sources, but here, it's totally believable.

"What's your story?" I ask. "Are you guys related?"

When I hear Tawny laugh, I understand the meaning of the word "guffaw" for the first time. "No, sweetheart," she says, and it comes out sounding like *sweet-hawt.* "Jada and I used to be married to the same man."

"Um, at the same time?"

She laughs again. "Ha! No, but that would have made it

more fun, wouldn't it, Jada? At least we would've had a little entertainment."

"Ron was handsome and rich as anything, but he was a *serious* snooze-fest," Jada explains. "Tawny married him first, and six months after they split up, he married me. We were divorced before the year was over." *Di-VAWCED.*

"Jada and I met in yoga," Tawny chimes in. "It took us six weeks of sun salutations before we figured out we were gossiping about the *same* boring ex-husband."

"And we've been besties ever since," Jada finishes, just as we hear a familiar voice behind us.

"*Miranda?* What the hell are you doing here?"

We turn to face Samir, and I hear Chuck hissing, "Get this, get this!" Three cameras converge on us like seagulls on a stray French fry.

Samir stares at us for a minute, taking in our Team Revenge T-shirts. "Oh my God," he says. "You have *got* to be kidding me."

Miranda opens her mouth, presumably to rattle off a witty comeback, but then she notices the girl standing beside Samir, and her cheeks start turning very pink. For a second I'm afraid she's going to lose it, but when she speaks, her voice is low and steady. "Funny, Samir, you told me you were auditioning with your *brother*," she says. "Once a liar, always a liar, I guess."

The girl is an Amazon—even in her flat running shoes, she's at least ten inches taller than me. My eyes are level with her boobs. She tucks her caramel-colored hair behind her ears like she's embarrassed by this whole scene and extends her hand to Miranda. "Hi, I'm Janine," she says. "Samir and I were scene partners for our Chekhov class last semester? I don't think we ever officially—"

"Yeah, I know who you are," Miranda says, her voice ice-cold. "I just didn't recognize you with your pants on." I suddenly remember her limerick: *He hopped in the sack with that ho Janine Black....* Oh God, this is even more awkward than I thought it would be.

Miranda doesn't shake Janine's hand, and it hovers there in the air for a few seconds, her violet fingernails shining in the sun. Finally, my sister turns back to Samir. "Good luck on the race," she says. "I would say 'May the best man win,' but that would require at least one of us to be a man." Then she links her arm with mine and steers me toward the other side of the field. Despite her calm façade, I can feel how tense she is.

Two of the camera guys follow us, and the other stays behind to get a reaction shot of Samir and Janine. "That was great," I tell Miranda quietly. "You totally threw him off his game."

Miranda lets go of me and shakes out her hands, like she can fling excess emotion off her fingertips like water. "I cannot *believe* he had the nerve to bring her here. God, I can barely think when he's around. Ninety percent of my brainpower goes into trying not to scream or punch him."

"You seemed totally in control," I say. "And all that energy is great. It'll give us an edge in the race." I give her arm a little squeeze. "I know how much this part sucks, but once the race starts, we'll get ahead of him, and then you'll barely have to see him at all. You can do this."

She takes a deep breath and lets it out slowly. "I can," she says. "I'm totally fine. Everything's fine."

Out of the corner of my eye, I spot Will walking past with the boob-grabby sound guy. He gives me a little eyebrow waggle—I guess he doesn't want to be obvious about knowing me, since we're being filmed. I eyebrow-waggle back.

Chuck's walkie-talkie emits a crackle of static and some unintelligible words, and he claps a bunch of times to get our attention. "All right, everyone, come on over here and stand in a semicircle," he calls. "Isis is on her way."

I have no idea who Isis is, but she sounds important, so we follow Chuck to the other end of the outfield. He assembles us in front of a banner strung between two poles, rolled up so we can't see what it says. The last team to arrive ends up standing next to Miranda, and I hear them introduce themselves as Zora and Aidan. They have exactly the same face, but Zora has a nose ring, dark eyeliner, and blue streaks in her dyed black hair, and Aidan looks more like someone who drinks a lot of chai and goes on road trips. If Zora is hard rock, Aidan is her acoustic version.

More garbled words hiss through Chuck's walkie-talkie, and then a tall, elegant woman comes striding toward us from across the field. Presumably, this is Isis. Her hair is cropped incredibly short, showing off the perfect shape of her head and the swanlike curve of her neck. She's wearing a filmy white top that contrasts beautifully with her dark skin, and she glides across the lawn in her stiletto heels, which somehow aren't sinking into the grass like a normal person's would. She radiates the kind of glow pregnant women are supposed to have, but without the inconvenience of actually growing another human inside her body. As she takes her place in front of the banner, everyone stands up a little straighter. A makeup artist rushes forward to powder her perfect nose.

Finally, when all the cameras are in place, the woman unleashes a radiant smile on us—God, she must bleach her teeth twice a day. "Hi, everyone," she says. Her voice is lower than I expected, purring and musical. "My name is Isis Everleigh, and I'll be your host. You are the best of the best, chosen from a pool of thousands of contestants, and I'm expecting some fierce competition as you circumnavigate the globe. Each leg of the race, you'll be sent to a different country, where you'll complete a series of challenges before finding your way to a check-in point for a rest. The last team to arrive at each check-in point will be eliminated, and the first team to complete the entire race will win . . . *one million dollars.*"

Everyone whoops and cheers at the mention of the prize. I picture myself and my sister pushing in front of Samir and Janine and crossing that finish line first, our hands clasped together as Isis beams down at us and says, "Claire and Miranda, you are the winners of *Around the World.*" For a moment, it feels possible, and a little flash of excitement zings through me, overpowering the nervousness churning in my stomach.

I grin at Miranda as Isis reaches out with her perfect, manicured hand and pulls the cord on the banner behind her. It unrolls with a satisfying zip, revealing the logo of the show we're going to win.

And then I register what I'm seeing, and I stop breathing.

The logo is a map, as might be expected from a race-around-the-globe show. But the map is pink, shaped like a heart, and flanked by two cartoon Cupids about to loose their arrows into the middle of the Atlantic Ocean. Across the bottom of the banner, in curling script, is the tagline: *Where in the world will you find your soul mate?*

Something is terribly, terribly wrong with this picture.

"Welcome, everyone," Isis says, "to *Around the World in Eighty Dates.*"

7

For about five seconds, there's dead silence. Then Zora says, "I'm sorry, *what*? You want us to *date* each other?"

Yup. That pretty much covers it.

As if her outburst has given the rest of us permission to speak, a chorus of heated, whispered conversations breaks out all around us. Miranda grips my arm hard enough to bruise, and I can feel that she's trembling. "Did you know about this?" she hisses.

"Are you *kidding*? Of course not! Do you seriously think I'd bring you on a dating show *now*? Do you think *I'd* audition for one *ever*?"

"Oh my God." Miranda rakes her fingers through her hair. "I can't do this, Claire. This isn't what I signed up for. Can we quit? What does our contract say? I skimmed over all those parts with the tiny type. Why didn't I read the whole thing? You're always supposed to read the whole thing! Do you think it said something about this?"

"I don't know," I say, and my voice sounds like it's coming from very far away. My sister's rare display of panic feeds my anxiety, and the whole world suddenly starts tilting beneath me. I struggle to come up with something reassuring to say, but I can't think of a single good thing about this situation. My sister may have to cozy up to the person she hates most in the world. And I, at the age of eighteen, have to go on my first few real dates with total strangers, some of whom are *Vegas strippers,* in foreign countries, on national television. This might actually be my worst nightmare.

We didn't rock the auditions. I didn't impress the casting team with my theory about reality TV being a great equalizer. Miranda's here because the producers want drama, teeth and claws and screaming fights, and maybe, if they're lucky, a dramatic, sappy reconciliation between her and Samir. And I'm here because I'm awkward and inexperienced and totally ridiculous in this context. I'm the one they'll underscore with sad tuba noises.

I am on this show for comic relief.

I taste acid at the back of my throat, and for a moment I'm sure I'm going to be sick. In a desperate attempt to distract myself, I look around the circle to see how the other teams are reacting. The African American stripper shouts out, "Hells yeah!" and high-fives the blond one, and the sorority girls giggle in unison. The geeky guys are whispering heatedly, and I catch the words "boobs" and "terrifying" and "never even had a girlfriend," which makes me feel a little better. I seek out Will's eyes, expecting to see my shock and dismay reflected there, but he looks infuriatingly calm. Did he guess the twist from the auditions somehow? Maybe all the signs were there, and I missed them. How could I have been so stupid?

Isis's soothing voice cuts through the chaos. "I know this is an unexpected development," she says, somehow managing to convey sympathy, superiority, and rabid excitement all at once. "But if everyone could calm down, I'd love to tell you more about our show. That's not the last exciting surprise I have in store for you today!" If this is what all her "exciting surprises" are like, I don't want to hear any more, but I don't think I have a choice.

"First of all," Isis says when everyone has quieted, "please turn and look at your partners."

We do, and my stomach twists at the scared-rabbit look in my sister's eyes. I want to be strong for her, to promise her we can still take down Samir, but I'm not sure I have any leftover strength to give. As Miranda stares back at me, her face softens a little, and I realize I must look as bad as she does. At least we're in this together.

"Now say good-bye," Isis instructs. "The person you're looking at right now will not be your partner as you race around the world."

I try to shout *"What?"* but all that comes out of my mouth is a breath. Across the circle, one of the strippers says, "Later, bro," totally impassive. Aidan mutters, *"Seriously?"*

Isis produces two pink silk pouches embroidered with the heart-map logo and the labels GIRLS and GUYS. "All teams will be composed of one girl and one guy," she explains. "I'll be randomly selecting your dates for the first leg of the race. At each check-in point, there will be a Proposal Ceremony, during which you will choose your own dates for the next leg in the order you arrived. We have some seriously steamy challenges in store for you, so look around and pick out the racers *you* think are hottest. You'll want to race quickly so you can snatch them up before someone else does! There will also be special prizes awarded throughout the race for making sparks fly! Let's get started—are you ready to meet your first dates?"

The strippers and the sorority girls cheer. "This is the worst thing ever," Miranda whispers. "What if I get Samir?" She sounds like she's going to cry.

"Odds are you won't, right? And it's not like you guys are going to pick each other at the Proposal Ceremonies, so you'll be safe after today." I grab her hand. "Listen, no matter who they pair us with, I'm still going to help you take him down. That's the reason we're here, and we're always going to be a team, okay?" Miranda nods, but she doesn't look reassured.

Isis reaches into her silk pouches and pulls out the first two names. "Claire?" she calls out, and I hold up my hand to identify myself. "Your partner for this leg of the race is ... Will."

Oh.

Oh.

The tight coil of fear in my stomach hatches into a swarm of butterflies on speed. I can feel my cheeks turning bright red as I think about doing "seriously steamy challenges" with Will Divine, and the fact that there are at least four cameras pointed at me doesn't help the situation. I feel a little light-headed—maybe all those butterflies are clogging up my brain stem. I bite my lip and look down so millions of viewers won't see the terrified excitement in my eyes.

"Please come stand next to your new partner, Claire," Isis says.

I give Miranda a quick hug and whisper, "Good luck, Mira," and then I walk across the circle to Will, feeling my sister's gaze on my back.

"Fancy meeting you here," Will says with a smile when I reach him, and I look up into those piercing eyes. He seems like he's pleased that I'm his partner, but maybe I'm just seeing what I want to see. If there really are going to be intimate challenges, he probably wishes he'd gotten one of the hot sorority girls. Or maybe Zora, with her edgy blue streaks, or statuesque Janine. Suddenly, my Team Revenge T-shirt seems childish and ridiculous.

"Isn't this insane?" I whisper. "My sister is going to kill me. I'm the one who roped her into auditioning, and now she's on a dating show with her ex. I feel awful."

"Maybe running away from him will give her incentive to race harder," he says. The adorable dimple in his right cheek peeks out at me, and I know that if it means keeping him as my "date," I'll race pretty hard myself.

While we've been talking, divorcée Jada has been paired with Will's friend Lou, and the blond sorority girl, Philadelphia, has been paired with Blake, the blond stripper. When Isis reaches into her bag again and pulls out my sister's name, I cross all my fingers and toes and pray she won't be matched with Samir. "Miranda, your partner for this leg of the race is . . . Aidan," she says. I let out my breath in a thankful rush as she moves to stand beside him, looking relieved.

The other stripper, Troy, whose dark skin is covered in geometric tattoos, is paired with cheating Janine. Vanessa, the other sorority girl, gets Steve, one of the nerds, and she stands a little apart from him, like the desire to attend Comic Con might be contagious. Samir is paired with Tawny. That leaves blue-streaked Zora to partner with Martin, the one I heard whispering about never having had a girlfriend. She's a good six inches shorter than he is, but she looks very intimidating; when they stand together, he crumples in on himself so much that she looks taller. The thought of the two of them doing sexy challenges together makes me cringe.

When we're all paired up, the cameras turn off for a minute while Chuck assigns us our crew people. For each leg of the race, each team will have a different camera operator and sound person, and we're not allowed to go anywhere they can't follow us, except to the bathroom. Today, our camera guy is Greg, who has an impressive mustache that curls up at the ends, and our sound person is a skinny, freckled guy named Terry. They look at me like I'm nuts when I ask them if they're excited about the race, and I realize that for them, this is just another normal day.

Isis walks around the semicircle and hands each team a long pink envelope embossed with the show's logo and sealed with Velcro. Then the cameras turn back on, and Isis says, "You each have your first instruction envelopes. Inside are your directions about where to travel first. As soon as I tell you to begin, you may open them and start racing. Who knows where in the world you'll find *your* soul mate?"

"You want to open it, or should I?" whispers Will.

"I'll do it," I say.

"May the forces of love and luck be with you. Ready ... set ... race!" Isis shouts, and the sound of ripping Velcro fills the air.

"Read the instructions out loud," Greg says, sticking his lens right in my face.

"'Drive yourselves to Los Angeles International Airport in one of the cars provided and fly to Surabaya, on the island of Java,'" I read, my voice trembling a little with nervous excitement. "'Once there, make your way by cab to Alun Alun Stadium, where you will receive your next instructions.'" There's a wad of cash in the envelope, which I tuck into my pack with my passport. I guess we're supposed to use it to pay cabdrivers.

"*Java?*" Will says. "Seriously? This is *awesome*. Let's go!" He high-fives me, and we turn and sprint for our packs. As nervous as I am about the unknown challenges ahead of me and about being separated from Miranda, there's another part of me that's sparking with excitement.

The race has begun, and we're off.

Except, as it turns out, we're not. When we're halfway to the stadium doors, heavy packs bouncing and jostling against our backs, Chuck raises a megaphone (where did that even come from?) and calls us back to the starting line. Some of the camera operators didn't get the shots they needed, so we're told to reseal our envelopes and enact the whole scene again. I guess this explains the Velcro. Isis repeats her cheesy tagline like she's never said it before, and we rip into our envelopes with feigned hungry curiosity. Will reads our instructions aloud this time, and then we sprint for our back-packs . . . only to be called back a second time. If this is what racing around the world on television is going to be like, we might never make it as far as the airport.

The fourth time is the charm. I'm jogging along half-heartedly when Martin and Zora sprint past us, followed by Troy and Janine. Only then do I realize this time is the real deal. "Oh my God, go go go!" I scream to Will, and we fly out the exit and run toward a row of waiting black cars with heart-map decals on the windows. Will hops into the driver's seat, but when I move to get in next to him, Greg tells me I need to sit in back so he can film both our faces. The sound guy crams in beside me.

"I don't know where the airport is," Will says to me. He does a quick search for a GPS, but of course there isn't one in the car. "Do you have a map of LA?"

"Yup." Miranda and I bought a bunch of maps in prepara-tion for the show, and I pull open my pack, proud of myself for being so prepared . . . until I realize that map ended up in my sister's bag. "Crap," I say. "You didn't bring one?"

"It's in Lou's stuff." Will rattles off a string of words that will definitely need to be bleeped out.

Miranda's coming out of the stadium now, and she slides into the driver's seat of the car at the end of the row. "There's my sister," I tell Will. "Follow her, okay?"

"Good call." Will pulls out of the parking lot behind Miranda. When she looks back to check her blind spot, I try to wave at her, but I'm pretty sure Aidan's head is blocking her view. She's smiling at something he said, and for a minute I want to be in that car with her so badly it hurts.

And then Will says, "I'm so glad I got you for this first leg. Can you imagine being paired with one of the sorority girls?" He catches my gaze in the rearview mirror, and those eyes make my brain feel like a Cadbury Creme Egg that's been sitting in the sun too long.

"Hey, just be glad both strippers are guys, so you'll never have to be with them," I say.

"I don't know. On a show like this, a certain willingness to take off your clothes could actually be an asset."

"There are other ways to get what you want," I say. I have no idea what I'm even talking about, but it sounds pretty good.

Will quirks an eyebrow at me. "I'm sure you know all kinds of tricks. We're going to kick some ass together, Claire Henderson."

I grin back at him, and when my sister's car pulls onto the highway and accelerates away from us, I'm surprisingly willing to let her go.

8

Will and I park in an airport garage and dash through the international terminal until we find an information kiosk. There's really no reason to run at this stage of the game—I can't imagine there are a lot of flights leaving for Surabaya, and everyone will probably end up bunched up at the gate—but it makes better television if we look like we're in a hurry. I can't believe how well Greg manages to keep up with us, given all the equipment he's carrying. His camera alone looks like it must weigh fifty pounds. By the time we reach the kiosk, Will and I are both breathing hard, but Greg doesn't seem winded at all.

"Can you tell us which airlines fly to Surabaya?" Will asks the woman behind the desk. She points us toward the Cathay Pacific counter, and we're off and running again.

Martin the nerd and blue-streaks Zora are already there when we arrive. I look for Miranda, but there's no sign of her. "Is anyone else here?" I ask Zora as Martin pays for their tickets.

"There are a couple teams over at the Singapore Airlines

counter," she says. Her voice is low and husky, like she spent last night screaming at a concert. "But the flights are supposed to land ten minutes apart, and we heard Cathay Pacific has better food."

Martin steps away from the desk, and we take his place. "How many seats are left on the earliest flight to Surabaya?" I ask.

The woman behind the desk gives me a cold, penetrating stare, like I've asked her what brand of tampons she prefers, then starts typing away on her computer. Her hair is slicked into a perfect black helmet, and her cheekbones are sharp enough to cut diamonds. Just looking at her makes me feel disheveled and sticky—she's probably never sweated in her life. "There are twelve tickets left," she says in a clipped accent I can't identify.

Since we have to buy tickets for ourselves and our crew, that's only enough seats for us and two more teams, and the rest will have to take a later flight or find a different airline. "Do you think we should check out Singapore Airlines before we buy anything?" I ask Will. "Just to see?"

Philadelphia and Blake burst through the terminal doors and jog toward us, followed closely by Steve and Vanessa. When all four of them head toward our counter, Will says, "We better be safe and go with these."

I've never been on an overseas flight before, and I wish I didn't have to do it without Miranda. But I slide my show credit card over the counter to the Ice Queen and say, "We'll take four, please."

"You can't reference us," Greg reminds me. "Tell her you want two, and then I'll turn the camera off and you can buy another two."

That seems convoluted, but I don't argue. "We'll take two, please," I say.

As we move away from the counter with our tickets, Blake and Philadelphia step up to take our place. "We need to go to Serbia," Blake says.

"I think it says Sur-*bay*-a," Philadelphia attempts to correct him.

"Is that in Italy? I thought Serbia was in Russia."

Will rolls his eyes at me, and I feel another surge of gratitude that I got him as my partner.

After we go through security, change our money into rupiahs, and get a snack, we still have three hours to kill. There's nothing interesting in the terminal, so we end up sprawled on the floor at the gate, playing hearts with Zora and Martin. Zora asks about my Team Revenge T-shirt, and I tell her about Samir. "Is Aidan your brother?" I ask her.

She nods. "We're twins, but we got adopted into different families when we were babies," she says. "We just found each other a year ago. We thought the race would be a good way to bond, but . . . not so much, apparently."

"Man, that sucks," Will says.

"What's your deal?" Zora asks him, and only then do I realize *I* don't even know why Will's here. The one time we had an extended conversation, I was too distracted by his trivia game—and, let's be honest, his face—to ask.

"Lou's my half brother, and our dad's the CEO of a pretty

major company," Will says. "Totally stereotypical bigwig, with the private jet and the expensive cigars and the country club membership and everything. He's been grooming me to take over the family business my whole life, but the thing is, I have zero interest in business, and neither does Lou. When we told him we wanted to start an arts nonprofit instead, he threatened to cut us off. So . . . we're here for the money."

"Wow," Zora says. "That's rough."

"My dad even has my future wife picked out, if you can believe it. She's the CFO's daughter. She's gorgeous, but she's literally the most boring person I've ever met. He's always trying to shove us together at company Christmas parties and stuff. Last time I saw her, she spent an hour talking about the problems she was having with her maid. I wanted to puncture my eardrums with a prawn fork."

I stare at Will, suddenly more intimidated by him than ever. I can't believe I didn't know any of this. I thought he was just a regular guy who went to NYU, and now it turns out he probably grew up vacationing on a private island. How could a childhood like that produce someone so *normal*? But now that I know what to look for, his backpack does look more high-tech than mine, and his jeans look more artfully distressed.

I try to picture myself on his arm at a black-tie company Christmas party, but the whole thing is too ridiculous for even my imagination. I'd probably trip in my high heels and fall in a chocolate fountain or something. The CFO's daughter would never do that. She probably has impeccable table manners, speaks twenty languages, and uses some sort of billion-dollar yak's-blood zit cream that makes her skin look like rose petals. How could I ever compete with someone like that, boring or not? I don't even know what a prawn fork *is*. She probably has her own monogrammed set.

I tune back in as Martin asks, "Which company does your dad run?"

Will gestures toward the cameras, then lowers his eyes. "I'd rather not say, if you don't mind. He's not a bad guy, and I don't want to get him into trouble. That's just not the kind of life I want, you know?" There's an undercurrent of pain in his voice, and it makes me want to reach out and put my hand on his cheek. I manage to restrain myself.

The gate agent announces that preboarding is beginning for flight 372 to Hong Kong with continuing service to Surabaya. My heart is suddenly in my throat as we get in line—I'm about to sit next to Will for twenty-five hours. What if we run out of things to talk about right away and I have to deal with an entire day of awkward silence? What if I fall asleep and drool on his shoulder or exhale horrible plane breath in his face? Would it help if I went to sleep with gum in my mouth? Probably not—knowing me, it would end up in my hair. Just in case, I rummage around in my pack until I find a piece, which I tuck into the pocket of my hoodie for easy access.

Greg turns off his camera to board the plane, and as soon as his lens cap is on, Will's friendly, easygoing demeanor disappears completely. He's strangely quiet as we make our way down the jet bridge and onto the plane, and maybe it's the horrible lighting, but I notice that he's starting to look a little green. "You okay?" I ask as we reach our row. "You don't look so hot."

That's a total lie. He still looks incredibly hot.

"I'm fine," he says, shoving his backpack into the overhead compartment. "Do you mind if I take the aisle?"

"No, I like the window." I scoot into my seat, and he plunks down beside me and stares straight ahead. When he doesn't say anything for a good fifteen seconds, I try, "This must be really different from what you're used to, huh?"

He looks confused. "What?"

"Flying coach." When he still doesn't react, I continue, "I'm sure this is nothing like your dad's private jet."

"Oh, ha. Right." But he doesn't elaborate. He just stares at the blank video screen on the back of the seat in front of him like he wants to be left alone.

As I turn toward the window and watch the waves of heat rising off the tarmac, it occurs to me that maybe Will was only acting sweet and flirty earlier because we were being filmed. After all, this show is centered on romance, so he probably knows he'll get more screen time if he's nice to me. Maybe he's even angling for one of those special prizes Isis mentioned for getting close to your partner. But the cameras will probably stay off during the flight, and if he's only pretending to like me, I'm in for an even more uncomfortable twenty-five hours than I'd feared. A knot of anxiety tightens in my stomach, and I start missing Miranda like crazy.

The moment the plane begins taxiing toward the runway,

a weird noise starts up nearby, like someone's taking quick, wheezy, gasping breaths. At first I think it's a fussy baby, but when I turn to look, I realize the sound is coming from *Will*. His eyes are squeezed shut, his skin has a clammy, grayish pallor, and he's digging his nails into the armrests so hard he's making little dents in the rubberized plastic. There's obviously something really wrong with him.

I touch his shoulder. "Will, what's the matter? Are you sick? Do you need a doctor?" There's always one on board in movies, but does that happen in real life? Are there enough doctors to go around?

"Not sick," Will whispers. "Just really hate flying."

I've never seen somebody have a panic attack before, but this must be what it looks like. And as scary as it is to see him fall apart, I'm relieved that his sudden withdrawn attitude has nothing to do with me. As the plane starts picking up speed, Will makes a low, terrified sound in the back of his throat, and when the wheels leave the ground, he gasps and crumples in on himself. Very gently, I loosen his death grip on the armrest and give him my hand to hold instead. He clamps his fingers around mine so tightly it hurts, but I grit my teeth and let him squeeze. His fingers are ice-cold and sweaty.

"What can I do?" I ask. "Do you want some water? Should I get a flight attendant?"

He shakes his head. "It's okay. There's nothing to do but wait it out."

"How long does it usually take for you to calm down?"

There's a small bump in the air, and he gasps again. "Depends," he says in a strained voice. "Sometimes half an hour. Sometimes more."

"How are you going to do this race if you're afraid to fly? We have to be on planes, like, every other—"

He winces. "Claire, you're *really* not helping."

Wow, I am officially the worst partner ever. "Sorry, sorry. Forget I said that. Maybe you could do deep-breathing exercises?" My fifth-grade teacher made us meditate together first thing every morning to "clear our minds and center ourselves," and although I've always thought it was kind of stupid, maybe there's something to it after all. I stroke the back of Will's hand rhythmically with my thumb. "Here, try it. Close your eyes. Now breathe in through your nose for three counts, then out through your mouth for five."

He tries it once, way too fast. "I feel really stupid."

"No, you have to do it slowly. I'll count with you, okay? In, two, three . . . Out, two, three, four, five. Good, that's it. Again. In, two, three . . ."

I coach him through a couple minutes of slow breathing, and by the time the plane levels off, Will's grip around my hand is starting to loosen. A bit of color has returned to his face, and a proud little voice in the back of my mind shouts, *I did that!*

"You're looking better," I say.

"I feel better. Thank you so much."

"Of course," I say. "Now that you know what to do, the rest of the flights should be easier, even if I'm not with you." The thought of him holding some other girl's hand as he tries to calm down makes me feel a bit sick, but I try not to show it.

"Keep distracting me," he says. "Ask me a question or something."

I'd really like to know more about Prawn Fork Girl, but that doesn't seem like an appropriate topic. "What's NYU like?" I ask instead.

"Not that kind of question. Something fun."

"Oh. Okay." I scour my brain for something Will might find clever. "Um, if you could choose a superpower, what would you pick?"

He doesn't hesitate even for a second. "The ability to transform things into cheese."

I laugh. "What? *Cheese?* Wouldn't you rather be invisible or something?"

"No, think about it. I could turn toxic waste into cheese and solve the pollution problem and hunger problem at the same time. And I could turn trash into cheese and sell it, so I'd be filthy rich. Plus, I'd always have a snack."

"You've given this a lot of thought, haven't you?"

"Well, duh. Who hasn't?" He smiles at me, and I see that his color is almost back to normal. "What would yours be?"

"Teleportation. My town is super boring, and I'd love to be able to pop over to Thailand for lunch or something and be back in time for calculus class."

"Ooh, that's a good one. And you'd win the race for sure."

"I wouldn't even need to do the race. I could just teleport into a bank vault, grab a million dollars, and zip back home." He laughs. "Okay, your turn for a question."

"Say we get off the plane in Surabaya and the airport's full of zombies. What's your survival plan?"

I love how effortlessly creative he is. "All I'd really have to do is run faster than you, right?" I say.

"Good luck with that. I did track in high school. I'm super speedy."

"Well, in that case, my plan is to hop on your back and kick you until you speedily carry me to safety. Maybe Greg would let me use his camera as a weapon. Seems like it would be good for bashing in zombie heads."

"I doubt you could even lift that thing. You probably weigh, like, forty-seven pounds."

"I'm not *that* small!"

"You're minuscule!"

"Then you shouldn't mind me riding you." The minute the words are out of my mouth, I feel my face turning bright pink. "Please tell me I didn't say that out loud."

Will smirks at me. "You want to ride me, huh?"

"That's not—" I sputter. "What I meant was—"

"Don't be embarrassed. I wouldn't mind."

If my face gets any redder, I'm pretty sure it's going to catch on fire. I look down so my hair swings in front of my cheeks and take a couple deep breaths of my own. "And *next question.* Um . . . if you could only eat food beginning with one letter of the alphabet for the rest of your life, which letter would you choose?"

"Ooh, good one." He thinks about it for a minute, and I take that time to concentrate on banishing my blush. "I'd choose P. I'd be able to have pizza and pasta and pad Thai and peanut butter. And pie, obviously."

"What would you put the peanut butter on?"

"Pumpernickel. With peach preserves."

I laugh. "Nice."

"What would you pick?"

"Maybe S. I'd have tons of variety if I could eat soup and salad."

He snorts. "That's cheating, unless all your ingredients start with S."

"Oh, yeah, and *pizza* isn't cheating at all. 'Cause 'cheese' and 'tomato sauce' totally start with P."

He grins at me. "Pomodoro and parmesan?"

The Question Game stretches on for hours—turns out we're in no danger of running out of things to say. Since we're flying west, it doesn't get any darker as night approaches, and the flight attendants eventually pull down our window shades and pass out eye masks to mimic night. But I'm too high on adrenaline to rest, and Will doesn't seem tired either, so we lower our voices to whispers and huddle closer together under our Cathay Pacific blankets. Our arms are barely touching, but every time he shifts and the sleeve of his T-shirt brushes my skin, shivery electric sparks fly all over my body. The other passengers drift off to sleep, and eventually it feels like Will and I are the only people awake in the world, alone together in the clouds.

When it's his turn for a question, he whispers, "Tell me a secret."

"What kind of secret?"

"Something nobody else knows."

Ordinarily, I'd never reveal anything personal to someone I'd just met. But there's something about Will that makes me want to tell him everything. I want him to know me inside and out.

I take a deep breath. "I'm scared," I tell him.

"Don't be. I'm not going to judge you."

"No, that's the secret. I'm scared."

He shifts a little closer, so his arm presses against mine all the way from shoulder to wrist. It's like he's saying *I'm here, you're safe* without any words. "What are you afraid of?" he asks.

"Just . . . the race in general, I guess. I mean, I was nervous enough when it was a *normal* race around the world—I'm not really one of those people who can jump into stuff without thinking about it, you know? I like to plan everything out in advance, and you can't do that here. And a dating show is, like, a thousand times worse. How am I supposed to do 'steamy challenges,' Will? I'm going to make a complete fool of myself."

"No you're not. Why would you say that?"

"I don't exactly get to practice a lot—I'm from this tiny town, and there's nobody good to date there. And now millions of people are going to get to see how insanely awkward I am in . . . those kinds of situations." My embarrassment makes me feel overheated, and I pull my blanket down around my waist, but then I feel too exposed and pull it back up.

Will turns so he can look me straight in the eyes. "Claire . . . you know there's nothing actually *real* about reality TV, right?"

"Yeah, of course I know that. The producers manipulate

the story and fabricate drama, and things are filmed out of order, and—"

"No, I mean, *everything*. You don't have to be yourself when the cameras are on. People come on these shows, and they get characterized as the nerds, or the daredevils, or the bimbos, but that isn't necessarily who they really are, it's just who they've become for the producers and the viewers. You can be anyone you want."

This probably should've occurred to me before now; maybe I'm not the reality TV expert I thought I was. But even if playing a character is an option, I'm skeptical I could ever pull it off convincingly. "I can't just become someone else like that. I don't have acting training like you do."

"You don't need acting training. All you have to do is play a version of yourself who isn't afraid. When the producers put you in a situation that makes you uncomfortable, you don't have to let them know they've shaken you up. Let Claire take a break, and let your fearless alter ego take over."

"You really think that would work?"

"Totally. You should name her. What's the strongest name you can think of?"

I picture a cartoon version of myself: taller than Janine, with glossier hair, dressed in giant, ass-kicking boots and wielding an enormous sword. That girl never lets anyone intimidate her. She eats steamy challenges for a snack.

"Dominique," I tell Will.

"Great. I love her already. When you get scared, let Dominique take the reins. She can handle anything. She'll do the whole race for you, if you want."

"Do you think the producers will buy it?"

"Why wouldn't they? It's not like they know anything about you. I mean, look at me—they totally loved my good-hearted-son-of-a-CEO character at the auditions. They ate it right up. People will believe anything you tell them, as long as you commit to it. All they want is a good story."

Now I'm *really* confused. "But . . . Wait, I thought . . ."

Will's eyes widen with delight. "You fell for the CEO thing, too?"

"I mean, I . . . um . . ."

"Oh my God, that's awesome." Will looks like he's trying to figure out a way to high-five himself.

I suddenly feel deeply stupid. "So your dad's not a CEO?"

"My dad's a math teacher. Do I look like I come from money?" He lifts his blanket and displays his navy blue hoodie, worn jeans, and sneakers, which have a tiny hole in the toe.

"I just thought you were, like, slumming or something. I mean, you said you and Lou were trying to get *away* from your rich family."

"Yeah, that's another thing. Lou and I aren't related. We're just friends."

A small bubble of hope rises in my chest. "So . . . there's no CFO's daughter?"

"There's no CFO's daughter. And there isn't anyone else, either."

His revelation makes my brain feel fizzy, like it's been marinating in a glass of champagne overnight. As I sit there staring back at him with a goofy grin on my face, I imagine the fictional CFO's daughter drowning in a chocolate fountain, a whole set of prawn forks sticking out of her flawless neck.

Will is available, and I'm going to make him mine.

9

By the time we land in Surabaya, I've been awake for thirty-four hours. The flight attendant cheerfully announces that it's seven in the morning local time.

"Is it Thursday, Friday, or Saturday?" I ask Will. Remarkably, he slept through the landing of our second flight and only woke up when the wheels touched down.

He messes with his hair under his hat, then pulls a piece of gum out of his pocket and shoves it into his mouth. He doesn't even have to rummage for it, and I wonder if he also worried about his bad plane breath in advance. Would a guy be concerned about that if he didn't find the girl next to him at least a little bit attractive?

"I think it's Friday," he says.

"But we crossed the international date line, right? Did we skip ahead or back?"

Will rubs his eyes. "I have no idea. Thinking about it makes my brain hurt."

We pull our packs down from the overhead compartment—somehow, mine feels like it's gotten heavier since yesterday—and stumble blearily into the airport. On all the race shows I've seen, it looks like the contestants zoom off the plane and straight into waiting taxis, but instead we're routed down an endless series of hallways and into the line for passport control. Disappointingly, the Indonesian airport doesn't look any different from an American one. I was hoping for palm-frond floors and walls made of orchids or something.

We answer some questions and have our passports stamped, and as we're heading into the arrivals area, I spot Miranda waving at me from the end of the line. She was always better at sleeping on planes than I was, and she looks fresh and rested, though Aidan is rubbing his eyes under his hipster glasses. I don't see Samir, and I pray he's way behind us instead of ahead. Part of me wants to wait for my sister to get through the line so we can talk, but as soon as I think it, Martin and Zora zip past us, and Will says, "Come on, we better move." He tugs me toward the exit, and I lose sight of Miranda.

The moment we step outside, the hot, wet air hits me like a slap. It's so humid that it feels like we've just walked into someone's mouth, and my shirt instantly starts clinging to my damp back. Will and I find the taxi line and toss our backpacks into the trunk of a blue-and-yellow car. I pray it'll be air-conditioned, but when we slip inside, it's even warmer. I wish I had changed into shorts on the plane.

"Alun Alun Stadium?" Will says, showing the driver our instructions. "Do you know where that is?" The guy nods enthusiastically. "Perfect. As fast as you can, please."

"What day is it?" I ask the driver, but he just says, "Yes."

Greg hops in beside him and somehow gets him to sign a release form agreeing to be on camera. Terry and all his sound equipment squish into the back with Will and me, and we're off.

Logically, I know there are lots of countries where people drive on the left side of the road, but that doesn't prepare me for the feeling of zooming into what looks like oncoming traffic. Every time a car flies by on the wrong side of us, I flinch. "Relax," Will says, giving my knee a little squeeze. As if I could possibly do that with his hand on my leg.

We drive onto a massive suspension bridge, the cables glinting red-orange in the morning sun, and as I gaze out the window at the sparkling water underneath, it hits my sleep-deprived brain with renewed force that I'm actually here. I'm hurtling through a foreign country with a cute boy by my side, competing for a million dollars. I've never even been to Europe before, and here I am in Indonesia. And for this one moment, I'm not even that scared, just proud of myself.

"Holy crap," I say to Will. "We're in *Java.*" I leave out the cute boy part.

"Welcome to the other side of the world, Dominique," he says. And then he *winks* at me. If this were a movie, I'd groan at how cheesy that is. But somehow it's totally different when someone does it to you in real life. I start to feel even more overheated.

"Aren't you dying in that wool hat?" I ask to distract myself.

"A little. But it's my lucky hat. I have to wear it."

"All the time? Or only when you're trying to win something?"

"All the time."

"Does it work? Are you actually luckier?"

He thinks about it. "I guess I don't really know, since I always wear it. But I bet my life would be worse without it."

"Or maybe your life would be exactly the same, only your head wouldn't be hot."

Will gives me a very serious look. "Do I really want to take that chance? Think of all the terrible things that could happen. What if I took it off and then our cab broke down, and we had to sit here in the middle of this bridge for hours while the strippers and the bimbos passed us?"

"Good point," I say. "Why don't you keep it on for now."

We wind through the streets of Surabaya, past storefronts shaded with slapdash, corrugated-metal awnings and topped with tiny apartments. All the roofs are made of red tile, and everyone seems to have a balcony, even if they don't have a front door. A man comes out to sweep in front of his shop and shoos away a couple of chickens. When we stop at a light, a woman passes in front of the car lugging an enormous basket filled with unfamiliar red objects. I think it's food, but I can't tell if it's produce or fish.

Eventually our cabbie pulls up beside a long, oval field surrounded by a tall iron fence, scrubby trees, and multicolored flags. "Alun Alun," he announces.

I don't see any sort of marker that indicates we're in the right place, but Martin and Zora are getting out of another cab farther up the block. "How much do we owe you?" I ask, pulling out our rupiahs. They're bright jewel tones, purple and blue and green. I hope we'll have some left over so I can keep one as a souvenir.

Our driver rattles off something in . . . Indonesian? I can't believe I don't even know what language they speak here. In any case, I don't understand it, so I fan out the money and extend it so he can pluck out the correct change. He extracts two bills, and I hope he hasn't taken more than the ride was worth.

"Thank you!" Will calls as we sprint away with our backpacks. Or, rather, Will sprints, and I shuffle along as quickly as I can. I swear this backpack has gotten heavier.

Now that we're out of the car, the box of pink envelopes at the other end of the field is hard to miss. Standing off to the side is a large crowd of locals who cheer when they see us and an American guy in a pink *Around the World* shirt, jabbering angrily into his phone. He must be one of the producers. Farther down the field are a couple guys in fringe pants and gigantic lion-head masks decorated with peacock plumes. They're performing a spinning, squatting dance while a couple musicians accompany them with bells and some sort of wind instrument that sounds like an out-of-tune oboe.

Will extracts a pink envelope from the box, rips it open, and reads the instructions aloud.

At the end of a wedding in the nearby Marquesas Islands, it is traditional for the guests to lie facedown on the floor while the bride and groom walk over their backs and get out the door.

In homage to this, one member of your team must crawl one hundred meters while the other team member rides on his/her back. The rider may not touch the ground at any time, or you must start over. When you have completed this task, the head lion dancer will give you your next instructions.

I stare at Will, sure he must be teasing me for the comment I made on the plane about riding him. "It does *not* say that."

"See for yourself." He holds it out.

It really does say that. I suddenly don't feel the least bit tired. "I seriously have to *ride* you?"

"Well, I could ride you, if you'd prefer. It doesn't specify which team member should be on top." His mouth quirks into a teasing smile, and that insane dimple peeks out at me.

I might die if this conversation goes on for one more second, so I try for the first time to channel Dominique. My kick-ass alter ego wouldn't let this situation embarrass her. There's nothing scary or intimidating about sitting on someone's back. "All right, I'm on top," I say. "Let's go."

Zora is already climbing onto Martin's back over by a pink flag in the grass, which seems to mark the starting line. There's another flag way down the field; it turns out a hundred meters is kind of a lot. "So . . . how do we do this, exactly?" I ask Will when we've joined them and shed our packs.

He drops down onto all fours. "Hop on, cowgirl."

Gingerly, I sit down near his hips, facing sideways. I don't even want to touch him with my hands, in case he feels how sweaty they are. "Is this okay?" I ask.

"Are you going to be able to hold your feet off the ground? I think you should straddle me."

Greg's right in my face with the camera, and I can imagine millions of viewers roaring with laughter at my expression. *Dominique straddles people all the time,* I remind myself. I take a deep breath, swing my leg around, and squeeze Will's hips tight between my thighs, then tuck my feet up under his perfect butt. "Sorry if I'm too heavy," I say. "Rest whenever you need to."

"Oh, please," he says. "My backpack is heavier than you. I got seriously lucky having you as my partner." I know he's talking about my weight, but I pretend he might mean it in other ways, too.

Nearby, Martin and Zora are trundling off. Zora's pretty small, too, but Martin's face is the color of strawberry jam, and there's a drop of sweat hanging off the end of his nose. I doubt it's from exertion—he's probably as mortified by this as I am.

Will starts crawling, and he's much faster than I expected. Ten feet into the ride, I give up on protecting my sweaty hands and brace them against his shoulders. "You okay up there?" he calls.

"I'm good."

I'm slipping to the left a little, and I lean the other way, trying to balance. "Hey," Will says as I overcorrect, "this might be easier if you lie all the way down on top of me."

"Lie on top of you?" Oh God.

"Like a piggyback ride, but horizontal." He stops for a minute and waits for me to reposition myself.

The suggestion kind of makes me feel like my head is going to explode, but Martin and Zora are way ahead of us now, and another cheer goes up behind us, signaling the arrival of a third team. Slowly, I lower myself down until my boobs are pressed flat to Will's back. I lay my cheek between his shoulder blades, breathing in the heat rising from his skin and the smell of his detergent and fresh sweat. I lock my arms around his torso for balance and wonder if he can feel how fast my heart is beating.

"Comfy?" he asks, and the vibrations of his voice rumble through my whole body.

"Ready when you are," I say.

Will was right—we're able to go a lot faster like this. I close my eyes as his body shifts and flexes under mine, and just for a second, I allow myself to imagine pressing this close to him because he wants me there, not because it's part of a game.

The ride ends way too quickly.

When we hit the finish line, Will lets out a whoop. "All done," he says, reaching back to pat my thigh. "You can get off now." I don't want to, but I do.

Will stands up, brushing the dirt off the knees of his jeans and rotating his wrists. His face is pink with exertion, and it makes him look cuter, if that's even possible. "Did I hurt you?" I ask him.

"Nah. You're like a tiny baby koala." He runs over to the lion dancer, who pulls a pink envelope out of the pocket of his fringed pants and hands it over. Will opens it and reads aloud:

> Make your way by cab to the Hotel Majapahit and find the swimming pool. In Java, it is traditional for couples to pay a fee of twenty-five rat tails to the Registrar of Marriage before their wedding. In homage to this, you must search the bottom of the pool for twenty-five rat figurines, which you may trade for your next instructions.

Rat tails? *Ew.* I make a mental note never to get married in Java.

"That sounds easy," Will says. "How hard can it be to find twenty-five figurines on the floor of a pool? It's not like there's anywhere to hide them."

We sprint back to the starting line to collect our backpacks and see that two other teams have arrived. Steve is already crawling with Vanessa perched cross-legged in the center of his back like a queen riding an elephant. Troy and Janine are having a little trouble with logistics; they're about the same height, and she can't seem to keep her mile-long legs off the ground, no matter how she contorts herself. I still don't see Samir at all—maybe Miranda and I won't have to do a thing to knock him out of the competition. Then again, my sister's not here yet either.

Just as I think that, a taxi comes screeching up to the curb, and Miranda and Aidan pile out with their camera crew. "Hey," my sister calls. "You guys need a cab? You can have this one."

"Yeah, thanks." I give her a hug as Will and our crew squish inside and start talking to the driver about our next destination. "How was your flight?" I ask my sister.

"Miranda, come on," Aidan calls.

"I gotta go," she says breathlessly. "I'll talk to you later." She blows me a kiss, and then she's gone.

I slide into the car next to Will feeling a bit let down—seeing my sister in tiny, rushed snippets is almost worse than not seeing her at all. "So, the driver knows where the hotel is?" I ask.

"He nodded and said okay when I showed him the instructions," Will says.

"I guess we're good, then." I pat his head. "Thanks, Lucky Hat."

But half an hour later, we're still driving around, and I swear the same droning song has been playing on the cab-driver's stereo the whole time. I have no idea where the hotel is supposed to be, but I'm starting to feel like we're going in circles. Did Miranda know how awful this cabbie was when she handed him off to us? I'm pretty sure she wouldn't try to sabotage me, but I guess I can't be certain, now that we're not technically a team. "Didn't we already pass that store with the blue awning?" I shout to Will over the music.

"I'm not sure. They're all starting to look the same." He leans forward. "Excuse me, sir? Hotel Majapahit?"

The guy nods. "Yes, yes."

"You know where we're going?"

"Yes." But then he does a U-turn, which doesn't exactly inspire confidence.

Will leans back and lowers his voice. "What do we do? Should we get out?"

"I don't know. Do you think we're really behind?"

"Maybe. But other people might have gotten lost, too."

We pull up beside another cab, and to my relief, our cabbie yells something out the window to the other driver. I don't understand any of it, but I assume (and hope and pray) he's asking for directions. Then he does *another* U-turn, cranking the wheel so hard Will flies into the sound equipment.

By the time we get to the hotel, we've been driving around for an hour, and I'm pretty sure I recognize the auto body shop down the street as one we passed five minutes from the stadium. Martin and Zora sprint out the lobby doors as we go to pull them open, and we spot Troy and Janine getting into a cab down the street. I can't believe they've managed to do two challenges in the time it took us to get here. "This sucks," I mutter to Will.

We ask the woman behind the front desk where to go, and she signs Greg's waiver and directs us toward the back of the hotel. The pool area is gorgeous, tiled in a warm terra-cotta color and surrounded by palm trees and potted ferns. We're the only ones here, except for a producer and a Javanese guy dressed in a sarong and holding a stack of pink envelopes. Cushioned beach chairs under canvas umbrellas line the edge of the pool, and when I see them, my exhaustion hits me like a punch to the face. All I want to do is curl up in the shade and let the soothing sound of the breeze rustling through the palms lull me to sleep.

Will approaches the edge of the pool and looks down into

the turquoise-blue water. "Oh God," he says. "Now I get why this is hard."

Every single inch of the pool's floor is covered with tiny animal figurines. There must be thousands of them. From here, I can pick out a few orange tigers, a couple of bright green parrots and frogs, and some white polar bears. But most of the animals are various shades of gray and brown, the same colors as rats.

"Are you kidding?" I say. Then something else occurs to me. "Oh God, I'm not even going to be able to *see* which ones are rats without my glasses." In the rush to pack for the race, it never even occurred to me that I'd need to buy prescription goggles.

"Can we tie them to your head somehow, so you can swim with them on?"

"There's an extra pair of shoelaces in my bag," I say. "I'll give it a shot. Why don't you go ask that guy where the swimsuits are?"

I've managed to craft a functional glasses-holding device by the time Will comes back empty-handed. "That looks . . . good," he says, then bursts out laughing. "I mean, you also look like the biggest nerd I've ever seen."

"Shut up, this was your idea. Where are the swimsuits?"

"There aren't any. The producer says we have to swim in whatever we brought."

I stare at him. "But . . . I didn't bring a swimsuit. They said we didn't have to. Do you have one?"

"Nope." He slips off his shoes. "Come on, we're wasting time."

I can't very well swim in my jeans, and my cotton shirt will never dry in this humidity. I start pawing furiously through my bag, looking for the sports bra and shorts I know I packed, but I can't find them. And even if I did, where would I change? Maybe I could go inside the hotel and find a bathroom?

"Claire, come on! What are you doing?" Will says.

"I'm looking for something to swim in, but I can't—"

And then I glance up, and my brain shuts off.

Will is standing in front of me in nothing but a pair of black boxer briefs. His torso is wiry but subtly muscular, and his smooth, damp skin glints in the Java sunshine. As I try not to stare at the chiseled lines leading down from his hip-bones, I hear Isis's voice in my head: *We have some seriously steamy challenges in store for you.*

For a second, all I can think is *Thank you, God.*

And then I think, *Millions of people are about to see my lucky smiley-face underwear.*

"We're wasting time," Will says. "We have to find those rats and get out of here. Just take off your clothes, okay? It's no big deal."

Maybe it's no big deal for him, but it is for me. I hate myself for my nerves and my modesty, and I know I'm wasting precious minutes. But if I'd known coming here would mean that *everyone I know* would get to see me strip on television, I never would have auditioned. I'm beyond exhausted, there's a camera in my face, Will is standing in front of me practically naked, and I'm suddenly so overwhelmed that I'm sure I'm going to cry.

"I just . . . I can't . . . ," I say, and my voice comes out so small it's almost inaudible.

"You can," Will says firmly. He grabs my shoulders and looks me right in the eyes. "The producers want you to make this into a big deal, but you're not going to let them win, are you? You're stronger than they are. You're going to do this challenge with your head held high, and it'll be over before you know it. Plus, you have absolutely no reason to be embarrassed about taking your clothes off. Trust me."

He doesn't say it in a flirty way, and that's what makes me believe he really means it. He's not trying to hit on me; he just thinks it's an empirical fact that my body is fit to be seen by strangers. I suddenly don't feel like crying anymore.

"Come on, Dominique," he says quietly. "Let's go swimming. Nobody else is looking. It's just you and me and the water, okay?"

If Natalie and I were watching this show at home and we saw some girl fall behind because she didn't want to swim in her underwear, we'd be disgusted. Nat would probably throw Cheez-Its at the television and shout, "Suck it up, wimp!" I'm sure none of the other girls will have trouble with this challenge—the sorority sisters are probably dying to get out of their clothes, and Miranda's always bragging about how she skinny-dipped in some reservoir in France. She won't expect me to face this challenge head-on, and I picture the respect that will dawn in her eyes when she hears how far her innocent little sister was willing to go to stay in the race. This is my first chance to prove her wrong about me, and I'd be stupid not to take it.

I slip out of my shoes and socks, then turn away from the camera, pull my shirt over my head, and unclip my mike. My bra is dark purple, which won't be see-through in the water, and I tell myself it's the same as a bikini. I wriggle out of my jeans and toss them onto a deck chair. And then I join Will at the pool's edge, holding my head high like Dominique would.

Who cares if I have a shoelace tied around my head like the biggest dork in the world? Who cares if my butt is covered in neon-colored smiley-faces? If I act like I'm the hottest thing ever, like nothing I'm doing is ridiculous or scary, maybe everyone else will be fooled.

"Cute undies," Will whispers. He takes my hand, his fingers warm and strong as they lace through mine, and we jump into the pool together.

Things are better once I'm in the water. Will scours the deep end for rat figurines while I take the shallow end, and we're far enough apart that I almost feel like I'm alone. After the exhausting, sweaty day we've had, the sensation of cool water against my bare skin is heavenly.

"Got one!" Will calls after a couple minutes. He holds a figurine up above his head.

"Let me see." I swim over, and he drops it into my hand. It's about the length of my palm, gray with a long pink tail. As I hand it back, I catch Will sneaking a peek at my chest, just like he did to Miranda at the auditions, and I suddenly like this challenge a lot more.

"Cool," I say. "Twenty-four to go."

Will runs his fingers through his spiky, wet hair—he

looks different without his lucky hat—and then his hand dips back into the pool and settles on my waist. "You doing okay with this?" he asks, low enough that I'm not sure Terry's boom microphone can hear him. He's so close I can feel his breath on my cheek. A little shiver goes through me, and it has nothing to do with the chilly water.

"Yeah," I whisper back. "Thanks." He smiles at me, and then he dives back down, and he's gone. I hope he's checking out my legs underwater.

My glasses-on-a-string contraption works surprisingly well, and over the course of the next half hour, I find ten rats. Will scrounges up the additional fourteen. As I towel off and struggle into my jeans, Will presents the rats to the man in the sarong and stands there in his dripping boxer briefs, waiting for our next instructions. While he's turned away, I can't help staring at the muscles in his smooth, tan back, but then I catch Greg filming my face and smirking, and my cheeks heat up as I turn away. But my embarrassment does nothing to squash my good mood—conquering my fear has invigorated me, and I smile and hum to myself as I pull on my shirt. If I could get through this, maybe the rest of the "seriously steamy challenges" won't be a problem.

Maybe I'm more ready for this race than I thought.

10

Just as Philadelphia and an already-shirtless Blake sprint into the pool area—I guess they didn't end up in Serbia after all—Will returns to my side with our next envelope. "Go ahead and read it while I get dressed," he says, pulling his lucky hat on over his wet hair.

The sound guy makes me wait while he reaches up my shirt and reattaches my mike to my wet bra, and then I rip the envelope open and read the instructions aloud.

> *Make your way by cab to the Pasar Pabean market. In nearby Malaysia, brides and grooms are forbidden to use the bathroom for three days after their weddings, a superstitious practice meant to ensure the health of their future children. In homage to this tradition of "holding in your water," so to speak, you must navigate this crowded marketplace and purchase one srikaya, one bakpao, and a quarter kilo of ikan asin, all while holding a shallow pan of water between you. If you spill it, you must return to the entrance to have your pan refilled. You may not set down the pan at any time. Present your purchases and your full water pan behind the market to receive your next instructions.*

I don't even understand half the words I just read. "What the hell is a *srikaya*? And a *bakpao*?" I say.

At the same time, Will says, "I'm sorry, people aren't allowed to pee for *three days* after they get married?"

I start giggling uncontrollably; I am so, so tired right now. "That doesn't even seem possible, does it?"

"I would just let it flow. Screw my future children. They can keep themselves healthy."

"I guess we should be happy *that's* not the challenge, right?"

As we run out the sliding doors and back into the hotel lobby, I catch Will glancing back at Philadelphia, who has just removed her shirt. It's not exactly surprising that he wants to see more boobs—he is a twenty-one-year-old guy, after all—but it makes me a little sad that my boobs weren't enough for him.

We manage to flag down a taxi, and the driver smiles and nods when we tell him where we're going. Will tries asking him what a *srikaya* is, but he just repeats the word and nods again, which isn't very helpful. A little while later, he drops us off in a small square in front of the market and extracts a few more rupiahs from the stack I hold out. We're getting low on cash—our hour-long ride to the hotel cost a lot, and it was impossible to haggle. I pray a *bakpao* isn't something expensive, like a television or a live cow.

The square is crowded with people carrying heaping shopping baskets and riding bicycles and mopeds, but the pink *Around the World* flag is easy to spot. A middle-aged woman in a long print skirt is waiting for us with a stack of pans and a bucket of water. Though there are no other teams in sight, some of them are probably inside the market already. I peer through the doorway, but it's too dark in there to make out anything but general chaos.

"Okay, let's strategize," Will says. "We should find someone who speaks English and ask them what this stuff is that we're supposed to buy."

There's a group of teenage boys loitering and smoking near the front of the market, and I point them out. "Maybe those guys?"

"Sure. Go for it."

I look down at my feet. "Um, maybe you could do it?"

"They'd probably be more likely to help a cute girl than some random white dude, don't you think?"

As much as I love that Will just called me cute, I feel anything but attractive right now. My butt is damp from the swimming pool, my hair is a bedraggled mess, and I have wet spots on the front of my shirt that make me look like I'm lactating. I don't even like to ask for help at the grocery store at home, where everyone speaks English and I look relatively normal. But I've wasted enough of our time already today. If I can strip on camera, surely I can ask a stranger what an Indonesian word means. "Fine," I say. "I'll be right back."

My palms start sweating as I approach the guys, and I wipe them on my jeans. At first nobody even notices me, but when the boys spot Greg and his giant camera, they all fall silent and look at me. I have no idea what to say, so I try "English?"

"Yes," says one of the guys. He's wearing a red baseball

cap and looks about my age. When he smiles into the camera, he reveals a gap between his front teeth.

"Can you tell me what *srikaya* is?"

His eyebrows furrow. I hold out the card and point to the word. *"Srikaya?"* I say again.

Comprehension dawns on his face. "Fruit," he says.

"What kind? What does it look like?"

He struggles for descriptive English words. "Bump . . . green?"

That doesn't sound like anything I've ever eaten, and there's no way I'm going to be able to find it based on that description. "Can you show me? Inside?" I point at the market.

He looks at his friends. One of them shrugs and says something in Indonesian, and the rest of them laugh. I wonder if they're talking about the wet spots on my boobs, and I cross my arms over my chest. Finally, the guy in the baseball cap says, "America? TV?"

"Yes," I say, hoping that's a good thing.

He nods. "Okay. We go."

"You know what these other two things are, too?" I point to *bakpao* and *ikan asin,* and he nods again. I breathe a sigh of relief. I did it.

I gesture for him to follow me. "What's your name?" I ask as we walk, hoping it won't be something impossible to pronounce.

"Taufik."

"Nice to meet you, Taufik. I'm Claire." I can't believe I'm having a more normal conversation with a random Javanese stranger than I managed to have with a bunch of Middlebury students a few weeks ago. Am I getting braver? Or is it just that I know Taufik won't understand a word I say if I start spouting media theory?

Will is standing over by the pink flag, and I bring Taufik over and introduce him. "He's going to come in with us and show us what we need."

"Nicely done, Claire." Will grins at me, and a warm feeling spreads through my whole body. Maybe I'd be more willing to talk to strangers if I got positive reinforcement every time. I'm like a puppy, and Will's smile is my liver treat.

While Greg presents a waiver to Taufik, I secure the instructions to my forearm with a hair band so I can read them hands-free. Then Will and I hold a water pan level between us while the woman in the print skirt fills it. It's only a little deeper than a cookie sheet, and as soon as we take a step toward the market, it jostles and splashes all over my chest. Now I look like I'm participating in a wet T-shirt contest.

"Oh God, I'm so sorry," Will says. But he doesn't sound that sorry, and I wonder for a second if he dumped the water on me on purpose. A tiny part of me hopes he did.

Taufik looks confused as we hold out our pan to be refilled. "We go to market?" he asks.

"Yes," Will says. "We have to bring this water."

"It's for a game," I try to explain, but I'm pretty sure he still doesn't understand.

Will and I carefully coordinate our steps this time, and we make it to the door without spilling. But once Taufik leads us inside, I lose hope that we'll ever be able to complete this challenge. The market is a dark, confusing rabbit warren of passageways, packed to the brim with shoppers. The roof is translucent, but it's so dirty that hardly any daylight gets through. Fluorescent lights hover here and there like UFOs, reflecting the red paint of the stalls and casting a ruddy glow over everything. A man carrying a massive basket of chili peppers comes barreling out of nowhere and nearly tramples us, and we struggle to keep the water pan level. Taufik disappears into the crowd, his red baseball cap bobbing farther and farther away, and I have to shout his name five times before he hears us and fights his way back.

"Slowly," I say, nodding to the water pan. Even inclining my head makes it splash.

After a while, Will convinces Greg to go ahead of us with the camera, effectively clearing a path for us. We pass massive white sacks full of spices, tables piled high with produce, crates filled with unrefrigerated eggs, and cookware dangling from hooks. Many of the stalls are selling things I don't even recognize. There's an overwhelming smell of seafood and spices and smoke and sweat. It's all pretty amazing, and I wish I weren't carrying this stupid water pan so I could actually look around.

Finally, Taufik pauses at a produce stall and holds up a baseball-sized object that looks kind of like a round, green pinecone. *"Srikaya,"* he announces.

"Awesome," Will says. "Claire, where's the money?"

"Crap. It's in my back pocket."

"Can Taufik get it out for you?"

I don't really want a random stranger sticking his hands in my jeans. "I can get it. Stay really still . . ."

Painstakingly slowly, I reach behind me and try to tug the rupiahs out of my damp pocket. I'm almost in the clear when someone knocks my arm from behind, and I lurch forward, dumping the entire tray of water down Will's front. I hear a gasp and a giggle behind me, and I whirl around to see Philadelphia and Blake. "Oh gosh, I'm *so* sorry," Philadelphia gushes, making her best innocent face. "It's so *crowded* in here!" Bizarrely, her eye makeup still looks perfect, even after swimming. Maybe it's tattooed on.

I feel my face go hot—she obviously hit us on purpose—but I know I can't afford to waste time by losing my temper. What she did is probably against the rules, but it's not like I have any way to report her. "Come on, let's refill this," I say to Will through gritted teeth. As soon as Philadelphia and Blake pass us, concentrating on their pan of water, I pay for the weird green fruit and stuff it into my pack. They move right past the stall without stopping, so they probably still don't know what they're looking for. I think about bumping them back, but that's not the kind of racer I want to be. I don't want to win by playing dirty, unless it involves Samir.

We push through the crowd to the entrance, Taufik and Greg at our heels, and the woman in print refills our tray. Just as we're about to head back inside, Miranda and Aidan sprint up, damp and out of breath. "Hey," my sister pants. "God, our driver got so lost on the way here." She looks down at my wet clothes. "I take it this isn't your first tray of water."

"Nope. But it helps if you get your cameraman to go in front of you. And watch out for Blake and Philadelphia; they'll try to slam into you on purpose."

"Thanks." She holds out her instruction card. "Do you know what any of these words mean?"

I pull our *srikaya* out of my pack. "This is the first one. We don't know about the others yet."

"Come on, Claire," Will urges.

Miranda looks slightly annoyed, but she says, "Go ahead. Good luck."

We trundle back into the market, and Taufik steers us down a different aisle, this one lined with enormous tubs of seafood on ice. Fish with the heads and scales on have always creeped me out a little, but these are arranged so nicely that they're actually kind of pretty. The floor is slippery with half-melted ice and slime, and the fishy smell is overwhelming. "We're going to reek for the rest of our lives," I say.

I expect Will to laugh and agree, but he has a frustrated look on his face and barely responds. "What's the matter?" I ask.

He shrugs a little, and the water pan tips dangerously. "I just don't think you should be giving hints to other teams," he says. "It kind of defeats the whole purpose of the race, you know?"

I get that cold, twisty feeling in my stomach that always happens when someone I care about is mad at me. "But . . . she's not 'other teams.' She's my sister."

"Claire, she's not your partner anymore."

"But she's the whole reason I'm here. I have to help her beat Samir. I promised her I would, no matter what."

"We haven't seen Samir all day. He's probably way at the back of the pack. Miranda doesn't need your help beating him right now."

"Well, yeah. But people form alliances on race shows all the time. What's the big deal if I have an alliance with Miranda?"

"Alliances help both teams. It's not like she's done anything for us."

"She gave us her cab after the first challenge!"

"Yeah, but that wasn't exactly a sacrifice. It's not like she needed it anymore. Plus, that guy was the worst driver ever."

Taufik calls out *"Ikan asin!"* and points at a large basket of crusty dried fish that look like they've been pounded flat with a mallet, eyes and all. I seriously do not want those inside my pack, but I smile and call, "Thank you! One quarter kilo!" Very precariously, I manage to pass him some money.

As Taufik haggles with the fishmonger, Will says, "Look, I'm not telling you to freeze your sister out or anything. But you have to race for yourself. Think about how you're going to look to the viewers if you keep helping her instead of trying to win."

"I'll look like a nice person."

"The race isn't about being nice. It's about winning."

I think back to my second audition, when I told Charlotte I wasn't racing for my sister. I was so cocky then, but maybe Will's right—now that I'm actually here, exhausted and soaked through and reeking of fish, I've slipped right back into my old supporting role. How am I going to make my sister see how competent I am if I don't stay focused and try to pull ahead? Plus, I can't let Will down when he's been so supportive. After all, he's my partner now.

"You're right," I say. "Sorry. I'll be more careful."

"I'm not trying to scold you. All I'm saying is, I bet there are things you could do with half a million dollars, too. You just have to believe you're worth it."

Taufik appears at my side with the bag of dried fish, and I motion for him to tuck it into the side pouch of my backpack. "Okay, we're almost done," I tell him. *"Bakpao?"*

He nods happily—either *bakpao* is something awesome or he can't wait to be finished with us. Judging by the dried fish, it's probably the latter.

It only takes about thirty seconds for a young woman with a basket on her head to crash into us and spill our water again. Taufik has started to get the hang of the game now, and he races back to the entrance, shouting for people to clear a path for us. When we get to the woman in print, Samir and Tawny are getting their pan filled. It gives me great pleasure to see that Samir is dripping wet and extremely pissed off. "God, hold it level!" he snaps at Tawny. "That means *parallel to the ground,* genius!" Then he turns to Will and me and asks, "Do you guys know what we're supposed to buy?"

I angle my body away so he won't see the fish and fruit in the mesh pocket of my bag. "Someone in there told us *bakpao* is pig intestines," I tell him. "We don't know what the other stuff is." I feel kind of bad when Tawny sincerely thanks us, but I can't worry about her right now. Samir has to go, and someone will have to go down with him.

With Taufik and our crew forming a protective little pod around us, we manage to make it all the way to the other side of the market without spilling. Taufik leads us over to a cart near the exit and proclaims, *"Bakpao!"*

Apparently, *bakpao* are big, pillowy dumplings. They smell heavenly, and when the guy behind the cart passes the warm, soft dough to Taufik, my mouth starts watering like crazy. He stares at it so longingly as he tucks it into the pocket of my bag that I tell him to get another one for himself, and he breaks into an enormous grin.

The exit is only a few feet away, and we move with exaggerated care through the jostling crowd. A pink flag is waiting for us just outside, and a bearded man nods as we present our water pan and our three items. When he holds out a pink envelope, I literally jump for joy.

Will rips open the Velcro and pulls out the instructions. On the card is a photo of a sculpture depicting an alligator trying to bite a shark. Greg leans in between us to get a close-up, and Will reads the text out loud.

> *Make your way by cab to this sculpture, which is the Cupid's Nest for this leg of the race. Hurry—one team's race around the world ends here!*

"What's a Cupid's Nest?" I ask.

Will shrugs. "I guess it's like the final check-in point? That's really stupid."

I hold the instructions out to Taufik, who is blissfully stuffing his face. "Do you know where this is?" I ask, pointing to the picture.

He swallows. "Surabaya Zoo."

"Is that far from here?"

"Not so far."

"Thank you, Taufik," I say. "You've been incredibly helpful." I reach for the second *bakpao,* and when the bearded check-in guy gestures that I can take it, I hand it to Taufik. He thanks me, and we run off to find a cab.

"I wanted that dumpling thing," Will grumbles.

"Yeah, me too, but he deserved it. We can always go back for the dried fish, if you want that."

"I'm hungry enough that that almost sounds like a good idea."

I shove his shoulder. "Stop being a baby. We're almost there."

As Taufik promised, the ride to the zoo isn't long, and I nearly weep with relief when I see Isis standing under an arch of pink flags near the base of the alligator statue. Even in the sticky Surabaya heat, she looks totally refreshed, like someone's been spritzing her with iced cucumber water every few seconds.

"Welcome to the Cupid's Nest, Will and Claire," she says when we reach her. "You're in fourth place."

We both cheer—that's better than I thought we'd done— and Will picks me up and spins me in a circle. I love the feel of his strong arms around me.

"How did today go for you two?" Isis asks.

"We wasted an hour because our cabdriver got lost, but otherwise it went pretty well," Will says. "Claire's a fantastic partner. I'm really lucky to have gotten her."

I feel my cheeks heating up, but I don't fight it—the producers will love it if I blush at Will's compliments. "He's pretty fantastic himself," I say.

"I'm so glad this race brought you together," Isis says in a voice laden with meaning. "Perhaps you'll have a chance for more steamy escapades together later on."

"I'd like that," Will says, and he takes my hand. Greg ducks down to get a close-up of our entwined fingers. There are so many emotions swirling through my head that I feel like I might shatter.

Isis points to a little plaza full of topiary shrubs and tells us to wait there until everyone else arrives. There's another *bakpao* cart in front of the zoo's entrance, and I collapse onto the low stone wall surrounding the plaza while Will goes off to buy some for us and our crew. The three teams who beat us are grouped together about ten yards away, and I know I should probably go over and chat with them, but I'm way too tired to move. When Will comes back with the food, I barely find the strength to gobble down two *bakpao*s before I fall asleep on my backpack.

As I drift into unconsciousness, hoping against hope that Miranda beats Samir to the checkpoint, I'm vaguely aware of Will gently tucking a folded sweatshirt under my head.

11

It seems like only a few minutes have passed before Will's shaking me awake again, but it must have been longer—when I slit one eye open, the sun's a lot lower in the sky. It vaguely occurs to me that I still have no idea what day it is. I swat Will away, and I hear him yelp as my hand connects clumsily with his face. "Sleeping," I mutter.

"Come on," he says, nudging me with his toe from a safer distance. "We have to pick our new partners, and then you can rest."

I struggle into a sitting position and peel his sweatshirt off my face. It feels like something flew into my mouth and died. "Who got eliminated?" I ask, trying not to breathe in his direction.

"Lou and that woman with the purple hair, whatever her name is. Jade, or something? They just got in a minute ago." He points off to the right, where Lou and Jada are sitting on a stone wall with one of the producers and doing their exit interview.

"It sucks that Lou's out," I say. "I'm sorry. Are you upset?"

He shrugs. "Nah. No big deal. I'll see him at home in a

couple weeks." His nonchalance surprises me—if my sister had been eliminated, I'd be devastated. But maybe it's different for guys.

Isis arranges us in a semicircle at the base of the alligator statue, and the camera people surround us, careful to stay out of each other's sightlines. Miranda waves at me, and I smile back at her, relieved that she's safe, but we're too far apart to talk. "Congratulations to all of you for completing the first leg of the race," Isis says. "I hope you've all enjoyed getting *very close* to your partners over the last two days. Before you select your new dates, I have a special prize to award. The team who bared the most skin on this leg of the race will receive five thousand dollars each!"

For a moment, I wonder if it could be Will and me, since we did the pool challenge in our underwear. Then again, everyone probably did that. Is it going to come down to who was wearing the skimpiest underwear today?

"The winner of the Bare Bod award is . . ." Isis pauses for dramatic effect. "Blake and Philadelphia! Congratulations!"

I must be really tired, because I only now notice that Blake still isn't wearing a shirt, and Philadelphia's in a sports bra and tiny shorts. Blake's wearing a silver pendant on a black cord that I hadn't noticed before, and when I see that there's a wire running between it and his waist, I realize it must be a microphone. The two of them whoop and hug, and Blake shouts, "Dude, that is awesome! I just took my shirt off 'cause I was hot, and now I get money! *Sweet!*" It's like he's forgotten he's a stripper and he takes off his clothes for money every day.

Isis arranges her perfect features in a more serious expression. "But now it's time for a bit of separation and heartbreak. You will choose your dates for the next leg of the race in the order you arrived at the Cupid's Nest. For this first round, the boys in each pair will go first, and next time, it'll be the girls. Martin and Zora, please step forward."

The last time I saw Martin, he was sweaty and shaking, but he looks way more confident now that he's come in first. Even his superhero shirt seems a little cooler somehow. "Martin, who would you like to spend the next leg of the race with?" Isis asks.

"Um, I'd actually like to stay with Zora, if that's, um, okay with her." Martin gives Zora a shy smile, just barely meeting her eyes. I can tell how afraid he is of being rejected.

"Zora, since you came in first as well, you have the option of rejecting Martin's proposal. What would you like to do?"

"I want to stay with him," Zora says. "Martin's the best." Martin looks at the ground, pleased and blushing and relieved. The viewers are going to love him.

As Isis explains that Martin and Zora will depart for the next leg of the race twelve hours after they arrived, I sneak a sideways glance at Will. Is he going to pick me when our turn comes? Have I been a good enough partner? I think we did pretty well together, and he did tell Isis he hoped we'd have more steamy times together. I try to think of something witty and cute to say when he chooses me, but my sleep-deprived brain is a total blank.

"Steve and Vanessa, please step forward," says Isis. "Steve, who would you like to spend the next leg of the race with?"

"I'd like to race with Miranda, please," Steve says without hesitation.

My sister looks surprised, though I can't imagine why—she's always picked early for things. "Oh," she says. "Okay."

"Miranda, Steve arrived forty-five minutes before you, so he's given you a significant lead," Isis says. "That's very flattering."

Miranda beams at Steve. "Wow, thank you. I'm happy to be your partner." She moves to stand next to him and touches his arm lightly as she says something in a voice too low for me to hear. He blushes, and the camera guys jostle each other to get a good reaction shot. She barely knows him, but somehow my sister's already managing to make Steve feel like a rock star. I wish I knew how to do that.

When it's Vanessa's turn, she chooses Blake, who's currently standing arm in arm with Philadelphia. "Bitch," I hear Philadelphia mutter. Before she relinquishes her big blond prize, she stands on her toes and kisses him possessively on the cheek, leaving behind a smudge of sparkly lip gloss.

It's Troy's turn now. He looks around at the remaining girls, sizing us up like he's at one of those restaurants where you get to pick your lobster live from the tank. "Okay, I'm not gonna lie," he says. "If I'm gonna end up carrying my partner around again, I'm gonna need someone a hellllllll of a lot smaller than Janine. Girl, you are *smokin'*, but you are freakin' *tall*. These guns have their limits." He pats his biceps, then flexes for the cameras. I feel sorry for whoever gets him.

The moment I think it, he points straight at me. "Claire, right? You're tiny. I'll take you."

Oh *crap.* Somehow it hadn't even occurred to me that this could happen. I'm not the kind of person who tends to get singled out by strippers, especially when there are girls like Philadelphia in the mix. As I stand there with my mouth hanging open, Isis prompts, "Claire, please stand with your new partner."

Before I do, I glance back at Will, and he gives me a sad little wave. "Bye, Dominique, I'll miss you," he whispers, and I know he definitely would've picked me if he'd had a chance. The cameras follow me as I walk over to stand next to Troy. "Thanks for choosing me," I manage to say, but it comes out sounding pretty unenthused.

Troy doesn't seem to notice. He wraps one of his giant arms around my shoulders and says, "Fasten your seat belt, baby. You're gonna have some funnnnn with Troy." With his free hand, he high-fives Blake, whose other arm is tucked snugly around Vanessa. Why couldn't Steve have picked me instead of Miranda? I could have handled a nice gentle nerd.

Janine's up next, and when she requests Aidan, Samir's eyes widen with outrage. "What the hell?" he sputters.

"Sorry, dude," Janine says. "Aidan's faster." Miranda smirks, and when Samir glances at her, she innocently picks at something on the front of her shirt, drawing his attention to the Team Revenge logo. I should be loving this whole exchange, but it's hard to concentrate when there are so many other things weighing on me. Like Troy's fifty-pound arm, for instance.

It's Will's turn now, and he says, "I'd like to race with the lovely Philly, please."

Philly? Seriously? Since when are they on a nickname basis? Doesn't Will remember that she's the one who spilled our tray of water on purpose? Then again, maybe that's why he picked her—if you know for a fact someone plays dirty, it's best to have her as an ally. It's good strategic thinking. But it still makes my stomach twist when she goes to stand next to him and takes his hand, twining their fingers together. At least Samir is last in place with Tawny, who looks extremely annoyed.

"I hope you're all pleased with your new partners," Isis says with a custard-sweet smile, though it's very obvious some of us aren't. "I'll see you next time for another episode of *Around the World in Eighty Dates.* Where in the world will you find *your* soul mate?" She says the tagline a couple more times in case the producers don't like the first take, and then the crew starts packing up their equipment.

"All right, everybody," Isis says. "There are two vans here to take you to the hotel. When we arrive, the producers will be doing interviews with you, so please don't jump in the shower or go to sleep right away. After that, we need to give our wonderful crew some time off to rest, and you must stay in your rooms *alone* until the cameras are up and running again. We wouldn't want our viewers to miss out on a single moment of your bonding time with your new dates! In the morning, transportation will be available from the hotel to the starting line every twenty minutes. You will depart twelve hours after the faster person on your team arrived at the Cupid's Nest. Anyone have questions?" Nobody does. We're all too tired to think straight.

I try to maneuver myself into the same van as Miranda, but she disappears into the rear one before I can reach her, and I'm herded into the one in front. I lean my head against the window, too tired to hold it up myself, and pain shoots through my neck—I must have twisted funny while I was sleeping on my pack earlier. I knead the knotted muscles with my fingers, trying to work out the kinks.

"You okay?" asks Troy, who has just slid onto the seat next to me. For a second, he seems more like a human than a caricature—his voice sounds gentler, and he's not drawing out all his vowels in that ridiculous way. But then he destroys the illusion by reaching behind me and touching the base of my neck with his giant hand. "Does your neck hurt? I can work on that for you, if you want."

I flinch away from him. "No thanks, I'm fine."

"Are you sure? 'Cause I'm reeeeeally good at—"

"Seriously, Troy," I snap. "The cameras aren't even on, so knock it off, okay?" It comes out a little louder than I intended, and Vanessa snickers behind me.

"Jesus, Claire, I'm just trying to help. I'm not going to give you cooties if I touch you." When I don't respond, he says, "Fine. Whatever. Enjoy that stick up your butt." He turns around to chat with Blake, and I ride the rest of the way in silence.

A producer hands me my key when I enter the hotel lobby, and I go straight to my room, drop my pack, and collapse facedown on the bed. Usually I'm one of those people who won't even sit on a hotel bed until I've removed the top blanket—I've seen those *Dateline* specials about germs—but right now I'm so tired I'd lie in a bed covered with other people's chewed gum.

I'm floating in and out of consciousness, dreaming about alligator-shark wrestling, when a producer knocks on the door and calls, "Claire? We're ready for you." I shuffle down the hall after her in a stupor, trying to tame my staticky hair. It feels like this day is never going to end.

There are two interview stations set up in a small exterior courtyard full of palm trees and orchids—just like I thought the airport would be—and the producer points me toward the one on the left. I expect to find Will chatting with a producer when I make my way around the backdrop, but instead, Miranda's sitting in the far chair. Her eyes light up when she sees me, and she jumps to her feet and hugs me fiercely. She smells like chlorine and fish and sweat, but underneath is the familiar, cocoa-butter scent of my sister. Out here in the middle of Indonesia, where everything is so alien, that smell and the feel of her arms around me are such a relief that I want to cry. Being with her feels like being home.

"Clairie," she says, close to my ear. "I'm so glad to see you. Are you all right?"

"Of course," I say, confused. "Should I not be?"

She pulls back to look at me. "I hated having you off on your own today, when we were supposed to be together. I wasn't sure you'd be able to—"

The producer cuts her off, and it's only then that I remember he's even there. "Hi, Claire, I'm Ken," he says. "I need to ask you guys some questions, okay? We're running on a tight schedule."

"Oh. Right." I manage to muster up a smile for him. "Hi there."

"Go ahead and sit down," Ken says, and I slide onto the folding chair next to Miranda's. She gives my shoulder a little squeeze, like she has to keep reassuring herself that I'm here and in one piece.

"Now, let's start at the beginning. How do you guys feel about the show's twist? Were you surprised to discover that the race has a romantic component?"

"Yeah, we were both pretty shocked," I say.

"Could you rephrase that for me, using a full sentence? Like, 'We were both pretty shocked by the twist'?"

Oh, right—when they air this interview, they'll edit Ken out. "We were both pretty shocked by the twist," I repeat. "It's safe to say we wouldn't have auditioned for the race if we had known it had a romantic aspect."

"Definitely not," Miranda agrees.

"And why is that?" Ken prompts. He obviously knows, but he wants Miranda to say it on camera.

"Samir is my ex-boyfriend, and he cheated on me with Janine," Miranda says. "They're pretty much my least favorite people in the world right now. The only reason Claire and I even came on the show was to prevent Samir from winning. But I thought it would be us against them, and if I'd known there was a chance I'd have to race *with* him, I would have stayed away for sure."

Ken nods. "Claire, how do you feel about the romantic nature of the show?"

While I'm considering how to phrase my answer, Miranda

144

starts talking again. "Claire doesn't have the same problem I do, obviously, but these kinds of challenges are going to be a bit of a stretch for her. I'm really impressed with her for getting through today. I was so worried about her."

I don't like where she's going with this, and my stomach twists uncomfortably. "I'm *fine*," I say. "Totally unscathed, see?"

"Why are you concerned about Claire's ability to do these challenges?" presses Ken, like I'm not even here.

"Well, I mean, she's clearly the youngest one on the race, and the show is more . . . mature than we were expecting. I'm sure everyone here was equally surprised by the twist, but the rest of us have probably had intimate experiences in the past, so it's not that big a deal. But if you've never really experienced romance before . . . well, this isn't exactly the best way to get your feet wet, you know? It would be so easy for her to get hurt."

I gape at my sister. "You don't get any say in how I 'experience romance'! And you don't know anything about my history with 'intimate experiences.' You've been gone for the last four years."

Concern flits over her face. "Did you date someone I don't know about?"

"No, but—"

"Well, that's what I mean, Clairie. Since you don't know what it feels like to be in a real relationship, it'll be easy to get confused here and start forming attachments, even though it's only a game."

"Miranda, I *know* it's a game, okay? Coming on this show

was my idea, not yours. I know how it works." I really wish we weren't having this discussion on camera. Ken is practically drooling, and none of this is his business.

"I'm just trying to protect you," Miranda says.

"I appreciate that. But I can take care of myself."

"Okay," she says, but she doesn't sound convinced.

Ken changes the subject. "Claire, what was your biggest challenge today?"

I sit up a little straighter and try to take back control of the situation. "My biggest challenge today was when we had to swim in our underwear," I say. "I was really embarrassed at first, but Will was super gentle and supportive, and it wasn't actually that bad once I got used to the idea. I think the only way to succeed on this race is to acknowledge your hang-ups and try to move past them. There are enough obstacles in our way already. We can't create more obstacles of our own." It comes out sounding much better than I expected.

Miranda's eyes widen. "You swam in your underwear?"

"Well, yeah . . . I mean, I wasn't going to swim in my jeans, and they told us there weren't any bathing suits. Wait, did you get one somehow?"

"No, but I made Aidan hold a towel up between me and my camera guy while I changed into shorts. Seriously, Claire, I'm *floored* that you had the guts to do that." She shakes her head in disbelief, and I smile. This part of the interview will balance out what my sister said about my naïveté and inexperience.

"Tell me why you're so surprised, Miranda," Ken says.

"Claire has always been super modest. There was this one

time I took her shopping for bras and I accidentally opened the fitting room door while she was changing, and she was so embarrassed that she started crying and wouldn't come out for forty-five minutes."

I cannot *believe* she's telling this story right now. Ten seconds ago, I was the ballsy little sister, and now I'm the girl who had the freak moment of bravery in a lifetime of shame. Even if Miranda is legitimately proud of me, I know the producers will edit this to make me look ridiculous. If they wanted me to be the show's comic relief, Miranda's playing right into their hands.

"I was *thirteen* when that happened!" I say, trying to keep my voice light. "I've changed a little since then, in case you haven't noticed."

"Yeah, but not only did you strip on TV, you stripped in front of a guy you clearly like," Miranda says. "For you, that takes guts. Way to go, Claire. Seriously."

I am going to *kill* her.

Of course, Ken digs his little claws into that like a kitten with one of those catnip-filled toys. "Is Miranda right, Claire? Are you interested in Will?"

I'm sure my raging blush is enough of an answer, but I try to defuse the situation anyway. "I mean, Will is great, but I barely know him."

"Do you think he's interested in you?"

I think of how Will told me I was worth half a million dollars and how he told Isis he hoped we'd get to do more challenges together. I think of how he sneaked a look at my chest in the pool and how he opened up to me on the plane. But those things are personal—if the network didn't get them on camera, they don't deserve to know. "I guess you're going to have to ask him," I say.

"How do you feel about your new partners for this next round?" Ken asks.

"I was really hoping to get someone else, honestly," I say. "I don't think Troy and I are very compatible."

"Why do you say that?"

"He's . . . um . . ." I try to come up with a nice way to phrase what Troy is, but I can't. "He's kind of sleazy. He started coming on to me in the van on the ride here, and he got really snippy when I told him to back off."

Miranda touches my shoulder. "Do you feel unsafe? We can talk to someone if you do, and maybe you can get special permission to switch partners or something."

When I was in kindergarten, our neighbor Alan Bracknell used to call me names all the time, and Miranda always chased him off our lawn for me. I was grateful to her back then, but it's sad that she thinks I need that same kind of protection twelve years later. I shrug her hand off. "No, it's *fine,* Miranda. He just grosses me out a little."

"What do you think of your new partner, Miranda?" Ken asks.

"It was really nice of Steve to give me a lead," Miranda says. "He seems a little intimidated by me, but once he relaxes, I think we're going to have fun. I wish I could give him to Claire—he's a total gentleman. I know how to handle pushy guys like Troy."

Ken asks a bunch more questions about the specifics of

148

our days, and then he tells Miranda she's done and asks me to come back in ten minutes to do another interview with Will. As I walk my sister toward her room, I debate whether I should ask her to show a little more respect for me on camera. But when she slips an arm around my shoulders and says, "I'm so glad we got to be together for a few minutes," I lose my nerve. I have so little time with her on this race, and it seems stupid to waste any of it fighting.

I squeeze her back. "I wish *you* were my new partner."

"Seriously. I hope I'll get to see a little more of you on this next leg, at least."

Her voice sounds friendly and warm, like she's really disappointed that our bonding trip hasn't worked out as planned. But the things she said in our interview make me wonder if she just wants to be near me so she can keep a closer eye on me. I promise myself that I'll keep racing like I did today, no matter who my partner is, so Miranda will see that my competence wasn't a fluke. She'll see that she doesn't need to protect me. She'll see that even ten thousand miles from home, I can take care of myself.

"Yeah," I say. "I hope you'll see a little more of me, too."

12

The next leg of the race begins for me at 1:07 a.m., and when my alarm goes off at midnight, I pack up my stuff and meet Troy in the lobby. He still looks exhausted—he probably went out drinking or something instead of resting. As the van to the starting line is about to leave, a chattering, giggling Will and Philadelphia pile in behind us, both clutching take-out coffees that didn't come from the hotel. I hate that they clearly got up early to spend more time together, despite the producers' orders not to leave their rooms.

"Hey." Will shoots me a megawatt smile as he settles down in the seat behind mine. "You get some sleep?"

"*I* certainly didn't," Philadelphia chimes in before I can answer. "*This* one snores like a chain saw, and I could hear him through the wall." She giggles and shoves Will's shoulder in a familiar way, as if they've known each other for years, and it makes me want to puke. I turn back around and concentrate on looking like nothing is bothering me.

Isis is waiting for us at the checkpoint, looking as fresh and rested as she did at the starting line in LA. Doesn't she ever sleep? We meet our new camera crew and get miked, and at exactly 1:07, Isis hands us our first pink envelope. I notice she has tiny *Around the World* heart-map decals on her nails. "May the forces of love and luck be with you," she says as I rip open the Velcro.

Fly to New Delhi, India, and make your way to the Lodhi Gardens, where you will receive your next instructions and complete a task of jumbo-sized proportions.

"India," Troy says, nodding slowly. "Sweeeeet. I hope we have time for some of those samoas."

"I think you mean *samosas*," I say. "Samoas are Girl Scout cookies." I can't even believe this guy—this is almost as bad as Blake's comment about Serbia being in Russia.

Troy shrugs. "Either one's fine with me. It takes a lot of nourishment to maintain this kind of hotness, if you know what I mean." And then he *kisses his biceps.* I've never seen anyone actually do that in real life.

Will, Philadelphia, Troy, and I all end up on the same Singapore Airlines flight that leaves at six in the morning, which should get us to New Delhi at three-thirty in the afternoon. Martin, Zora, Blake, and Vanessa are already at the gate, sprawled on the floor with magazines, but Miranda and Steve are nowhere to be found. As soon as the sorority sisters see each other, the room gets noticeably colder, and Philadelphia suctions herself to Will's body like a big blond leech. "Take a walk with me, babe?" she coos, tucking a strand of his hair back under his lucky hat. I know she's probably just trying to prove to Vanessa that she doesn't care about being separated from Blake, but watching Will head off down the hall with her feels like having my organs rearranged. I steer Troy in the opposite direction to look for some food.

When our flight is finally called, I find that we're seated two rows behind Will and Philadelphia. It's close enough that I can hear the rise and fall of their voices, but I can't tell what they're saying, even if I strain. When I lean out into the aisle, I can see a sliver of Will's arm and half of his right shoe, but that's it. I wonder if he's feeling calmer about take-off, now that I've taught him the deep-breathing exercises. Does he trust Philadelphia enough to tell her about his fear of flying? For all I know, he's keeping calm by gripping *her* hand right now.

Troy sees where I'm looking and gives me a sly smile. "Oh, *that's* why you've got such a stick up your butt," he says. "I get it. What, you worried he's going to join the mile-high club with her or something?"

I lean back quickly, my cheeks flaming. Of course he would choose now to start being perceptive. "No," I mutter, though I suddenly wonder if I should be worried about that.

"Maybe we should slip into the bathroom together for a while," Troy says. "Make him niiiiiiice and jealous."

"Um, thanks anyway, Troy, but I really don't want to talk about this."

He shrugs. "Whatever. But this is a game, girl. He's playin' it. You gotta play it, too." He shoves his earbuds in and turns toward the window.

Troy and I don't whisper secrets in the dark. We don't

snuggle close together under our airline blankets. Even as we change money, buy a New Delhi map, and eat breakfast during our layover in Singapore, we barely speak. We're like strangers who happen to be near each other for eleven hours, and by the time we get to India, I'm incredibly lonely.

The moment we disembark onto the burning hot tarmac, I jog to catch up with Will, leaving Troy behind. "How'd you do?" I ask him.

Philadelphia shoots me a dirty look. "How'd we do with *what*?"

For a second, Will looks confused, but then he shoots me a small smile. "Pretty good, thanks to you," he says, dropping his voice so Philadelphia can't hear. I struggle to suppress the goofy grin that wants to explode all over my face—he didn't even tell her. She can flirt with him all she wants, but she can't make him open up to her like he did to me.

"Don't you have your *own* partner to bother?" Philadelphia links her arm through Will's and pulls him ahead, and he turns around and mouths "Later" to me.

The cabs in front of the airport are black with yellow tops and green stripes on the sides, and we pile into one with our crew. Troy makes no effort to tell the driver where we're going, so I lean forward and say, "Lodhi Gardens?"

I have no idea how many people speak English here, and I'm incredibly relieved when he says, "Okay."

"We gotta get there fast fast fast," Troy chimes in. *"Rápido!"*

I stare at him. "Seriously? Did you just say that?"

"What? It's a race."

"*Rápido* is Spanish, Troy. We're in *India*. That is so ridiculously offensive."

He shrugs. "Whatever. *You* talked English to him. I don't get how that's different."

We pull into traffic, and just like that, I forget all about Troy. I've never gotten carsick easily, but driving in India tries even my high tolerance. I'm pretty sure we're supposed to be on the left side of the road, but we weave back and forth so much that I'm not entirely sure which side the cabbie's driving on. He leans on the horn constantly, and we whip around mopeds, jeeps, motorized rickshaws, children, and stray dogs like we're in some sort of horrible race-car video game. Skinny white cows with horns and humps appear out of nowhere and wander across the road, and we nearly plow right into them a couple times. I grip the strap above the door with both white-knuckled hands and stare at the road in front of us, thinking *Stop!* and *Move over!* as loudly as I can, as if I can control the driver with my mind. "He took your '*rápido*' to heart," I mutter to Troy.

"Told you he'd know what I meant," he says, completely missing the point.

In the few brief moments I'm not terrified, I try to take in our surroundings, which are noisier and more colorful than anyplace I've ever seen. Women in bright saris fly by on the backs of motorcycles, the jewel-toned fabric whipping in the wind. Merchants line the roadsides in front of crumbling storefronts, peddling everything from vegetables to electronics. I see one man prostrate on a prayer mat in the middle of a traffic island and another having his beard shaved on a street corner. Monkeys climb around on the telephone poles and nobody pays them any attention, as if they're as ubiquitous as the squirrels back home. I ache to have someone next to me whose hand I can grab as I shout, *Look at that, and that, and that!*

By the time we get to the Lodhi Gardens, I'm so grateful to stop moving that I want to kiss the filthy ground. I hold out a handful of rupees so the driver can extract what we owe, and he takes a couple of bills, which bear Gandhi's face. Then we put on our packs and sprint through the gate and into the gardens. My shoulders are killing me from yesterday, and my pack feels heavier than ever. For a second, I wonder if I should've taken Troy up on his inappropriate offer of a massage.

As soon as we step inside the gardens, it's like we've passed through an invisible force field that repels the Delhi chaos. Everything inside the park is gorgeous and serene and neatly manicured, and the traffic noises fade away under the sounds of chirping birds and rustling branches. The heat even seems a little less oppressive in here. I finally feel like I can breathe, and as I stand still for a minute in the middle of a stone walkway, my shoulders start to relax.

We choose what looks like the main path, and we haven't been walking long before we see a large domed structure that looks like a temple. It's made of stone in various shades of red and tan and brown, surrounded by a crumbling protective wall. A smaller, triple-domed building sits off to one side, and people recline on the steps near its arched doorways, basking in the afternoon sunshine. It's so beautiful and ancient-looking that it makes me lose my breath. But there's no sign of a pink flag or a challenge anywhere.

"Maybe we should go around the back?" Troy suggests. "If it's a jumbo-sized challenge, we'll need a lot of open space, right?" It's weird to hear something so logical come out of his mouth, but I follow him.

And there on the lawn behind the building, draped in pink blankets printed with the *Around the World* logo, are seven elephants dressed in decorative headpieces. They're majestic and wise-looking, and they are definitely jumbo-sized. Childish glee bubbles up in me at the sight of them—I was obsessed with elephants as a kid, and my well-loved stuffed one, Grumby, still sits on my bed at home. I can't believe I get to hang out with real, live ones up close. Finally, a story I actually *want* to tell my friends.

"Dude, those things better not poop on me," Troy says, completely ruining the moment.

As we get closer, I see that each elephant has a pattern of flowers stenciled onto its cheeks and the front of its trunk. Samir and Tawny are standing on either side of one of them, filling in the petals with bright neon paints as if their elephant is a coloring book. It's infuriating that they've managed to pull ahead of us even though their flight was later—they must have had a shorter layover. Two of the elephants are already fully decorated, and I'm pretty sure the one with the blue toenails is Miranda's—that's the shade she prefers for her own toenails.

We choose a girl elephant with spotted markings on her ears, and her handler gives us our next pink envelope. The instructions inside read:

In India, grooms traditionally ride decorated elephants to their wedding ceremonies. When you have correctly decorated your elephant's face and painted its toenails, its handler will give you your next instructions.

I happily gather our paints and brushes and return to Troy. "This is so cool," I say. "Don't you think?"

He shrugs. "I guess."

I decide to ignore him—I won't let anything ruin my elephant bonding time. "Hi, beautiful girl," I whisper to her, patting her trunk. She blinks at me slowly with one enormous, thickly lashed eye and flaps an ear in my direction. I decide to name her Aruba, but I don't say that out loud. I can only imagine how Troy would react.

Will and Philadelphia show up just as I'm starting to apply paint to Aruba's left cheek, and Philadelphia lets out a piercing squeal. "Oh my God, can you even believe how *adorable* they are?" she gushes, bounding up to the elephant beside ours. I try to catch Will's gaze so we can share an eye roll, but he's not paying any attention to me. He just takes the brush and paints Philadelphia offers and gets to work. Maybe he's too focused on the elephants and didn't even see me standing here.

I turn my back and try my best to ignore them, but they haven't been working ten seconds before Will shouts, "Hey! No fair!" When I glance over, there's a streak of blue paint dripping down his tan forearm.

Philadelphia widens her eyes in mock innocence and giggles. "Oopsie! Sorry, I guess I can't tell the difference between you and the elephant. Your skin looks so similar."

I search Will's face, hoping to find annoyance there, but he just smiles mischievously, dips his brush in pink, and edges closer to her. "You naughty, naughty girl," he says, and the warmth in his voice stabs me right in the gut. Then he lunges at Philadelphia, and she shrieks with laughter as he swipes a dripping pink line from her shoulder to her elbow.

I hate that he's touching her on purpose, even with a brush. I hate that he actually seems to be having *fun* with her. For a second I consider ostentatiously flirting with Troy to show Will I don't care, but there's no way I could make that look believable. So I just grit my teeth and try to tune them out as best I can. Painting a live animal is harder than it looks, anyway, and I need to concentrate. Maybe it's just me, but I'm pretty sure Aruba looks annoyed, too.

Way before I'm finished, Troy abandons Aruba's right cheek and moves around to start painting her trunk. "You're not done already, are you?" I snap. "You have to actually paint inside the lines, you know. You can't just slosh it on like you're Jackson Pollock or something." As if Troy would even know who that is.

"Yeah, I knew," Troy says. He dips his brush in orange and starts painting.

Maybe he doesn't understand what "inside the lines" means. I sigh and move around to Aruba's other side, ready to point out what he's done wrong. But Troy's flowers look perfect, way better than mine. He's even managed to do shading on a few of them. "Whoa," I say. "You're really good at this."

He gives me a sarcastic half smile. "Imagine that. A stripper with actual skills."

"No, I didn't mean—I'm just really impressed that—"

"Whatever, Claire. Just keep working."

We don't speak again, except to say "pass the pink" or "here's a clean brush." When I finally finish my side, I start on Aruba's feet—her nails are massive and crusty and kind of gross, but they look a little better once I've spruced them up with pink and green. Will and Philadelphia are now loudly trying to remember the lyrics to the "Pink Elephants on Parade" song from *Dumbo,* and when our handler forks over our next envelope, I'm not sorry to leave. I hate that their flirting has ruined the one and only chance I'll probably ever get to touch an elephant.

"Those guys are freaking annoying," Troy mutters as we move off to the side to open our next instructions, and for the first time, I actually agree with him about something.

Make your way by taxi to Shahwilayat Goat Farms. In some parts of India, it's thought that any baby girl born with a tooth already protruding through her gums is possessed by a ghost. In order to exorcise that spirit, she must marry a goat in a special ceremony. In homage to that, you must search a herd of goats for the one that has a wedding ring tied around its hoof. Present your ring to the farmer to receive your next instructions.

Troy wrinkles his nose. "Uh, she has to marry a *goat*? Do you think she's gotta do *other stuff* with it?"

Leave it to him to go there. "*Ew,* Troy! It's obviously

symbolic. I can't believe you even thought of that." I start heading toward the exit.

He jogs to catch up to me. "How is that not the first thing you thought of?"

"'Cause I actually have some respect for other cultures? 'Cause I'm not totally warped? 'Cause I think about other things besides sex?"

"Thinking about sex doesn't make you warped. Everyone thinks about sex. *Not* thinking about it makes you a prude."

"Not thinking about sex with *goats* makes me a prude?" A couple of women in saris look up from their conversation and stare at us, and my cheeks heat up. I pray they don't understand English very well.

Troy rolls his eyes. "I don't know why I'm even talking to you. Let's just find a taxi, okay?"

The goat farm is a fair distance north of the city, which means a long trip on the terrifying Indian roads. The sections of New Delhi we've seen so far were crowded and noisy, but as we approach the outskirts of the city, the poverty we start to see is so disturbing it makes my chest ache. We drive down street after street where malnourished kids and bony dogs forage through ten-foot-tall trash heaps for bits of food. There's a pervasive smell of burning rubber, intensified by the heat. When we stop at an intersection, children swarm around the car and try to cram their stick-thin arms through our barely open windows. I know nothing's going to happen to us, but I still cringe away from their cupped, begging hands, and then I immediately feel guilty about it. The driver's face is totally impassive as he honks to scatter the kids, and they disperse like a flock of mangy pigeons.

When we finally arrive at the goat farm, a boy who looks a few years younger than me leads us into a giant dirt pen. I expected forty or fifty animals, tops, but there must be more than two hundred of them in here. They're actually pretty cute—small and white, with chocolate-brown faces and droopy ears—but they all look exactly the same, and they're constantly in motion. I have no idea how we're going to keep track of which ones we've already searched. The air is heavy with the smells of hay and manure, and though it's nearly seven o'clock in the evening, it must still be ninety degrees. When Troy strips off his shirt, I don't even blame him. Our sound guy immediately rushes in to give him one of those microphone necklaces.

"What is it with all these stupid animal challenges?" Troy mutters. "I thought this show was supposed to be *sexy*. How am I supposed to be sexy in a field of goat crap?"

Being sexy isn't exactly our biggest problem right now. "How are we going to find this dumb ring?" I say. "There's no way to keep track of the goats."

Troy's quiet for a minute, running his hand over his closely shaven head, and then he says, "What color is your toothpaste?"

"I'm sorry, what?" Is this the beginning of some kind of weird pickup line? "Um, white, I guess?"

"That won't work. We can use mine." Troy rummages through his pack until he finds his toothpaste, which is the blue gel kind. "After we search each goat, I'll put a dab of this on its butt, okay? Then we'll know which ones we've already done."

I stare at him. "That is . . . weirdly brilliant."

A slow smile dawns on Troy's face, and then he looks straight into the camera. "Let the record show that Little Miss Snooty-Pants called me brilliant. Ohhhh yeeeeahhhh." He starts doing this stupid gyrating dance, and I roll my eyes. I don't understand this guy—it's like every time he does something smart, he immediately has to do something idiotic and prove that his brief brush with intelligence was a fluke.

Troy may not be my favorite person, but I have to admit that his method totally works. We check the goats systematically, me searching the hoofs and Troy dotting on the toothpaste and moving the animals along, and about halfway through the herd, we find a little gold ring attached to one of their hoofs with a clear elastic band. I jump up and give Troy a high five, which leaves my hand smelling like manure and peppermint. I'm filthy and my back hurts from crouching down, but for the first time in hours, I'm happy.

That is, until we open our next envelope.

It's time to take a trip to the LOVE SHACK! A LoveMobile will meet you at the farm's entrance and transport you and your date to a secret location, where you will have a full hour alone! Though we'll still be able to hear you when that door closes, no one will be able to see you! So let loose, give in to all your deepest desires, and let those sparks fly!

When I finish reading, Troy says, "Awwww yeeeeahhhh, *that's* the kind of challenge *I'm* talking about." When I look up at him, my horror must be evident on my face, because he bursts out laughing. "Come on, baby. Let's go make some sparks fly." Then he leans very close to me and lowers his voice. "Don't be afraid. I won't bite. Unless you ask verrrrrry nicely."

I swallow hard. Troy already thinks I'm a prude, and he'll never let me live it down if he thinks the idea of spending an hour alone with him in the "Love Shack" makes me legitimately nervous. I'm sure my face is saying too much already. "Thanks, but no thanks," I say, forcing an eye roll. "Let's get this over with."

A producer points us toward the vans, which have tinted windows and giant pink heart decals on the sides. As we climb into the back and set off on the bumpy, swerving ride, I feel a little like I'm being kidnapped. My stomach ties itself into a series of tight knots, and this time it's more than just motion sickness. This is going to be so, so awkward. Objectively, I know the challenge is cheesy and ridiculous. The producers can't really expect that we're going to hook up in their Love Shack. So why can't I laugh the whole thing off, like I'm sure everyone else is doing? What if my sister is right and I'm taking everything too seriously because I don't have any romantic experience?

You can do this, I tell myself. *Let Dominique take over. She can handle an hour alone in a room with a stripper. This is pretty much a daily routine for her.* But I know I'm going to make a fool of myself somehow, no matter who I pretend to be.

"Dude, are you okay?" Troy says. "You look awful."

"Gee, thanks," I snap.

"No, I mean, you look like you're gonna hurl. Are you gonna hurl? Please don't do it on me."

I shake my head. "I'm fine, just a little carsick." Maybe he'll stay far away from me once we get to the Love Shack if he thinks there's still a possible threat of vomit.

A producer is waiting to meet us when we arrive, and he ushers us into a restaurant and leads us through to a tiny private room in the back. In one corner is a table set with a basket of strawberries, a pot of melted chocolate, and a bottle of what looks like champagne but is probably sparkling cider. Piled in another corner is a bed-sized heap of pillows in shades of pink and red and gold. The room smells strongly of incense, and dozens of pink candles cast a flickering glow over everything. Next to the pillows, I spot a large bottle of massage oil. There's low music with a strong beat playing in the background, the sort I imagine might be used to underscore porn.

"Welcome to your very own Love Shack," says the producer, and his tone makes me suspect he thinks this whole setup is as ludicrous as I do. "Your hour alone starts now. Your camera crew won't be in here with you, but your mikes will remain on. If you choose to remove any clothing, please do not remove your mikes, or we'll have to stop the timer while we send your sound guy in to reconnect them. Before we begin, I need you both to sign these release forms agreeing that the network is not liable if you contract a sexually transmitted disease while on our show. Do you have any questions?"

"I'm sure we'll be fine," I say before the conversation can get any more disturbing. It's bad enough that our sound guy is now swapping out my microphone for the necklace kind, like it's a given that I'm going to take off my shirt.

"See you in an hour," the producer says. "Enjoy yourselves." He closes the door behind him, and my stomach turns over as I hear the lock engage.

I cross my arms, then uncross them and wipe my hands on my filthy jeans. I feel intensely awkward standing here in the middle of the room, especially because I'm positive there's a hidden camera somewhere—they would never let us go unfilmed for an hour. The pile of pillows in the corner actually looks kind of inviting, but after that mention of STDs, I'm not sure it's safe to touch anything. I set down my pack and perch on the very edge of one the straight-backed chairs, absently rubbing my aching shoulders.

Troy sits down across from me. "You sore?"

"Yeah, kind of. It's fine."

"You know, I could help with that. There's even massage oil over there."

I must be even more tightly wound than I thought, because that one little comment is all it takes for me to snap. Before I can stop myself, I'm yelling. "Troy, knock it off, okay? Stop making stupid innuendoes, stop coming on to me, and stop trying to *touch* me! Just because we're stuck in this ridiculous room together doesn't mean I'm actually going to *do* anything with you, okay? I'm sorry if you have some sort of weird expectation because this turned out to be a dating show, but I'm not going to take off my clothes. If that's what you were after, you should have picked Philadelphia as your partner."

Troy rolls his eyes. "I don't want you to take off your clothes. Trust me." He says it like the very thought disgusts him, which is actually kind of insulting.

"Then why do you keep feeding me cheesy pickup lines and getting pissed at me when I reject you?"

Troy shoves his chair back and starts pacing around the room. "Oh my God, Claire, I'm not pissed that you're rejecting me! I don't want to hook up with you. You're covered in paint, and you smell like goats, and you're *way* too young for me. Not to mention the fact that I'm *gay*."

I blink at him. "Wait, seriously?" Suddenly, nothing makes sense.

"Yeah, seriously. Is that a problem?"

"I mean, no, of course it's not a problem. But if you like guys, I *really* don't get why you're pissed at me right now!"

"I'm pissed because you've been acting like a judgmental asshole all day! The second you looked at me, you wrote me off as a moron!"

"Well, aside from the toothpaste idea, it's not like you've done much to change my opinion, Troy! 'Can we get some *samoas* in New Delhi?' 'Come on, Indian cabdriver, drive *rápido*!' 'Yeeeeah, baby, fasten your seat belt, you're gonna have funnnn doing steamy challenges with Trooooooyyyy.'" I stand up and imitate his stupid gyrating dance to drive my point home.

"I'm *playing a character*! This is a *television show*! The producers wanted a big, stupid frat boy, and that's what I'm giving them, okay? You could at least *try* to see past the surface."

Somehow, even though I know Will's CEO-dad story is fake, it never occurred to me that other people's backstories might be, too. How did that not cross my mind until now? Then again, it doesn't change the fact that Troy's advances, real or not, are grossing me out. "Fine, play an idiot for the cameras if you want," I say. "I don't care what image you present. But leave me out of it, okay? If you don't even *want* to touch me, stop offering to *massage* me! The fact that you're gay doesn't make it less creepy!"

"I'm a licensed massage therapist, Claire! You said you were sore, so I was trying to help you! But that was obviously a mistake. Don't worry, I won't make it again." He puts his hands up in sarcastic surrender.

I stare at him. "You . . . *what*?"

"You don't even believe me, do you? 'Cause someone who looks like me couldn't possibly have a real career, right? I mean, how could I think actual thoughts when all my blood is being diverted to my giant pecs?"

"No, I just . . . you're not screwing with me right now? You really went to school for massage therapy?"

"Want me to prove it? I can name every muscle in your body. Ready?" He grabs my forearm and starts pointing.

"*Brachioradialis. Extensor carpi ulnaris. Extensor pollicis longus. Extensor digitorum communis . . .*"

I yank my arm away. "Okay, God, I believe you. But . . . wait, are you even really a stripper? Or did you make that up, too?"

"I strip to pay my student loans. Drunk bachelorettes tip really well, okay?"

This is becoming more fascinating by the second. "What about Blake? Is he a massage therapist, too?"

"Blake's in business school."

This totally explains the bizarre way Troy has been acting all day, trying to offset every smart idea with idiotic, testosterone-fueled behavior. His intelligence isn't a fluke. He's trying to cover it up. I try to think of something to say, but my mind is reeling, and all that comes out is an inarticulate "Wow."

"Yeah. Wow."

"Hey," I say. "I'm really sorry."

He shakes his head. "It's okay. I guess you couldn't have known." He stops pacing and plunks himself down on the pillow heap.

"I could have been less of a jerk, though," I say, and he doesn't argue.

We're both quiet for a minute, and then I say, "You know they're recording everything you tell me, right? So you've blown your cover now."

"It doesn't matter. They won't air any of this, except maybe the part where you're shrieking at me not to touch you. They want me to seem dumb and horny and uncomplicated."

"Why do you have to act how they want? You're already on the show, it's not like they can do anything to you now."

"Are you kidding? They're still totally in charge. If they don't like what I'm doing, they won't give me any airtime, or they'll manipulate things so I get eliminated earlier. Stuff like that happens all the time. And I want that million dollars. Prancing around in a G-string is starting to get really old."

"Yeah, I can see that." I take a strawberry and bite into it, then hold the bowl out to him. "Want one?"

"Sure. I'm starving."

We pass the bowl back and forth until all the berries are gone, and neither of us says anything the whole time. I know I should be thinking deep thoughts about the mismatch between surface appearances and interiors, but the only thing running through my mind is *I'm locked in a room in India, eating strawberries with a stripper masseur. How is this my life?*

I finally ask, "Do you think anyone's really going to hook up in here? Do you think anyone already has?"

This clearly hasn't occurred to Troy, and his face changes. I laugh as I watch him struggle out of the pillow heap while trying not to touch anything with his bare hands. "Probably not. But . . . just to be safe."

He sits back down in the chair across from mine, and we stare at each other awkwardly. "So, what now?" he asks.

It would be easy to sit here in silence for forty-five more

minutes, listening to the porny music and reading magazines. But the producers have put us in this room to bond, so maybe we should just give in and get to know each other. After all the stupid assumptions I made about Troy, I kind of feel like I owe it to him. So I pour him a glass of sparkling cider and extend it like an olive branch. "Tell me," I say. "If you could only eat foods starting with one letter for the rest of your life, which would you pick?"

And amazingly enough, the rest of our hour flies by.

13

The moment we're released from the Love Shack, the producer sits us down for a quick interview in the main restaurant area while another guy sweeps into the back room to prepare for the next couple. "So, how did you enjoy your date?" our producer asks, totally deadpan.

"Our date was niiiice," Troy says, waggling his eyebrows and slipping seamlessly back into the role of a meathead. "When things get hectic, it's always good to take some time out with a lady friend, if you know what I mean. And Claire's quite the little wildcat when you get her riled up." I feel like I've actually made a friend over the last hour, and it's sad to see him disappear again.

"Claire, did you learn anything about Troy that you didn't know before?" the producer asks. "Aside from the obvious. We'd prefer you not talk about that."

Troy nudges me as if to say, *See?*

"Troy has hidden depths," I say, and I give my best mysterious smile.

"Good job," the producer says. "Here are your next instructions."

This is probably our last challenge for today, and I give a little sigh of relief. If I could get through an hour in the Love Shack, I can get through anything. Then it'll be a brand-new leg of the race, and I'll get a brand-new partner who isn't actively trying to look like an idiot. Maybe I'll even get Will back.

Troy reads our instructions aloud.

Make your way by taxi to the Saubhāgya Ballroom. Before an Indian wedding, it is traditional to throw a sangeet party, during which family and friends of the bride and groom entertain the couple by performing songs and dances. When you arrive at the party, you will don traditional Indian clothing, and then you will have three minutes to entertain the wedding party with your sexiest dancing. Bring your hottest moves!

Troy grins at me. "Hellllll yeah! Sexy dancing? I am *alllll over* this. Let's go!"

Every time I think I've reached my maximum level of discomfort, the producers find a way to push me one step farther, so it figures they've finally landed on the one thing I hate most in the world. As we start our treacherous journey back toward the center of the city, all I can think about is my ridiculous, failed attempt to dance at Miranda's graduation party. It was humiliating enough that I couldn't do what came naturally to everyone else when I was an anonymous body in a sea of strangers. And this time, people will actually be paying attention—I'll be front and center, showcasing my paralyzing performance anxiety for a wedding party, a bunch of producers, and millions of viewers. Will it count if

I stand in the middle of the stage, frozen with terror, while Troy sexy-dances around me? In front of all those judging eyes, will I even be able to stay on my feet for three minutes, or will I just keel over in a mortified heap?

"What's up with you?" Troy says. "Why do you have that pinched-up look on your face again? Sad our time in the Looooove Shack is over?"

I don't want him to know how afraid I am, so I just swallow hard and say, "Um, I don't really dance."

Troy shrugs. "No biggie. Just pretend you're at a party and do whatever you usually do. Trust me, once I turn on my moves, nobody's gonna be looking at you, girl."

If only Troy knew that the parties I go to usually consist of popcorn and movie marathons.

Way before I've managed to slow my racing heart, we arrive at the hotel where the ballroom is located. Even all the way down the hall from the party room, we can hear the thumping beat of Bollywood music, and when Troy pushes open the door, my knees go weak. Since this is a pre-wedding party, I wasn't expecting that many guests. But the room is packed with hundreds of people, all grouped around a make-shift stage where three women in blue saris are performing a choreographed routine. Off to the side, I spot Samir and Tawny, dressed in their Indian outfits and waiting for their turn to entertain the crowd. Samir is in a red embroidered robe that falls past his knees, tight gold pants, and a sparkly scarf, and Tawny is wrapped in a hot-pink sari. Both of them are bopping their heads to the music, and neither one looks remotely nervous.

A small redheaded producer leads Troy and me toward two makeshift dressing rooms made of folding screens on the far side of the room. Troy disappears into one of them, and the producer directs me into the other. "When you're done getting dressed, stand where Samir and Tawny are now and wait your turn, okay?" she shouts over the music. I don't trust my voice not to tremble, so I just nod and slip behind the screen.

And miraculously, like the universe knows exactly what I need right now, there's my sister. I launch myself into her arms, ignoring the tiny woman who's dressing her in a forest-green sari, and Miranda's hand automatically flies up and starts stroking my hair. "What's wrong? What happened? Did Troy do something to you?"

I shake my head. "I can't dance in front of all these people, Mira," I say close to her ear. "I can't dance at all, in front of anyone, ever. You know how I get in front of crowds."

I feel her sigh. "Yeah, I know how you get. But you have to do this, babe. You don't have a choice."

"I don't think I can." Now that someone I trust is finally here next to me, I feel like I'm about to cry.

"I know it's scary, but you're strong," she says. She rubs my back in the same comforting pattern my mom always used to do when we were little—*circle, circle, pat pat pat.*

"I'm not. Maybe I should just quit now, before I make a complete fool of myself."

And just like that, the patting stops. Miranda pulls back, holds me at arm's length, and stares into my face. I expect to see sternness there, but weirdly, she looks a little desperate.

"You can't quit," she says. "How could you do that? You're the one who convinced me to come here, and now you want to back out on me? Because of *this*?"

"Miranda, I—"

"It's not like you have to bungee jump or eat live bugs or something. All you have to do is stand on a stage and move around for a couple minutes. You don't even have to do it *well*. This is not a big deal, Claire."

"It's a big deal to me," I whisper.

"I know, and I'm sorry. But you keep telling me you can take care of yourself, and I need you to do that now, okay? You're going to get through this." She squeezes my shoulders and gives me a quick kiss on the cheek, her hair a cocoa-scented whisper against my face. "It'll be over before you know it."

And just like that, she's gone.

I stare after her, openmouthed. I guess I shouldn't be surprised—of course she can't stay and talk this through with me while the clock is running. But if the two of us really are a team, like we promised each other at the starting line, shouldn't I be her priority right now? I understand that she wants to beat Samir to the checkpoint, but I'm almost certain there are several teams behind us, so it's not like she has to pass him to stay in the game. We'll have plenty of chances to get ahead of him later. Miranda's always implying that I need my hand held, but now, when I actually *do,* she's not willing to help.

The woman who was dressing my sister touches my arm, and I jump—I forgot she was there. "Clothes off," she orders.

I undress mechanically, and when she hands me a purple shirt and underskirt, I put them on without a fight. The shirt ends just below my rib cage, but when I try to pull it down to cover my stomach, she slaps my hands away. Then she starts wrapping me in yards and yards of purple and gold fabric, folding it into my waistband, pulling it over my shoulder, then pleating the remaining fabric and tucking it in near my belly button. She doesn't use any pins or fasteners, and I'm afraid the whole ensemble is going to fall apart the second I move. But when I test it, it feels surprisingly secure.

The woman glues a ruby-colored *bindi* to the center of my forehead, slips a few gold bracelets onto my arms, and surveys her work. I guess I must look acceptable, because she gives me a little shove, and I stumble out of the dressing room and into the crowd.

Troy is waiting for me with our crew, wearing a cream-and-gold robe that looks great against his dark skin. "Whoa," he says, looking me up and down. "Fancy."

I smooth the fabric of my sari, trying not to show how much my hands are shaking. "Yeah. I'm a little worried it's going to fall off, though."

He shrugs. "No big deal. I usually take my clothes off while I'm dancing."

Against my will, I smile a little. "Try to keep them on this time, okay?"

"I can't make any promises, baby. These abs can't be contained for long."

Samir and Tawny pass us on the way back to the dressing room, and Samir accidentally-on-purpose bumps me with his shoulder. "Too bad I can't stick around to watch *you* two dancing together," he snorts. "*That's* going to be a hot mess."

Did Miranda mention to him that I have a thing about dancing? Or is he just trying to rattle me? I try to think of a snappy comeback that'll rope him into an argument and slow him down so my sister can pull ahead. But I'm not great with comebacks even at the best of times, not to mention when I'm so nervous I can barely breathe. Before I can say anything at all, he's walking away.

Miranda and Steve take their places onstage, and the whole crowd whistles and cheers. Steve looks a little fidgety, but my sister's totally calm and composed, as if she performs dance routines in a sari every day. Before I manage to fight it back, a wave of jealousy and anger consumes me. Why did she have to take so much in the genetic lottery? Did she really need *all* the coolness, all the poise, every ounce of fearlessness? Couldn't she have left the tiniest bit for me? Miranda didn't even want to come on this show in the first place, and everything is still so *easy* for her, while I have to struggle for every accomplishment. And because my sister is the way she is, she'll never even understand how hard this is for me or how much I've already overcome.

"I guess we should go up there and wait," Troy says, breaking my train of thought. "You ready?"

I am the opposite of ready. For a second, I consider finding the redheaded producer and telling her I'm done, that the race is more than I can handle. Miranda doesn't need my help to beat Samir; if I left right now, she'd be absolutely fine. But quitting would only cancel out the small amount of headway I've made and show my sister that she's been right about me all along. This dancing challenge might be a massive failure, but I have to at least try, if only to prove I'm not a helpless little girl who spends her life cowering inside her comfort zone.

I give Troy a tiny nod, and he starts pushing through the crowd. The stage feels like it's physically repelling me like the wrong end of a magnet, and I have to fight to take each step forward. If I can barely make myself walk, I have no idea how I'm going to make myself dance. But before I know it, I'm standing in the wings and awaiting my three minutes in the spotlight.

My sister looks fluid and gorgeous as she whirls around the stage, shimmying her hips to the peppy Bollywood beat. She's not even doing anything sexy, but she looks so comfortable in her own skin that she's captivating to watch. I glance over at Steve, expecting him to look as awkward as I will—maybe it'll make me feel better. But he's doing this goofy, ridiculous move that involves hopping from side to side and doing a wave motion with his arms, and he's so committed to it that it's hilarious instead of embarrassing. The bride, who's sitting front and center, laughs uproariously and claps her hennaed hands, and the groom seems to be recording the performance with his phone.

Way too soon, the music ends, Steve and Miranda bow, and it's my turn.

I'm so terrified now that I feel oddly removed from the world. Troy walks out to the center of the floor, confident and sure, and my feet follow against my will. Miranda says something to me as she hurries past, but my head is full of a strange rushing noise that blocks out all other sounds. As I stand in the middle of the stage and stare out into the enormous audience, my vision starts to tunnel, and tiny sparks wink to life around the edges. I realize I've stopped breathing, and I take a giant gulp of air and forbid myself to pass out. There's only one thought in my mind, and it blares over and over, loud as a siren.

I can't do this. I can't do this. I can't do this.

The music starts, and I hear the thumping bass as if it's coming from underwater. Troy starts dancing, lifting his robe to display his rippling abs and swiveling hips, and everyone goes insane. I watch with detached interest as he flexes his butt cheeks one at a time. Then I see a guy in a yellow robe point at me and laugh, and I realize how ridiculous I must look, rooted to the spot like I'm playing freeze tag. I order my body to move, even just a little, but I'm way past being able to control my limbs. They don't even feel like they belong to me anymore.

The redheaded producer is frowning at me from the corner of the room, and her eyes stay locked on me as she says something into her walkie-talkie. Maybe she's calling in reinforcements to coerce me into dancing. If I don't start moving right this second, she'll probably refuse to give us credit for this challenge. Maybe she'll start the music over from the top. Maybe she'll make me dance alone. My cheeks feel wet, and I realize with horror that I'm crying. This is, without a doubt, the most humiliating thing I have ever experienced.

Just as I'm considering fleeing the stage and hiding under

a rock for the rest of my life, I feel a hand on my shoulder. I flinch away, sure someone has come to reprimand me. But it's only Miranda, still dressed in her sari and bangles. "What are you doing up here?" I try to say, but I'm not sure any sound comes out.

She doesn't offer an explanation. Instead, she gently turns me to face her and takes both my sweaty, shaking hands in hers. And then she starts to dance.

It's simple at first, just an easy side-to-side bounce. I try to forget about all the people staring at me and concentrate on my sister's face—her bright blue eyes, the tiny constellation of freckles sprinkled across her left cheekbone, the dimple in her chin—and feeling slowly creeps back into my limbs. I start to shift along with her, moving my feet back and forth, and she squeezes my hands to let me know I'm doing okay. When her shoulders and hips start to move, I try to copy her as best I can, and she smiles and nods encouragingly. Then she lets go of one of my hands so she can spin me around, and an unexpected laugh flies out of my mouth.

I'm actually doing this. I'm *dancing*. On a stage, in front of people. My body's not as fluid as Miranda's by a long shot, but I'm moving to the beat, and it feels . . . well, it feels kind of *good*. Nobody's booing or laughing or throwing things at me. And incredibly, I realize I'm actually having fun.

Now that I've started, dancing feels like something I've always been able to do, a skill that's been locked away inside me for so long I forgot it was even there. I jump up and down and bop my head back and forth, and Miranda grins and does the same. Troy shifts over to the left to make more room for us, and we spin forward to fill the space. As Miranda links her arm through mine and starts doing silly Rockette kicks, the crowd and the cameras cease to exist for me altogether, and I suddenly remember how my sister and I used to dance around her bedroom to the Backstreet Boys when we were little. Miranda was the only one who could ever make me feel that free and uninhibited, like I could stop overthinking everything and just enjoy being alive.

And for a few short minutes, as we spin around this stage on the other side of the world, it seems possible that some-day I could learn to be this way all on my own.

When the song ends, Miranda turns me toward the bride and groom and holds my hand up like I've won a boxing match, and the whole room erupts in applause. Everyone's cheering us on, even the redheaded producer. After a few seconds, I turn and look at my sister, who gives me the most gigantic grin I've ever seen. I smile back so hard my face hurts.

I can barely hear her over the noise of the crowd and the adrenaline pumping through my blood, but I see her mouth form the words "You did it."

And for the first time in as long as I can remember, being myself feels like enough.

14

It's nearly midnight by the time Miranda, Steve, Troy, and I find Isis at the Cupid's Nest in front of India Gate, which looks sort of like an Eastern-style Arc de Triomphe. We check in—Miranda and Steve are third, and Troy and I are fourth, by two minutes—and then my sister and I look around for a place to rest until the other teams show up. There are no benches on the vast plaza, so we finally plunk down on the ground and prop ourselves up with our packs. "So, other than the dancing, how'd your day go?" she asks.

"I'm just glad it's over," I say. "Mira, thank you so much. Seriously. I don't know what I would have done without you up on that stage."

"Don't worry about it. It was no big deal."

"It *was* a big deal. I was totally freaking out up there, and you—"

"Clairie," she says, cutting me off, "you're the one who said we're a team no matter what, remember? If you need me, I'll be there for you, okay? And I know you'll do the same for me."

I can't think of a situation in which Miranda would need

my help, but I nod. "Of course I will. But every minute counts here, so I appreciate the sacrifice."

"We'll just regroup and race faster tomorrow." Miranda leans back against her pack and stretches her arms over her head as we watch Janine and Aidan jog across the plaza. "God, I'm so sore from squatting down in that stupid goat pen," she says.

"Troy could help you with that."

She snorts. "How? By taking his clothes off to distract me?"

"No, apparently he's a licensed massage therapist. One of the many strange things I learned today."

"What? How is that even possible? He seems dumb as a brick."

"Actually, he's bizarrely smart. He says he's been acting like a idiot on purpose because that's what the producers want."

"Huh. Crazy."

We sit quietly for a minute, absorbing that and watching the tourists taking late-night strolls, and then Miranda says, "Hey, you want to play the Limerick Game?"

"*Yes.* That's *exactly* what I want to do right now."

"You first. Do Troy." She looks down at her watch and times out a minute.

When it's time, I clear my throat and recite:

"There once was a stripper named Troy,
Who acted quite dumb as a ploy.
He took off his pants,
Did a butt-shaking dance,
And said, 'Viewers, I hope you enjoy!' "

Miranda laughs. "Nice," she says. "My turn."

"Do Isis."

She thinks for a second. "No fair. Nothing rhymes with 'Isis' except 'crisis.' Which is kind of ironic." We both look over at our host, who's dressed in a crisp linen suit without a single wrinkle. A crisis wouldn't dare get close to her.

"Yeah, you're right. Do Steve instead."

When a minute has elapsed, she says,

"There once was a fellow named Steve,

Who everyone thought was naïve.

But he's sharp as a tack,

Not a geeky sad sack—

He has proven that looks can deceive."

"Oh, reeeeeally," I say. "What happened during *your* hour in the Love Shack? Did the sparks fly?"

My sister laughs. "Oh God, wasn't that the most ridiculous thing you've ever seen? And no, of course nothing *happened*. We just ended up having a ton in common, which was surprising, you know? I thought he would, like, babble on about Dungeons and Dragons for an hour, but we actually spent most of the time talking about Russian novels. And he's really funny. I was totally impressed."

"That's awesome, Mira. I'm glad you guys had fun."

"I'm going to pick him again for the next leg, if I can. He was a great partner."

That makes me think of Will, and I scan the plaza for him, but he's still nowhere to be found. I haven't seen him since the elephant challenge this morning; Philadelphia's probably slowing him down with all her inane flirting. If she gets him eliminated, I will seriously gouge out her eyes with my fingernails, glitter eye shadow and all. I bet that would boost ratings.

"What're you looking at?" Miranda asks.

"Nothing. Just trying to see if anyone else has gotten here yet."

"You suck at lying. You're looking for Will, aren't you?"

I shrug. "Okay, so what if I am? He should be here by now." Miranda gives me a look, half knowing and half concerned. "*What?* Spit it out."

"I just don't want you to get too attached to him, that's all."

"I'm not *attached* to him. I just like him, okay? If you and I can't race together, we should race with other people we like, right? You like Steve. I like Will."

"I don't like Steve the same way you like Will. Steve and I both know it's a game. I'm afraid that maybe you forget about the game when you're with Will."

I think about how he looked at me when I was in my underwear, how his hand felt as it settled against the skin of my bare waist. "Well, not everything *is* a game, okay?"

"It is when you're on television."

"He *likes* me, Miranda. He does. You haven't seen what he's like when we're alone and the cameras are off. The stupid 'steamy challenges' are a game, but that other stuff is real."

"I mean, I can't tell you for sure that it's not. But you

should try to keep your defenses up, or you're going to get hurt."

"I don't need to defend myself from him!" A couple walking by turns to stare at us, and I lower my voice. "Do you not believe someone could like me that way? Is that the problem?"

"Claire, no. But he's an actor, and this is a show. I have a lot of experience with actors, and I know what they're like. Trust me."

"You can't assume that all actors suck just because *one* of them does! Will isn't like Samir!"

She sighs. "Listen, I hope you're right. And if you want to race with Will, I can't stop you. But we're not *actually* here to find our soul mates, okay? We're here to—"

"I *know* why we're here," I snap.

"I'm just trying to help you."

"Fine."

"I don't want you to think that—"

"I said *fine,* Miranda."

"Okay. Good."

Awkward silence stretches out between us, so thick and palpable I feel like I could poke it with my finger and watch it wiggle like Jell-O. I want everything to go back to how it was ten minutes ago, and I think about asking her for another limerick topic, but now the atmosphere is all wrong for our lighthearted game. I suggest finding something to eat instead, and we wander around the plaza until we find a food stall. Neither of us says much of anything as we eat our *pakoras.* I tell myself everything's still fine, that we're

186

just tired. But Miranda's words grate on me, and I don't start to feel better until I spot Will and Philadelphia checking in with Isis. As soon as he spots me, Will smiles and waves. I know my sister's wrong about him. There *is* something real going on between us. She'll see.

It's nearly two in the morning by the time Isis assembles us for the Proposal Ceremony, and by that time, everyone is tired and cranky. Blake and Vanessa arrive last and are swept away for their exit interview, and I hear Vanessa telling the producer they "got a little sidetracked in an alley for a while, but it was *totally* worth it." I take my place across the semicircle from Will. Philadelphia is still clinging to his arm, but I just smile, knowing I'll probably get to separate them any minute.

"I hope sparks flew for everyone in the Love Shack today," Isis says. I have no idea how she delivers these lines with a straight face. "Before you choose your dates for the next leg of the race, I have a special prize to award. The bride and groom enjoyed all your performances enormously, but they agreed that one couple had the hottest moves of all. And that couple, who will receive the Sexy Strut award of five thousand dollars each, is . . . Will and Philadelphia!"

Will lets out a whoop, and Philadelphia screams and jumps into his arms. Her legs wrap all the way around his waist like they belong there, like they've been there before. I suddenly feel a bit sick. Thank God I didn't have to watch them dance together.

"Congratulations," Isis says. "How did you feel about your performance today?"

"Will and I are *such* a great team," gushes Philadelphia. "I honestly can't believe I got *paid* to dance sexy with him. I would have given *you guys* money to do it."

Isis lets out a practiced, tinkling laugh. "I'm glad you enjoyed doing it as much as everyone enjoyed watching you. It's thrilling to watch you connect with your partners in meaningful ways." She claps once. "All right! Now it's time to choose your dates for the next leg of the race! We'll start with the girls this time. Zora, you're up first again—congratulations. Who would you like to spend the next leg of the race with?"

"I'd like to stay with Martin," she says. "This partnership is obviously working for us. Don't mess with success, right?"

Martin lets out his breath in a rush, revealing how nervous he was that he might have to race with someone else. "Definitely," he says, nodding hard. When Zora reaches out and takes his hand, he goes red all the way to the tips of his ears.

"Next up is Tawny," Isis says. "Who would you like to spend the next leg of the race with?"

"I'd like to race with Troy," she says, shooting Samir a dirty look. "It'll be a relief to race with someone who actually respects me as a human being."

Troy waggles his eyebrows. "Ooooh, baby, I will respect you like you've *never* been respected before." He moves to stand next to her and wraps an arm around her shoulders, and Tawny giggles like a twelve-year-old. I've got to hand it to Troy—he is really good at staying in character.

Samir is next, and when Isis asks who he'd like to race

with, he smiles at her, the kind of smile that says *I know something you don't know.* "I'd like to race with Miranda," he says.

Oh *no.*

I feel my sister tense beside me, and I instinctively reach for her hand, but she's not paying any attention to me— she's staring at Isis with her mouth hanging open. "No," she finally sputters. "I, um, I reject Samir's proposal."

"I'm sorry, Miranda," Isis says, "but you don't have the option of rejecting him. Samir arrived at the Cupid's Nest before you."

My sister looks totally bewildered. "But . . . I can't race with *him.*"

"Those are the rules, I'm afraid. Your only other option is to withdraw from the race. You don't want to do that, do you?"

"No, I don't want to do that." Miranda's voice is quiet, but there's an undercurrent of fury that makes the hairs on my arms stand up. She whirls around to face Samir. "What are you doing? Did they tell you to pick me?"

He blinks innocently. "I'm sorry, who's *they*?"

"I don't know, the network. The producers. You can't seriously want to be my partner."

Samir shrugs. "Why not? You broke up with *me*, Miranda. I never had a problem with you. I'm not the one who wanted our relationship to end."

"If you didn't want our relationship to end, you should've stayed out of *her* pants!" Miranda stabs a finger in Janine's direction. All around the circle, people start murmuring, and

189

I realize it's still not common knowledge that Miranda and Samir used to be together. I wonder if the producers really did tell him to pick her. If I were the story editor, that's probably what I would have done.

"Nobody told me to do anything," Samir says. "I never even got to talk to you after that night you ran out of the graduation party. You didn't return any of my calls. So when you showed up on the race, I thought, hey, maybe this'll be a good opportunity to get some closure." He sounds so genuine that I suddenly see why a bunch of agents came to see him act at Middlebury. He's really, really good.

"You have *got* to be kidding me," Miranda mutters. She presses her fingertips to her temples and closes her eyes.

"Miranda, please stand next to Samir," Isis says.

For a second, I consider asking whether I can take Samir instead. But Miranda wouldn't want me to rescue her. She'd hate it if I implied she wasn't strong enough to handle this herself. She would want me to stay on task, concentrate on the race, and do everything I can to move to the front of the pack. As long as one of us is ahead of Samir, we'll be winning. So I just whisper, "I'm so sorry, Mira. Are you—"

"I'm *fine*," she says, but her voice cracks a little, and I can tell she's working hard to keep it together. As she moves across the circle, her hands ball into fists, and she stands as far away from Samir as she possibly can.

Steve chooses to race with Janine, and then Isis says, "Claire, you're up next. Who would you like to spend the next leg of the race with?"

"I'd like to race with Will Divine, please," I tell her.

190

As soon as Will moves away from Philadelphia and takes his place beside me, I feel stronger, more capable. This is how things are supposed to be. With Will supporting me and cheering me on, I'll be the fastest, most efficient racer I can be. Not to mention that the steamy challenges will be way more fun.

"Hey there, Dominique," he says. "I'm so happy to have you back."

It feels like my chest is going to shatter into a million joyful pieces, but I try to keep my smile in check. It feels cruel to be happy when my sister's so upset. But I do allow myself one quick glance into his gorgeous blue eyes as I whisper, "Me too."

Philadelphia is left with Aidan—it takes about twenty seconds before she has her hands twined in his hair—and we're done for the night. We pile into the show vans, which sweep us through the dark Delhi streets and drop us off at a modest-looking hotel. As I'm waiting for the producer to hand over my room key, Will nudges me with his shoulder.

"Hey," he says quietly. Then he pulls a tiny notebook out of his bag and starts writing something down, like I'm not even here.

"What are you—" I start, but he puts his finger to his lips and gestures to his microphone—the cameras aren't on right now, but we're still wired for our interviews. When Will holds up the notebook, it says, *Want to hang out later and strategize? Room 217.*

There's no possible way to strategize when we don't even know what country we'll be in tomorrow, and my mind automatically starts making a list of other things we could do alone in Will's room. I take the notebook from him and write, *Won't we get in trouble?*

I won't tell if you won't.

I smile, trying not to look like I care *too* much, and give him a little nod. He grins, slings his bag over his shoulder, and heads toward the stairs.

Two minutes ago, the only question on my mind was *How can I make Miranda feel better?* But suddenly, that question is surrounded by a flock of other questions with brighter feathers, beating their wings and competing for my attention. What should I wear tonight? Do I have time for a shower? How soon can I go over to Will's room? How late is too late to knock? What if someone sees me sneaking down the hall? How long will he let me stay?

And what will happen when that door swings closed behind us?

15

I barely have time to drop off my pack in my room before I'm called back out for my daily wrap-up interviews. As a producer leads me through the hotel lobby, I try to think of comforting things I can say to Miranda about the Samir situation. Should I remind her that at least she'll be working with someone she already knows, so she'll be able to compensate for his weaknesses? That she won't have to suffer through any awkward getting-to-know-you small talk? That maybe she actually *will* come away from this with some closure about her relationship? None of that sounds remotely convincing. The truth is that being with Samir is going to suck, and there's really nothing I can do about it except sympathize.

But when I reach the producer's makeshift studio in the hotel's outdoor restaurant, Miranda's not even there; Troy's waiting for me in the other chair. The redheaded producer from the banquet hall is interviewing us, and she introduces herself as Tessa. "Where's my sister?" I ask her.

"Happy to see you, too," Troy says, and I roll my eyes at him.

"We'd like to talk to you with Troy first," Tessa says breez-ily. "Sit down and let's chat about your day, okay?"

Troy and I spend half an hour recapping how we felt about the various challenges. I spend the whole time won-dering if Miranda's all right—not to mention what's going to happen when I get to Will's room—and I'm totally dis-tracted and incoherent. When Troy finally leaves and my sis-ter comes out to take his place, I jump up to hug her. "I'm so sorry, Miranda," I say. "Are you okay?"

"I'm fine," she says automatically. But she doesn't return my hug, just pats me quickly with one hand before she pulls away. A small knot of uneasiness forms deep in my stomach—Miranda is a pretty huggy kind of person. She won't look directly at me as she sits down, but I can tell she's been crying.

"I wish I could do something to help," I say.

When she finally meets my eyes, I'm shocked by how des-perate she looks. "I wish you'd wanted that a couple hours ago," she says.

What does *that* mean? What could I have done hours ago to prevent this? But before I can ask, Tessa says, "Let's chat about what happened back in the ballroom today. Can you describe the situation for me, Claire?"

I don't really want to rehash my meltdown—it'll only help the producers personify me as incompetent. But maybe I can spin it so the focus is on our sisterly love, not my hu-miliation. "Miranda was amazing," I say. "I have a pretty seri-ous phobia of dancing in public—I always feel so stupid and self-conscious, even if nobody's looking at me. And this time

194

it was much worse, because *everyone* was looking at me, and I totally froze. But then Miranda got up onstage with me, and it was like the fear just melted away. When I concentrated on her, I was able to do the challenge. I actually kind of had fun. She's my knight in shining armor." I expect my sister to smile at least a little, but she doesn't.

"What made you get up there and help Claire, Miranda?" asks Tessa.

I assume Miranda will repeat what she said on the plaza an hour ago—that we're a team no matter what, that she'll always be there for me, that we'll make up our lost time tomorrow. But instead she says, "I mean, it's not like this has never happened before—I've pretty much spent my whole life jumping in to help Claire when things get too overwhelming for her. And usually it's fine, and I don't mind doing it. But I guess everything's different when you're on a TV show, and I probably should have realized that helping her today could have serious consequences."

I blink at her. "What are you talking about? What consequences?"

"'*What consequences*'? Do you seriously not see this disaster of a situation I'm in?"

I don't even understand what's happening. Of course she's pissed about the whole Samir thing—she has every reason to be—but none of that is *my* fault. "Why are you blaming me for this? I didn't make Samir pick you!"

"No, but if I'd left the ballroom when *I* was done dancing instead of waiting for you, I might've beaten him to the check-in point, and then he wouldn't have been *able* to pick me." She makes a dismissive gesture with her hand. "Whatever, it's not your fault you needed help. I just wish it had worked out differently. This next leg of the race is going to *suck*."

"Miranda, he was already ahead of you! Even if you hadn't waited for me, he still would've gotten there first."

"Maybe. But I gave up what little chance I had to beat him," she says. "There's a big difference between a three-minute lead and a six-minute one."

I can't believe that after all I've overcome today, Miranda's *still* making me look helpless and weak, like all I ever do is drag other people down. I never even asked her to stay with me in that ballroom; that was her choice, and now she's throwing it all back in my face.

"What happened to 'It's no big deal'?" I say. My voice cracks, and I hate how young I sound.

"I said that before the Proposal Ceremony. At that point, I didn't *know* it was a big deal."

"So now you regret helping me? Is that what you're saying?"

"I mean, I'm glad it made you feel better. Of course I don't regret that. But maybe I'm not even helping you when I jump in like that. Maybe I'm just preventing you from learning to do things for yourself. It probably would've worked out better for both of us if I'd left you alone up there."

It's like she's scouted out my body for weak spots and aimed a kick at the softest one. I've made so much progress on this race, and she's dismissed it all with a couple of sentences. I open my mouth to defend myself, but I'm so stunned that I have no words.

"*Good,*" Tessa says. "Thanks, girls. We've got everything we need for today."

I stumble out of the restaurant in a daze, still holding on to a slight hope that Miranda will apologize to me as soon as we're out of range of the cameras. But she doesn't, so I guess she really meant everything she said. Does she think *I* should be apologizing? I'm about to do it, just to get rid of this fog of resentment between us, but the words catch in my throat. I didn't do anything wrong. Miranda has no right to blame me for the choices she makes.

When I turn down the hallway toward the stairs, she starts heading to the lobby instead. "Where are you going?" I say. "It's three in the morning."

"I need to walk around and clear my head."

For a minute, I consider offering to go with her. Maybe I really *do* owe her for slowing her down today, and this would be a way to make amends. But it doesn't seem fair that all the stuff she just said about self-sufficiency should apply only to me. If Miranda doesn't have my back anymore, she can't expect me to reach out to her, either. Waiting in room 217 is a boy who respects me and supports me and doesn't see me as a child or a burden, and I'm not giving up my time alone with him. I've earned it. Miranda can deal with her own problems.

"I'm going to sleep," I say.

"Fine. I guess I'll see you tomorrow."

I feel a little guilty as I head back to my room. But not *that* guilty.

I take a quick shower, trying to concentrate on the night ahead and let all my thoughts of Miranda fade away. When I get out, I blow-dry my hair—I tell myself it's because I want it to look nice on camera tomorrow, but really I just want it to be shiny for Will. I wish I'd brought something cute and flirty to wear, but I don't even own anything like that, so I pull on my shortest shorts and a plain pink tank top, which I tug down as low as I can to emphasize my minimal cleavage. I brush my teeth, just in case, rub on a little lip gloss, and pout at myself in the mirror. Not effortlessly sexy by any stretch of the imagination, but at least it's a slight improvement.

Will's room is on the same floor as mine, and it only takes about thirty seconds to find it, but I'm so nervous someone's going to catch me sneaking down the hall that every tiny sound makes me jump. He answers the door in a clean T-shirt and a pair of low-riding basketball shorts, his hair damp and messy from the shower. I want to tangle my fingers in it like Philadelphia did to Aidan.

"Hey," I say. I'm going for breathy, but I end up sounding like I've been jogging.

He breaks into a dimpled smile. "Hey! You came!"

I push into the room before he even has a chance to move out of the way, and my shoulder bangs into his. "Um, come on in," he says, confused and laughing, as the door shuts behind me. "Are there wolves in the hall or something?"

"What?"

"You launched yourself in here like you were being chased. I mean, I know I'm irresistible, but ..."

"I just didn't want anyone to see me," I say, pretty sure my cheeks are now the same color as my tank top.

He shakes his head. "Why do I always have to be everyone's dirty little secret?"

I don't love the implication that this isn't his first secret tryst on the race, but I ignore it. "*You've* got nothing to complain about—I'm the one putting my million dollars at stake by wandering the halls."

"I believe you mean *my* million dollars." He grins at me. "Sit down."

There's a pile of clothes and a wet towel on the only chair in the room, so I perch on the edge of his bed. He flops down beside me and lies on his back, his head pillowed on his arms. "Oh my God, I'm so tired," he says.

"How'd your interview go? How was the delightful Philly?" I put air quotes around her name with my voice.

Will rubs his eyes with the heels of his hands. "She's a piece of work, isn't she?"

Just hearing him say those words rounds out all the sharp corners of the day. Will may have flirted with Philadelphia for the cameras, but he was just acting, like Troy. All my worrying was for nothing. I scoot farther onto the bed so I'm leaning against the headboard and try to suppress a silly grin.

"I don't know how you even got through a whole leg of the race with her," I say.

"Hey, it can't have been much worse than your day with

Troy the Beefcake." He does some goofy muscleman poses, and I laugh. I kind of feel like I should defend Troy, but I don't want to say anything positive about another guy in front of Will, in case he takes it the wrong way.

"Let's just say I'm really glad to have you back," I say.

"Likewise, Dominique." He rolls over and grabs the remote off his nightstand. "You want to watch something?"

"Sure," I say, and my heart leaps to attention. I've never snuck into a boy's room before, but I've seen my fair share of romantic comedies, and it's pretty obvious what's going to happen next.

Will scrolls through a couple news channels until he finds a movie that involves a lot of things blowing up. There aren't any subtitles, but it doesn't matter—it's not like we're actually going to pay attention to the television. He switches off the lamp "so we can see the screen better," stuffs a pillow under his head, and makes himself comfortable. I remember what I've learned from watching *Speed Breed* and try to make my body language as welcoming as possible: legs crossed in his direction, hand resting on the covers between us, head inclined toward him, lips slightly parted. I don't think I could be any more obvious if I stood on the bed and screamed *Kiss me!* through a megaphone. I keep my eyes on the screen, not even registering the movie, and I wait.

But nothing happens.

And nothing happens.

And when I finally steal a glance at Will to see what's taking so long, he's *asleep*.

Seriously? We're finally together in a room with a bed,

all alone and far from the cameras, and he's chosen to spend this time with me *unconscious*? I try to tell myself he didn't mean to nod off—we've both had a long day, and I'm exhausted, too. We'll have the whole flight tomorrow to hang out and talk. But talking isn't what I want to do, and I feel totally cheated. This isn't how tonight was supposed to end.

I'm about to get up and tiptoe back to my own room, where I'll spend the rest of the night stewing in frustration and disappointment. But then it occurs to me that I really have no reason to leave. Who would know if I just stayed here tonight? It's not like anyone's going to come looking for me, and I can always sneak out early in the morning. If Will wakes up and finds me next to him, he'll assume we both fell asleep watching the movie.

After the evening I've had, I deserve this.

Will sleeps with one arm flung over his head, legs spread out on top of the covers like a starfish. I carefully curl up on my side of the bed and watch the slow rise and fall of his chest. A streetlight shines through the curtains, highlighting the curve of his stubbled cheek, the straight slope of his nose, the dark hollow of his throat. A lock of his damp hair has fallen over one eye, and very tentatively, I reach out and brush it back. When he doesn't react, I let my hand rest on the pillow next to his head, close enough to feel his breath on my fingers. But after a few minutes, that isn't enough. My whole body aches to get closer to him.

So slowly it's almost imperceptible, I start inching my way across the bed. There's less than a foot of mattress between us, but the trek takes several long minutes, and by the time I'm close enough to feel the warmth of his skin, my heart is pounding like I'm about to commit a crime. I worry it might be loud enough to wake him. It's probably loud enough to wake the whole hotel.

I spend another few minutes psyching myself up for the final approach. Then, in a rare moment of reckless bravery, I roll toward Will and drape my arm across his waist. There's a thin stripe of bare skin between his T-shirt and his shorts, and I thrill at the warmth of it against the inside of my wrist. He shifts a little in his sleep, and I freeze, praying he won't turn away. But he just sighs, and then he's still. My arm moves gently up and down as he breathes.

When I'm certain he's still deeply asleep, I scoot my hips a tiny bit closer, then slide my top leg over so it tangles with his. Now the whole length of our bodies is pressed together, and I think I might faint from the feel of so much contact at once. I rest my cheek against his chest, close my eyes, and try to relax enough to sleep, knowing I'll regret it tomorrow if I don't. But I can't bear to let myself drift off. Every moment I spend unconscious is a moment I'll be unaware of how close together we are.

I finally sink into sleep as the sun starts to rise, painting the ceiling of Will's room in shades of watercolor pink, and I dream of kissing the edge of his hairline, the fragile curves of his eyelids, the dimple in his cheek, the tip of his nose. In my dream, he wakes and smiles just as I'm hovering a breath away from that gorgeous mouth. "Don't stop," he whispers against my lips.

And I don't.

16

I wake up around eight, glowing from my dreams, and tiny fireworks go off in my brain when I discover it wasn't all my imagination—I really *am* in bed with Will Divine. We've shifted in our sleep, and now Will is curled around me, his stomach pressed to my back, his knees against the undersides of my thighs. I can feel his breath stirring the hairs at the nape of my neck. I never want this to end, but I know I need to get back to my own room before anyone finds us. I'm careful not to wake him as I slowly, gently free myself from his arms and climb off the bed. Before I go, I turn to look at him one last time, marveling at the way the morning sun catches in his long eyelashes. I wish I had my phone with me so I could take a picture.

I start missing him even before the door clicks shut behind me.

Humming and dancing and grinning at myself in the mirror, I pack up my stuff and get ready for the day. I'm so buzzy and happy that I don't even remember Miranda and Samir have the same start time we do until I spot them in the lobby. My sister has dark circles under her eyes, but she looks determined and stoic, like she's done crying. "How are you holding up?" I ask, hoping she'll say she's sorry about last night. My good mood has made me benevolent, and I'm ready to accept an apology if she offers one.

But she just shrugs. "Tired. I didn't really sleep."

I spot Samir across the lobby, looking perky and awake. "Have you talked to him at all?"

"Just for a second. He's so infuriating—when anyone else is around, he acts all innocent and vulnerable, like he wants me back or wants closure or whatever, but the second no one's looking, he just smirks at me. The whole point of coming here was to mess with his head, and he's the one messing with mine."

Part of me wants to ask *What can I do to help you?* But according to her, we're supposed to be fending for ourselves now. I try to make my voice sound supportive but detached. "Well, it's only one day. You can get through this."

"I know I *can.* I just hate being on the same side as him. It sucks that I can't even do anything bad to him without sabotaging myself." She sighs deeply, and then a little crease appears between her eyebrows. "You look . . . rested."

"Yeah, I slept pretty well. Maybe you can get in a nice long nap on the plane. You should buy some Tylenol PM or something at the airport." I try to tamp down my glow so she won't ask any more questions. "Should we go wait outside for the van?"

"I guess."

Will joins us as we're standing out front with Janine and Steve, and he winks when he sees me. "How'd you sleep?" he asks, totally innocent. I can't tell whether he knows I was in his bed most of the night.

I try to match his tone. "Pretty well. You?"

"I slept like a dead person," he says. "I was trying to watch this movie, but I guess I crashed in the middle. I totally didn't mean to . . . it was super entertaining. Next time I'll try harder not to miss the end." He looks straight at me, like he's trying to send me a telepathic message, and I smile to show him I accept his apology. Just knowing he wants there to be a next time sends a little shiver down my spine.

Nobody speaks on the ride to India Gate. I try to tell Miranda good luck as she heads off with Samir to get their first pink envelope, but she barely acknowledges me. Steve and Janine head out ten minutes later, and then it's finally our turn. Isis introduces us to our new cameraman and sound guy, who immediately sticks his hands up my shirt to attach my mike. It's weird how even after just a few days, it's starting to feel routine to have random guys clipping things to my bra. I guess you can get used to anything.

When he's done, Isis blesses us with her standard "May the forces of love and luck be with you," and Will rips open our instructions and reads them aloud.

Fly to Athens, Greece, and make your way to Mikro Kavouri Beach, where you're in for some finger-licking good times.

If I'd gotten these instructions with Troy yesterday, I'm pretty sure that phrasing would've turned my stomach. But as long as I'm with Will, I'm up for anything.

"Greece," he breathes. "That is so awesome. Come on! Let's go!"

I love his boyish enthusiasm—it almost makes me forget about Miranda and Samir. Even the insane ride through the camel-and-monkey-and-cow-filled Delhi traffic doesn't seem so bad, now that he's the one next to me in the cab.

The earliest flight out is at six in the evening on Qatar Airways with a two-hour layover in Doha, and all twelve of us end up on the same flight. As soon as we're on the plane, I remind Will to do the breathing exercises I taught him, and when I offer him my hand, he takes it eagerly. I was hoping for a continuation of the Question Game, but staying up most of the night has left me sleepier than I thought, and I drift off the moment we reach our cruising altitude. Even with the help of a large coffee in the Doha airport, I don't feel fully alert again until we're standing in the customs line in Athens. I hate that I've missed out on so much valuable time with Will, but honestly, last night was worth it.

We stumble out into the cool night air—somehow it's midnight again—and find a cab. Our driver seems to be in the mood to practice his English, and he asks a million questions about the race as we zip down the highway. When he gets tired of that, he serenades us with some of his favorite American songs, all of which are by Lady Gaga—it turns out her music is way more entertaining when sung by a pudgy Greek man. He finally lets us off at the beach around one in the morning, shakes our hands, and gives us his card in case we ever need a cab in an emergency. "Wherever you are, I come for you like the wind!" he promises.

We follow a winding path between a bunch of beach-side hotels, but when Will finds the rickety gate that leads out onto the sand, it's latched and locked. He pulls a tiny LED flashlight out of his bag and reads the sign. "The beach doesn't open until sunrise," he calls.

A couple teams are spreading out their sleeping bags and settling in to wait for dawn, and I spot Troy a little farther down the fence, alternating between sets of crunches and push-ups. Miranda and Samir don't seem to be here yet. Maybe she's off burying his dead body in the sand somewhere.

"What do you want to do?" I ask Will. "Should we nap?"

He shrugs. "I slept on the plane, so I'm okay. How about you?"

"I'm actually feeling kind of wired."

"You want to walk around?"

I know we'll only be killing time, but it *almost* feels like Will just asked me on a date. "Definitely," I say.

Our crew guys look exhausted, and since our walk isn't race-related, Will convinces them to rest instead of tagging along. He acts like he's just being nice, but it seems like he wants to be alone with me. We leave our packs with the cameraman and head back up to the road. Will keeps his hands deep in his pockets, but he walks close enough to me that our arms occasionally brush. Neither of us speaks as we amble through the nighttime streets, looking at the darkened storefronts and cable car tracks in companionable silence. This unhurried time feels like a gift.

"Hey," I finally say to Will as we turn down a cobblestone

sidewalk that's shiny and wet from an earlier rain. "Why are you really here?"

A crinkle of confusion appears between his eyebrows. "Um . . . because the beach is closed?"

"No, not here on this street. I mean here on the race. Why'd you try out? You're not really a CEO's son who's trying to escape some evil corporate destiny, so what's the real story?"

He shrugs. "I just wanted to. That's all." But he doesn't meet my eyes.

"Oh, come on. You're totally hiding something. People don't just randomly try out for reality shows. You must've had a reason."

He's quiet for a minute, and then he says, "It's kind of embarrassing."

"I'm, like, the queen of embarrassing. I can handle it."

"I know you can *handle* it, but—"

I cut him off. "When we were on the plane to Java, you made me tell you a secret, and you never told me one back, so now you owe me. It's only fair."

He sighs. "Fine. But you can't judge me."

"I'd never judge you."

"Okay. So, one of my friends is a PA for this show, and when she started working on it back in the winter, she told me all about it. And I mean *all* about it."

It takes me a second to figure out what he's saying, but then my mouth drops open. "You *knew* this was a dating show?" No wonder he didn't look surprised when Isis revealed the twist at the starting line.

"Yeah. Please don't tell anyone. They'd probably fire my friend."

"I won't. But . . . I'm sorry, you seriously came here to meet *girls*?"

"I knew you'd laugh at me." He looks down at his shoes.

"No! No, it's just ... you couldn't meet girls at home? You're in college. In New York City. There are literally four million women there. And you're"—I make a vague gesture up and down his body—"*you*. You can't possibly have trouble meeting girls." This is more than I intended to say, and I'm blushing like crazy, but I'm pretty sure he can't tell in the dark.

"Well, I also wanted a free trip around the world, but it didn't hurt to know that I'd get to meet some extremely kick-ass women. I mean, sure, there are a lot of *attractive* girls at school, but it's hard to find someone who's interesting past the surface, you know? I wanted to find someone deep and adventurous and brave, who's willing to step out of her comfort zone and try new things, even if it scares her." He looks right into my eyes. "And I have."

I'm totally speechless. Nobody has ever called me a kick-ass woman before. Nobody has ever called me deep or adventurous or brave, either. Is that really what Will sees when he looks at me? Is that what millions of viewers will see when they watch the show? Even if I don't feel like that girl, is it possible I've started to become her without even noticing?

After a few seconds, when I still haven't said anything, Will drops his eyes again. "I told you it was embarrassing."

"*No*. It's not. Not at all." I reach out and touch his arm.

I want to thank him for the compliment, but you can't really say *Thanks for noticing how awesome I am.* So I settle for "I'm glad you, um, found what you were looking for."

"Me too." He smiles. "Ready to keep walking?"

He links his arm through mine, like he's more comfortable touching me now that he's told me how he feels, and he leads us to the left. We haven't seen any other people up until this point, but on the corner of the next block, we spot a restaurant that's still open. It looks exactly like a restaurant in Greece should look—the outside is painted bright white, and the plaster walls are crumbling slightly at the corners to reveal the bricks underneath. The planters out front overflow with red flowers that are blooming so enthusiastically it's almost indecent. Even though it's the middle of the night, the place is jam-packed, full of flickering candlelight and music and laughter. I tiptoe closer and peer through the window.

There's some sort of party going on; most of the tables have been removed, and couples are dancing in the middle of the parquet floor. Many of the women look a little unsteady in their heels, and waiters in black circulate through the crowd with bottles of wine, compounding the problem. Best of all, everyone is wearing masks sparkling with sequins and adorned with ribbons and feather plumes the colors of tropical birds. It's a real, live masquerade party, straight out of a movie. This place looks like my heart feels right now— glittery and bright and whimsical.

"That looks like so much fun," I whisper to Will.

"We should go in."

"I'm sure it's someone's private party. They'd realize they don't know us right away and throw us out."

"Maybe not if we were wearing these." He holds up two masks.

I gape at him. "Where did you get those?" Tonight feels so magical that it seems possible he's conjured them out of the air.

"They were in the planter. Someone must have left them when they went home."

One of the masks is small, covered in plain black sequins, like a really shiny bandit mask. The other is shaped like a butterfly and decorated with iridescent blue and green feathers. Three gorgeous peacock plumes swoop up from beside each eye hole, and I trace their softness with my finger.

Will holds it out to me. "Here, try it on."

I slip the elastic band around the back of my head. It takes a minute to get the mask settled over my glasses, but when it's in place, I feel more like the kick-ass woman Will was describing earlier. "How do I look?"

"Dazzling." He puts on the bandit mask. "And me?"

"Kind of like . . . a bank robber from a Broadway musical."

"In a good way, I assume."

"How could that possibly be bad?"

He smiles and holds out an arm to me. "So, shall we?"

I thought we were just playing, but I realize now that he's serious about crashing this party. "Will, we can't *actually* go in. I'm wearing yoga pants. You have a Batman logo on your shirt. This is, like, a fancy-rich-people party. We don't belong here."

"Don't be ridiculous. The mysterious Lady Dominique belongs anywhere she damn well pleases." He takes my hand, does an exaggerated bow over it, and presses his lips to my knuckles. I feel it through my whole body, and I giggle.

"Okay, seriously, though. We're just going to waltz through the front door? Someone's going to notice. See that big guy with the clipboard? He might be a bouncer."

Will shrugs. "Then I guess we better find the back door."

Before I can protest, he grabs my arm and leads me around the back of the building, where there's a parking lot full of cars and catering vans. "That probably leads to the kitchen," he says, pointing at an unmarked metal door in the corner. "Follow me." Tiptoeing like he really is a bank robber, he slinks through the shadows toward the door and tugs on it. It's locked, of course.

"Let's just wait here for a few minutes and see if anyone comes out," he whispers. "I used to work for a catering company, and we were always forgetting stuff in the van." He crouches down against the restaurant's back wall and gestures for me to sit beside him.

"We really don't have to do this," I say. "We could get in trouble. What if the network finds out and sends us home?"

"How could that happen? Nobody here knows who we are. They don't know we're from the race. If they catch us, they'll toss us out, and we'll be right back where we are now, only with a good story. What do we have to lose?"

He's right. I love that he's not content with pretending and playing it safe and looking in on adventures from the outside. It's frightening to be with someone who's always testing the limits and pushing things to the next level, but it's also totally thrilling. I want more than anything to be worthy of this, to be that brave girl Will thinks I am. So I crouch down next to him, close enough that our shoulders are touching, and we wait for our opportunity to slip into the unknown.

Will's hat must really be lucky, because barely five minutes have passed before a frazzled-looking guy in an apron emerges and jogs toward one of the vans. Will's on his feet in a flash, and he manages to catch the kitchen door. Before I have time to make a conscious choice, I'm slipping inside behind him.

The kitchen is at least fifteen degrees warmer than the outside air, and it's swarming with a chaotic mob of caterers opening bottles and plating appetizers. Will leads me behind a rolling rack of silver trays and pulls me back down into a crouch. "Can you see the door to the dining room?" he whispers.

I peek around the edge of the rack and see a server pushing through a set of double doors on the other side of the room. "I think so," I whisper back. "But there are, like, twenty people between here and there. We can't exactly make a run for it."

The doors slam open, and a red-faced man storms in and starts shouting in Greek. I don't understand a word he's saying, but it's obvious none of it is friendly. I grip Will's arm and squeeze farther behind the rack. "That guy is going to eat us," I whisper.

A slow smile spreads across Will's face. "Don't worry, everything's fine."

The voice is getting closer now, and a few feet from us

a metal tray crashes to the floor so hard it must have been thrown. "Will, I *really* think we should go."

He shakes his head. "No need. It's time for Plan B."

Before I can ask what Plan B is, Will grabs my shoulders, pulls me out from behind the rack, and presses me up against a refrigerator in full view of the entire catering staff. And then his arms are around me, and his mouth is on mine.

Will Divine is kissing me.

My brain's first reaction is to panic—I'm so completely unprepared for this—but my body has other ideas. Before I've even processed what's happening, I'm pulling him closer and kissing him back, just like I did in my dream last night. His hand slides up my spine and cradles the back of my neck, and I fear I might melt into a Claire-shaped puddle on the floor. His mouth is soft and urgent, teasing my lips apart, and he tastes like peppermint. Nerve endings I didn't even know I had ignite like matches as my fingers slip under his hat and tangle in his hair. I never, ever want this to stop.

Not nearly enough time has passed before I hear the angry Greek voice again, and a pair of rough hands separates us. My mask has been knocked askew, but out of half an eyehole, I see Angry Catering Guy, flecks of spit flying from his mouth as he bellows at us in Greek. I look around frantically, unsure which way to run.

But Will seems totally calm, even as Angry Catering Guy grips him by the front of his T-shirt with fingers thick as salamis. *"Miláte angliká?"* Will asks innocently. It means "Do you speak English?"—it's the one Greek phrase we got our cabdriver to teach us on the way from the airport to the beach. I have no idea how Will was able to remember it under pressure.

Angry Catering Guy looks confused for a second, and then his face turns the color of a boiled beet. "Stupid kid!" he sputters. "No! No kiss here! *Out!*"

He shoves us toward the dining room. Will grabs my arm, and we stumble across the kitchen, through the doors, and straight into the party.

"Yes!" Will whisper-screams. He pumps the air with his fist, then picks me up and spins me around. "That was brilliant! *You* were brilliant! Well played, Claire."

I wasn't playing, I want to say as he sets me back on my feet, and for a second, I worry that the kiss was just a ploy, not a romantic gesture. Maybe he would've kissed anyone with that same passionate intensity if it meant getting into the party. Then again, I'm not sure it's possible to fake those kinds of feelings. Maybe he'd been wanting to kiss me since we started off on our walk, and he was just waiting for the perfect dramatic moment. The way he's looking at me now, his eyes full of excitement and tenderness, makes me believe it was real.

I hope my mask covers enough of my face that he can't see how flustered I am. "Good Plan B," I say, still a little out of breath.

Will reaches out and unwinds a strand of my hair from the peacock plumes on my mask. "Sorry, I tangled you up a little."

He certainly did. "That's okay," I breathe.

His lucky hat is slightly askew where I pushed my fingers under it. I think about fixing it for him, but I like being able to see the evidence of our kiss on his body, so I leave it as it is. A word pops into my head to describe how I feel as I gaze at him: *smitten.* It's hardly my fault. Whole religions have been founded around divine beings smiting things.

Will smiles as he looks around the room. "This party looks even better from the inside, huh?"

I've been so focused on him that I haven't even bothered to look around. But it *is* pretty amazing. There's a live band in the corner, a guitarist and a drummer and a guy playing what might be a mandolin, all of them singing in warm, caramel-rich voices. There are about a billion candles on the bar and the small tables lining the edges of the room, and the orange glow makes everyone look young and beautiful. The smells of meat and fried cheese and alcohol waft through the air and vie for my attention.

Quietly, Will slips his hand into mine and holds it tightly. Before this moment, he's only ever held my hand to quell a panic attack, but it feels natural to do it just for the sheer pleasure of pressing our palms together. It feels like something we do every day.

Someday, I hope it will be.

A waiter glides by, lithe as a shadow, and puts a glass of red wine into my hand like I'm just another guest. I don't really like wine, but I hold on to the crystal goblet anyway—it makes me feel more sophisticated, more like I'm part of things. I know I'm an impostor here, among all these elegant Greek women and laughing men in expensive suits. But at this moment, with the candlelight dancing on my face and my fingers twined with Will's, I feel like I could belong anywhere.

17

We return to the beach just in time to see the sky brighten into a mural of pastel colors over the ocean. As the rest of the teams begin to pack up their sleeping bags, I lean against the wooden gate next to Will and stare out at the waves, happier than I've ever been. Though I know it's a cliché to watch the sun rise over the ocean with someone you've just kissed, that doesn't make it any less romantic. I wish he'd kiss me again now, but I understand why he'd be more hesitant in front of the cameras and the other teams. So I press my shoulder against his, knowing I'm starting my day right where I should be, and wait for that first perfect sliver of sun to slip over the horizon and bathe us in gold.

But it doesn't come. The sky is pretty light now, and I finally say, "So . . . where is it?"

"Where's what?"

"The sun."

Will stares at me. "Seriously? We're facing west, genius."

So much for romance. I try to think of a snappy comeback so he'll think I was kidding, but before I can, a Greek man with a droopy mustache arrives along with two producers.

I'm grateful for the distraction, and we move away from the gate so he can unlock it. When he pulls a stack of pink envelopes out of his back pocket, all twelve of us pour out onto the sand and surround him like puppies eager for our breakfast. Miranda's standing near me, and I try to catch her eye, but she avoids my gaze like I'm not even here.

Well, fine. If that's how today is going to be, I'll ignore her right back. If she wants self-sufficient Claire, that's what she'll get. I turn my back to her as I rip open our instructions, just to make a point.

Before a Greek wedding, it is traditional for a bride to pull a teenage boy into her lap and bite a biscuit ring hanging around his neck. In this challenge, the male competitor must wear a pastry ring around his neck, and the female competitor must eat it off of him without using her hands. You must complete this challenge while riding double on a horse. Proceed five hundred meters north along the beach, where you will find your pastries and mounts.

For a second, I stand there considering the summer I was supposed to have, serving soy chai lattes to the yuppies of Braeburn. In my wildest, weirdest dreams, I could never have imagined that I'd end up on horseback on television, licking pastry crumbs off Will Divine. I so wish I could press pause and call Natalie.

"Do you think these bizarre wedding traditions are even real, or is the network just inventing stuff to make us look stupid?" Will asks as we head up the beach.

I automatically reach for my phone so I can look it up before I realize it's in New York, not in my back pocket. "I miss the Internet," I say.

"In any case, this is totally unfair. How come I don't get any pastry? I'm starving."

"They must know you're watching your girlish figure," I say, and he sticks out his tongue at me. It's amazing how relaxed I feel right now—four days ago, I would have been dying of embarrassment at the thought of this challenge. Maybe I still would be if I were paired with someone else. But things are different with Will, who has welcomed my closeness even off camera. Now that he's shown how much he genuinely likes me, this doesn't seem scary at all.

Will and I choose a brown horse with a white star on its nose, and he stays with its handler while I retrieve our pastry ring. I'm not sure what to expect, but they turn out to look like necklaces sculpted from glazed pretzel dough. There's some confusion as the producers distribute them— apparently, Tawny needs a special gluten-free ring—but I finally return to Will with the pastry. It's still warm and dripping with honey, and it smells amazing. "So, I guess I should just . . . put this on you," I say. "You might want to take your hat off."

Will tucks the lucky hat into his pocket, then pokes at the dough to test its consistency. "Oh God, this is really sticky."

I'm not sure what comes over me, but I suddenly want to see how far I can push things between us. "Maybe you should take your shirt off, too," I say.

If Will is surprised by my boldness, he doesn't show it.

He just smiles and says, "You're in charge," then peels off his shirt and tosses it onto his pack. The other day at the pool, I was careful to look away before he caught me staring. But this time, I unabashedly drink in the sight of his bare torso, which glows in the early-morning sun. He's so gorgeous I can barely stand it. I slip the ring over his head and settle it against his collarbones, letting my hands linger against his skin a little longer than necessary.

A couple other teams are already up on their horses, the girls behind the guys. Janine's having no trouble taking bites out of Steve's pastry necklace, since she's eighty feet tall, but Zora is much shorter than Martin, and she can't even reach his neck unless he leans way back in the saddle. They barely seem to be staying on their horse as their handler leads them down the beach at a slow walk. "I think I should go in front and face you," I say.

"Ooh, smart. Are you okay riding backward?"

"I trust you to keep me from falling," I say.

We explain to our handler what we want to do, and he helps us up into the double saddle. I can't put my feet in the stirrups in this position, but Will grips my legs tightly with his and holds onto the pommel behind me, and once I put my hands on his waist to steady myself, I feel pretty secure. When the horse starts walking, rocking us gently back and forth, I can feel Will's muscles shifting under my hands as he works to balance us. His face is very close to mine, and he stares right into my eyes—if I leaned forward a few inches, I could close the gap between us. I have to work very hard not to look at his mouth.

"Ready when you are," he says.

I lean forward and take my first bite of the dough necklace. It's soft and sweet, and it melts in my mouth like a croissant. When I lick a drop of honey off Will's neck, he draws in his breath sharply, and I feel intoxicatingly powerful. I can tell how hard his heart is beating, and mine speeds up in response.

"No, God, Samir! See how Claire's doing it?" I hear my sister's voice say behind us. "Why don't you ever listen to me?" She sounds like she's on the verge of tossing him off their horse and into the ocean, and for a second I feel bad for her. But that doesn't dampen my excitement that she's just held me up as an example on camera for the first time. The pastry in my mouth suddenly tastes even more delicious.

I make the challenge last as long as I reasonably can, but when I see Miranda and Samir getting off their horse, I hurry up and take my last few bites. When I finish and smile up at Will, he's looking at me with wonder in his eyes. "That was *hot*, Dominique," he whispers. But until he says it, my brave, sexy alter ego hadn't even crossed my mind. I haven't needed her today—it's always been plain old Claire up on this horse. And Will Divine *still* thinks I'm hot.

Our handler helps us down and hands us our next envelope, and I rip it open as Will pulls his shirt and hat back on.

Make your way by train to Corinth. At the station, choose one of the marked Around the World cars and drive yourself to Acrocorinth, where you will find the ruins of the Temple of Aphrodite. Here, you must snip a small lock of your hair as a sacrifice to the goddess of love and fertility, then make a private romantic wish.

There's a new buzz of intimacy between Will and me now, and I wonder if our crew guys can feel the electricity zinging through the air as we crush into a cab and head toward the train station. I know I'm probably getting a little ahead of myself, but as we board the train to Corinth, I can't help daydreaming about the future. Will has one more year at NYU, but Braeburn's only four hours from the city, and we could easily visit each other on weekends. And during the week, we could Skype and email and text. If we wanted to, we could make it work. Will sits with his thigh pressed against mine, and every time he smiles at me, heat rushes through my body. If it weren't for the cameras, I'm pretty sure we'd be all over each other right now, regardless of all the Greek strangers around us.

The ride to Corinth is so beautiful the scenery doesn't even look real. There's a steep drop-off alongside the tracks that leads right down to the ocean, which is the same bright blue as Will's eyes, and if I squint I can see a smattering of islands shimmering in the distance. At the station, we buy a road map and choose one of the cars waiting for us in the parking lot. Will slips behind the wheel, and I climb in back to navigate, wishing I could sit beside him and hold his hand. Not all the street signs have English transliterations, so we get lost a few times, but we eventually find the turn-off to Acrocorinth and creep up the steep hill toward the massive citadel perched on top.

It's a good thing we choose to leave our packs in the trunk, because even the climb from the parking area to the first gate is shockingly steep. We pass through two more huge gates, and then we're inside, zigzagging up through the crumbling ruins. The sandy stone walls and turrets look like they're growing straight out of the rocky hillside, and flowers have taken root between the stones, adding bright, startling flashes of red and yellow and purple. Will and I are too out of breath to talk as we climb, but after everything that's happened last night and this morning, I still feel like we're connected even when we're silent. The sun is warm and the breeze is perfect, and for a while, it's easy to forget about the cameras and imagine that we're out hiking together just for fun. When Martin and Zora pass us on the way back to their car and give us a friendly wave, I wonder if they can sense how things have changed between us.

The view from the summit is totally worth the effort— miles and miles of ocean and city and distant mountains are spread out before us like a patchwork quilt. A single pillar of the ancient temple stands at the peak of the hill, and a producer in a pink shirt has set up a makeshift studio at its base. Miranda is sitting across from her, making her wish, and Samir is waiting off to the side, meticulously picking tiny pieces of lint off his shirt. "You want to go first or should I?" I ask Will when the two of them start heading back down, ignoring both us and each other.

"You can go," he says, so I climb the slope and snip a small piece of my hair into the wooden bowl at the base of the pillar. Then I sit down in the folding chair across from the producer, a woman with a million tiny dreads and lipstick so dark it's almost black.

"Hi, Claire," she says. "What I need from you is a wish that has to do with love or romance. It can be anything you want, but the more specific you are, the more exciting it'll be for our viewers. For example, if there's another racer you're interested in, now would be a great time to mention it. Do you need a minute to think about it?"

"No," I tell her. "I know what I want to say."

"Great. The camera's rolling, so go ahead whenever you're ready."

I look straight into the lens. "I wish that Will Divine and I can be a real couple once this race is over," I say, loud and clear. "He's the most amazing guy I've ever met, and he seems to like me, too. I want him to be my boyfriend." It's the first time I've voiced that thought out loud, and it feels terrifying and wonderful in equal measures.

The producer beams at me. "That's perfect, Claire. You're all set. Go ahead and send Will up."

Will's gone for a lot longer than I was. He and the producer seem to be having a heated discussion, but even when I edge closer, I can't hear what they're saying. Finally, the producer hands him a pink envelope, and he climbs back down. "What took you so long?" I ask.

"Oh, nothing. She just wasn't happy with how I phrased my wish at first."

He tears open our instructions, but I'm not quite ready to be done with this topic yet, even though I can see Tawny and

Troy making their way up the hill. "What did you wish for?" I push, hoping it was about me.

He gives me a mysterious smile. "If I told you, it wouldn't come true."

"I don't think that rule applies when you've already said it out loud."

"If you're so sure, why don't you tell me what *you* wished for?"

"Fine," I say. "I wished for the power to turn anything I wanted into cheese."

He laughs. "That was your wish about love and romance?"

"Maybe. Cheese is very romantic."

"I'll tell you my wish when you tell me your real one."

I'm right on the brink of doing it, but I'm suddenly not sure if I should—I don't want to say too much too fast and risk scaring him away. Our new dynamic feels fragile as an eggshell, and I'm worried I might break it if I squeeze too hard. So I just shrug and say, "I'll tell you later."

"Same goes for me, then." Will pulls out our next instructions, and I'm a little disappointed that he didn't try harder to weasel my wish out of me.

Drive yourselves to the Ancient Stadium in Corinth, where you will run a relay race using golden apples, one of the symbols of Aphrodite. You must travel up and down the field four times, passing off your golden apple each time. The first team member will begin with the apple under his or her chin. After the first lap, the apple must be passed to the second team member's

chin. For the third lap, the first team member must hold the
apple between his or her knees, and for the final lap, the apple
must be passed to the second team member's knees. You may not
touch the apple with your hands at any time. If you drop your
apple, you will incur a three-minute penalty, during which you
must sit down and remain silent.

"Now they really *are* just trying to make us look stupid," Will says as we start our descent.

"I don't know, I think it sounds kind of fun," I say. Then again, I'm so giggly and buoyant right now that picking dead flies out of a kiddie pool with tweezers would probably sound fun.

I expect the stadium to be a structure with walls, like a football stadium, but it turns out to be a wide, flat field surrounded by scrubby trees. In the middle of the grass, Miranda and Zora are doing hilarious ducklike waddles with golden apples clenched between their knees as a crowd of locals cheers them on. At the stadium gate, a man who's about as wide as he is tall hands us our "golden apple," which is made of plastic and is lighter and more slippery than a real apple. He also hands me another pink envelope, but instead of the regular logo that's usually printed on the front, this heart-map is circled in red and slashed through with a line. Inside are two hot pink cards and an explanation.

Attention, racers! This challenge is a HEARTBREAKER! If you
spot a team waiting out a penalty during the relay, you may
swap your own partner for either penalized racer, who will

become your new partner for the rest of this leg of the race. You must start the relay over with your new partner. Each person may initiate only one swap. Are you cruel enough to break your partner's heart?

Well, *this* clearly doesn't apply to me. Why would I want to switch partners when I have Will? "You're not going to trade me in for Philadelphia, are you?" I ask jokingly as I hand him his card, and he laughs and rolls his eyes. I'm pleased to discover that thinking about her doesn't make me feel the slightest bit insecure anymore. I tuck my Heartbreaker card into my back pocket and forget about it.

The field is divided into lanes, with little Venus-on-a-clamshell statues marking the boundary lines. Each lane also has a referee with a whistle and a red flag. We pick a lane, and Will asks, "You want to go first?"

"Sure." I tuck the apple under my chin, and I'm off.

My neck starts to sweat against the plastic almost immediately, and the apple threatens to slip, so I slow from a run to a smoother speed-walk. Will trots along next to me, cheering me on. I'm only about a quarter of the way across the field when I hear the shriek of a whistle. "Who has a penalty?" I ask, careful not to move my chin too much.

"Your sister," Will says. "Keep going. You've got this."

I manage to make it to the end of the lane and circle the statue without dropping my apple. Will moves in to make the transfer, and we both tip our heads to the right, as if we're about to kiss. I pray I haven't made the apple too sweaty to hold. "I don't have a very good grip," he says when he manages to grab it. "Could you nudge it in there more tightly somehow?" I end up using my nose like a seal with a ball, to help him reposition the apple, and the whole thing is so ridiculous that we both end up giggling hysterically.

We set off in the other direction. Miranda and Samir are still sitting down in their lane, waiting for their penalty to be up, and I notice that my sister is staring at me very intently. I shoot her a sympathetic smile, but she doesn't smile back. When her referee blows his whistle and lowers his red flag, she and Samir leap to their feet, and Miranda tucks her apple back between her knees. But before she's taken three steps, it shoots forward like it's been launched from a slingshot and rolls across the grass.

"*God,* Miranda, what's *wrong* with you? When did you get so freaking *clumsy?*" Samir snaps as they sit back down. I hate that he's yelling at her, but I have to admit I'm surprised, too. My sister's usually really coordinated.

Will has no trouble keeping the apple in place under his chin. He reaches the end of the lane just as Tawny and Troy arrive, and he slowly crouches until his face is level with my thighs. I brace my hands on his shoulders, squat, and stick out my knees, and after a minute of awkward maneuvering, I manage to grab the apple between my legs. It stays there for a total of eight steps, and then it bounces off my shin and rolls into the next lane. Martin drops his apple at almost the same moment, and both our referees blow their whistles and raise their red flags.

"Sorry, I thought I had it," I say.

"Don't worry," Will says. "It's no big deal. You're doing great."

Miranda's penalty ends moments after I sit down, and she immediately raises her pink Heartbreaker card high in the air. "I want to switch partners!" she yells.

Her referee jogs over, followed by a producer. "Who do you choose as your new partner?" he asks.

I expect her to pick Martin—it would be the best strategic move, since it would knock him and Zora out of first place. But instead she says, "I choose Claire."

If this had happened while we were in Java, I would have been thrilled and flattered that my sister wanted to be with me. If it had happened yesterday, when I was with Troy, I would have been relieved. But everything is different now, and for the first time, the thought of racing with my sister actually makes me unhappy. This swap benefits her, but it doesn't help me at all. Miranda knows how much I like being with Will. Is she trying to separate us on purpose, as payback for slowing her down yesterday?

"That's not even allowed," Samir says. "The teams have to be boy-girl, right?"

Miranda shoves her card in the producer's face and points at the small print. "It says right here that I can swap my partner for *either* penalized racer. I want Claire. I can have Claire, right?"

The producer takes a step back, obviously put off by her aggressive tone. "Yes, same-sex partners are allowed for this challenge. Claire, Miranda is your partner for the rest of this leg of the race. Samir, your new partner is Will. Please join him in the far lane."

Samir looks anguished. "I have to race with a *guy*? Are you *kidding* me?"

"I can't believe she's separating us," I say to Will. "This sucks."

"She's probably just intimidated by the hazardous level of awesome radiating from our lane." He reaches out and squeezes my hand. "Thanks for an amazing morning, Dominique."

I'm not sure if he's referring to the kiss or the pastry licking or the fact that we're near the front of the pack. But in any case, he looks genuinely sorry to be separating from me, which makes me feel warm all the way through. I hang on to his fingers for as long as I can. "We'll be back together soon," I say. "There's probably just one more challenge after this one. I'll try to beat you to the finish line so I can pick you for the next leg."

He gives me a sly smile. "Oh, please. As if you could possibly beat me. This is my million dollars, after all."

"Claire, let's go!" Miranda calls. She sounds incredibly pissed, so I smile at Will one last time and run off to join her. I haven't even made it to her lane before Tawny drops her apple and Will swoops in to steal her, leaving Samir to partner with Troy.

"Look how pissed Samir is," I whisper to my sister gleefully.

"Let's get this stupid relay over with," she snaps, like I haven't said anything. "Roll your pants up above your knees.

The apples are less slippery if they're against bare skin." She starts doing the same with her own.

If Miranda and I hadn't been separated at the starting line, would she have been this bossy and demanding for the whole race? And why is she so pissed *now,* when she's successfully gotten rid of Samir? For a minute, I consider using my Heartbreaker card to steal Will back as soon as I have the opportunity—I shouldn't have to put up with my sister's attitude when *I'm* the one who deserves to be upset. But Samir could pull ahead if we waste any more time, and neither of us wants that. I can suck it up for one more challenge.

I tuck the apple under my chin and set off across the field as fast as I can. "Do *not* drop that, or Samir will steal me back," Miranda calls after me, like I'm planning to sabotage her or something.

As we do our first transfer at the other end of the field, I realize this isn't the first time my sister and I have played this game. Our hometown used to have a lot of festivals with relay races when we were kids, and Miranda was always my partner, since I was too shy to interact with the other kids. Even though I'd forgotten all about those games until this moment, my muscles remember exactly how to work in sync with my sister's. It only takes one smooth motion for her to grab the apple from me with her chin. Of course, those ridiculous, fumbling, giggling transfers with Will would have been well worth finishing the race a few minutes later.

Samir keeps a close eye on us the whole time, ready to steal Miranda back the moment we screw up, but we get through the first three laps without dropping our apple. The last swap is pretty difficult, but when I lie on my back and Miranda stands over me, balancing herself with my hands, we manage the knee-to-knee transfer. She waddles quickly down the field, and when she crosses the finish line, I expect her to cheer or at least crack a smile—she's safe from Samir for now. But she just gives me a businesslike high five and snatches the next envelope from our referee.

Make your way to the Pegasus fountain in Korinthos Square, where each team will find a wheelbarrow full of pomegranates. At Greek weddings, it is traditional to smash pomegranates on the ground—the scattering of seeds symbolizes fertility and abundance. You must smash your pomegranates until you find the one that has a small Around the World in Eighty Dates flag in the center, which you may exchange for your next instructions.

Miranda grabs her pack and dashes toward the car, and I have to sprint to keep up with her. Before she slides behind the wheel, she pulls a map out of her bag and shoves it at me harder than necessary. "Navigate," she says.

"I have my own map. Why do you always assume I'm not prepared?"

"Just hurry and tell me which way to go, okay?"

We talk of nothing but left and right turns until we arrive in Korinthos Square—the air in the car is so thick with our unaired grievances that it's difficult to breathe, let alone speak. The plaza around the Pegasus fountain is sunny and bright and full of laughing locals with drinks and ice cream, and it seems impossible that such carefree people could exist in the same dimension as my sister and I right now. Six wheelbarrows full of pomegranates are spaced at regular intervals around the fountain, and a small crowd has gathered around the one where Martin and Zora are enthusiastically smashing fruit. The juice seeps into the tan paving stones, making dramatic, bloody stains.

We pick the first wheelbarrow we come to, and Miranda snatches a pomegranate and throws it with both hands. It's overripe, and it explodes against the ground, sending a shower of red juice onto my shoes. I smash the next one, and it's surprisingly cathartic to watch seeds and pulp fly in all directions. After I throw a few more, unleashing my physical anger starts to loosen my tongue, and I turn to my sister. "So, is there anything you want to say to me right now?"

She doesn't even look at me. "Um, not really. What are you talking about?"

"How about 'I'm sorry'? That would be a good start."

Miranda smashes another pomegranate, then stomps on it violently when it doesn't break all the way open. "Seriously? You think *I* owe *you* an apology?"

"Yeah, I do, actually. You knew how much I wanted to be Will's partner, and you saw how well we were doing together, but you just swooped in anyway and split us up like you were totally entitled."

"I *was* entitled," she says. "Swapping partners was the whole point of that challenge."

"You could just as easily have chosen Martin or Zora, and that would've been the more strategic move if you wanted to get ahead of Samir, because—"

Miranda throws a pomegranate so hard half of it flies up and hits me in the leg. "I didn't want Martin or Zora, Claire! I don't care about *strategy* and *getting ahead* right now! I'm having the crappiest day ever, and I just wanted to get away from Samir and find a partner who might actually understand what I'm going through and sympathize with me a little! But I guess that's too much to ask for from you, isn't it? I kept dropping that stupid apple on purpose and waiting for you to step up and separate us, and you just ignored me and carried on with your happy little lovefest!"

Oh God, of *course* she was dropping the apple on purpose. I probably should have picked up on that. But after the fuss Miranda made about the dance challenge, her anger seems completely unfair. "That is such a double standard! Why would you expect me to help you when you just made this huge deal yesterday about how pissed you were that you helped me?"

"Because even if it hurt me, I did it anyway!"

"But I didn't *ask* you to, Miranda! That was your choice! You can't decide to do me a favor and then hold it against me!"

My sister grabs a whole bunch of pomegranates and throws three in a row, *splat splat splat.* One of them is so ripe that it squishes in her hand, and the bright red juice drips down her forearm like she's just ripped out someone's heart. "You're the one who said we were allies no matter what, and

I was trying to be a good team member and actually *look out* for you. But I guess that doesn't work both ways if it means spending two seconds away from your precious Will Divine."

I shush her—Will and Tawny have arrived and are throwing pomegranates on the other side of the fountain. "He has nothing to do with this. Leave him out of it," I hiss.

"How can I? This whole race is about *him* to you. I stupidly thought you were here because you actually cared about *my* feelings. But now you're too busy making goo-goo eyes at Will to even ask me whether I'm all right!"

Will and Tawny let out a cheer—somehow they've found their pomegranate flag already. When Miranda sees me looking at him, she hurls a pomegranate directly at my foot. "You've known him all of one week, Claire! Is that really where your loyalty lies?"

"Are you seriously talking to *me* about loyalty?" I yell. "You sell me out every time we get in front of a producer! 'Doing romantic challenges is going to be a *huge* stretch for Claire. There's no way she can possibly deal with intimate situations.'" *Smash.* "'I've spent my entire life jumping in to save my incompetent baby sister when things get too overwhelming for her.'" *Smash.* "You told that stupid fitting room story on camera! What were you *thinking*? Can't you see how they're going to use that to portray me as a naïve idiot?"

"It's not like I made any of that stuff up, Claire!"

"But none of it matters! It's not holding me back! We've been on this race for six days now, and there were literally five minutes that freaked me out! I'm not the scared little kid I was when you were seventeen, okay? And if you'd made any effort at all to know me since you went away to school, you'd realize that!" There are hot, angry tears spilling down my cheeks now, and I don't even bother to wipe them away. "God, what is it going to take for you to stop patronizing me long enough to actually *see* me?"

"I'm not trying to patronize you, I'm trying to protect you!"

"But that's the thing, Miranda—I don't need your protection anymore! I'm so sick of you babying me all the time and acting like I can't take care of myself! Are you really that surprised that I'd rather spend time with Will, who actually respects me and treats me like an adult? *You're* the one I need protection from!"

Miranda throws another pomegranate, which explodes all over my shins—there's so much red juice on me that I look like I've spent the day in a slaughterhouse. "If you want to be treated like an adult, then try thinking about someone besides yourself for once, Claire! I've just spent an entire day with my *cheating ex-boyfriend,* who I can barely *look at* without feeling like I'm going to throw up, and you've made zero effort to reach out to me! Didn't it occur to you that I might be upset? My entire life just fell apart, and I'm in the middle of nowhere, and I can't even talk to any of my friends. You're my only ally out here, and you've basically abandoned me for a *crush.* I would *never* do that to you, no matter what distractions some stupid TV network threw at me. I don't see how it matters if you can swim in your underwear or dance in front of a bunch of people if underneath it all, you're just a selfish child."

I feel like I've been kicked in the soft place under my ribs, and for a moment, I'm speechless. "Miranda, that's not—" I start.

"I don't want to hear it," she says. "If you want me to believe you're so different from how you used to be, show me you've grown up in a way that actually *matters.*"

She hurls another pomegranate, and when it breaks open, a bright pink flag peeks out of the bloody ruins. "Let's go," she says, snatching it up. "We're done here."

18

We exchange our flag for an envelope and learn that the Cupid's Nest for this leg of the race is the Temple of Apollo. Miranda doesn't even look at me as she stalks back to the car, and when we get there, she grabs the map off the backseat and figures out the way to the temple herself, as if to prove how little she trusts me. I sit in the back, stewing in her words, awash in hurt and anger.

When we finally scramble up the hill to the temple, we find Isis standing under her usual arch of pink flags. She's wearing a pink skirt that matches the flags exactly, and for some reason I find this intensely annoying. "Welcome to the Cupid's Nest, Miranda and Claire. You're in third place," she says, and we both nod. We should be happy—we're improving every leg of the race, and we've beaten Samir, which means Miranda's safe from him at the Proposal Ceremony. But neither of us is in the mood to celebrate.

"You two don't look very pleased," Isis says in her usual astute way. "Was this leg tough for you?"

I'm about to attempt a diplomatic answer, but Miranda

snaps, "It's all on tape. Figure it out for yourself." She turns and storms off to the other side of the ruins, leaving Isis with her perfect mouth puckered in a tiny, silent O. I think about following her, but I decide to give her some time to cool down. I turn away from Isis before she can ask me any more insipid questions and head off in the other direction to find a place to wait.

The ruins of the temple are pretty amazing—only a few columns are still standing, but the ground is strewn with huge broken plinths, like everything was left exactly where it fell when a giant toddler knocked it over. The sky is a shockingly deep blue, and mountains loom in the distance. But I can't enjoy any of it with Miranda's cutting words playing on repeat inside my head. Show her I've grown up "in a way that actually matters"? What does that even *mean*? Over the last week, I've proven I have all kinds of adult qualities: strategic thinking, adaptability, focus, self-reliance, the ability to overcome my fears and do what has to be done. Don't any of those things matter to her? Why can't she see them, even when they're right in front of her face? How dare she call me selfish when the only reason I'm even here is for *her*?

I comfort myself with the thought that I'll soon be back with Will, who sees who I really am. He beat me to the check-in point, so he'll be able to pick me at the Proposal Ceremony, and I'm certain that he will. When we're back at the hotel tonight, maybe I'll sneak into his room again and tell him about my fight with my sister. He'll know just what I should say to her—he's good at understanding how people

239

work. And then he can wrap me up in his arms and comfort me, and we can finish what we started at the masquerade party last night.

Everyone arrives within an hour, so it isn't long before Isis calls us together for the Proposal Ceremony. Philadelphia and Aidan are eliminated, and a producer takes them off to do their exit interview. I should be thrilled to see Philadelphia go, but I have too much on my mind to care very much. Miranda reappears from wherever she's been sulking and stands next to me, but she doesn't look at me. I can't wait until I can move away from her hostility and take my place next to Will.

"Before our Proposal Ceremony, I have a special five-thousand-dollar prize to award," Isis says. "This prize goes to the racer who made the most romantic wish at the Temple of Aphrodite today. The winner of the Passionate Plea award is . . . Claire!"

Normally I'd be ecstatic to win five thousand dollars, but now I have to work to look happy and excited. "Thank you so much!" I say, forcing a smile onto my face. "Um, you're not going to reveal my wish, are you?"

Isis lets out one of her tinkling-bell laughs. "No, we'll let you reveal it in your own time." She winks at me, and I have to make a concerted effort not to roll my eyes.

It's the boys' turn to pick their partners first, and nobody is surprised when Martin chooses to stay with Zora. "Will, you arrived second," Isis says. "Who would you like to spend the next leg of the race with?"

Across the circle, Will looks at me, just for a moment, and

I'm so sure he's about to say my name that I start to move toward him. But then his gaze shifts to my left, and he says, "I'd like to race with the gorgeous Janine, please."

Wait, *what*? I freeze in my tracks as my brain scrambles for an explanation. Will's good at playing the game, so there must be some way this will benefit both of us. Maybe he heard Miranda and me fighting about him during the pomegranate challenge, and he doesn't want to come between us—after all, he refused to sit with me in the holding room at the very first audition for the same reason. I try to catch his eye again, hoping for a smile to reassure me that he has my best interests at heart. But he's staring straight at Janine's mile-long legs in her skin-tight running pants as she glides over to him. "I'm so glad you finally chose me," she purrs, squeezing his arm.

Will gives her a dimpled smile, the one that was meant for me, and his hand settles into the small of her back. "I'm so glad I finally got a chance to choose you," he says.

My heart turns to stone and plummets toward my feet, ripping holes in all the other organs in its path. This isn't a strategic ploy or a well-hidden kindness. Despite all our easy intimacies and obvious sexual tension, despite the fact that he kissed me, told me I was hot, and called me a kick-ass woman, Will Divine doesn't really want me after all. He wants Janine.

What did I do to make him change his mind? I *know* there was something real blossoming between us; it was obvious just a few hours ago. I run through all our interactions, all our glances and fleeting touches and flirtatious banter, desperate to figure out where I went wrong. But now all I can hear in my head is Will's voice saying, *Claire, you know there's nothing actually real about reality TV, right? People will believe anything you tell them, as long as you commit to it.*

And then I remember Miranda saying, *I'm afraid that maybe you forget about the game when you're with Will.*

I did forget. I didn't want to believe that all the affection and respect and support he showed me could be anything less than genuine. But Will lied to everyone about being a CEO's son to get on the show, and there's no reason to think the things he told me were any more real. Will's not here to find his soul mate—he's here to win a million dollars, just like everyone else. Flirting to gather allies is such an obvious, basic strategy, and if I had bothered to look past the smoke screen of dimples and compliments and bright blue eyes, I would've been able to see it coming a mile away.

How could I have been so gullible? And didn't he feel guilty manipulating me when it was obvious how much I genuinely liked him? Maybe there's nothing real about this show, but I'm a real person with real emotions. Doesn't he have a conscience? Or is he so distracted by the money that compassion and empathy mean nothing to him?

And just like that, everything Miranda said to me earlier clicks into place, and I suddenly feel sick to my stomach. I'm just as guilty as Will is. I've spent every minute of this race single-mindedly trying to prove to my sister how strong and independent I am, how well I can strategize and complete challenges and plot revenge. But this isn't the time or the place for that. Miranda was betrayed by someone she loved, and she must feel ten thousand times more helpless and confused and shattered than I do right now.

My sister doesn't need revenge. She needs compassion. Miranda has told me over and over that she's fine, that she can handle things alone, but she shouldn't have to. That's the whole point of having a sister.

Miranda elbows me hard, and I realize Isis has been saying my name. "Claire, who would you like to spend the next leg of the race with?" she asks.

I'm so humiliated that it's hard to fathom going forward with the race at all. Just knowing Will is in the same hotel, on the same plane, in the same *city* as me will make it impossible to concentrate. I can't believe Miranda has managed to make it this far with Samir right next to her, squeezing drop after drop of lemon juice into her open wound. All she wants is to get away from him, and I finally understand exactly how she feels.

I remember what she said back at the hotel this morning: *I just hate being on the same side as Samir. It sucks that I can't even do anything bad to him without sabotaging myself.* And a tiny spark of hope ignites in me. I know how to turn things around for both of us.

"I'd like to race with Samir," I say.

Miranda grabs my arm and digs her nails in. "What are you doing?" she hisses. "You're going to *help* him?"

"Samir, please stand next to Claire," Isis says, and he does, looking totally perplexed.

"Are you trying to get back at me for separating you from

Will or something? Oh my God, Claire, why are you being so immature about this?"

I want so badly to tell her what I have planned, but I can't say anything in front of Samir and all the cameras. Later, during our interview, I'll explain everything. But for now, I just say, "Trust me. I know exactly what I'm doing."

And for once, I actually do.

* * *

𝓘 𝒶𝓇𝓇𝒾𝓋𝑒 𝒻𝑜𝓇 my daily wrap-up interview with Ken the producer, ready to share my new plan with Miranda. But Will is sitting in the other chair, and when he smiles warmly at me, my chest does this painful swelling, squeezing thing. He looks so happy to see me that I wonder for a minute if I misread all the signs and he really *does* care about me.

It's a game, I remind myself. *He's acting. Pull yourself together.* God, I can't even be trusted to look at his face for three seconds without relapsing. I'm a disgrace to reality television, not to mention the entire female population.

"Hey," he says, as if nothing has changed. "Fancy meeting you here."

My cheeks are heating up, and I look down at my feet, so embarrassed I can't even meet his eyes. "Hi," I say. He reaches out to touch my shoulder, but I pull away and sit down on the edge of my chair, as far from him as possible.

Ken starts asking questions about our day, and I keep my answers short. It hurts just to be near Will, to realize I've lost something I never really had, and I want to get this interview over with as quickly as possible. Will keeps trying to engage me and get me to laugh, and when I make no effort to hold up my end of the conversation, he finally says, "Hey, Dominique, what's the matter?"

It occurs to me that Will has never once called me by my real name while he was flirting with me, and my stomach twists. "My name is *Claire*," I say quietly.

"Yeah, I know what your name is. I'm just trying to lighten the mood. What's going on with you tonight? I thought—"

"*I* thought you actually liked me," I say, and I'm horrified to hear my voice crack. "I can't believe what an idiot I was."

A crinkle appears between his eyebrows. "What are you talking about? Of course I like you! I had an awesome time with you today. You were a kick-ass partner."

"Not so kick-ass that you had any trouble ditching me."

He looks genuinely confused. "When did I ditch you? Miranda stole *you* during the Heartbreaker round. I didn't want to switch partners."

"I'm not talking about that! I'm talking about Janine! I thought we were so good together, and I thought . . . and then you were just . . . you just . . ." But all the sentences I want to say are too humiliating, so I leave them hanging unfinished in the air.

Will stares at me like I'm speaking another language. "Claire, we're on a TV show. We're not getting married. You're acting like I cheated on you or something. We'll race with other people this round, and maybe we'll get to be together again later. I didn't mean to hurt you by picking Janine. None of this is personal. You know that."

I hate that both Will and Ken are looking at me with sympathy, like I'm a little girl who has just discovered the Tooth Fairy isn't real. I'm so tired of looking pathetic and ridiculous and weak. Starting tomorrow, this is all going to change.

"I'm sorry if you thought—" Will starts.

I hold up my hand. "I get it. Just stop talking, please, okay?"

And he does. The fact that he doesn't try harder to make things right with me says more than any words could.

When Ken sends Will away shortly after that, I expect him to call someone to bring out my sister. But instead he says, "You're done for now, Claire. Have a good rest, and make sure you're at the starting line on time tomorrow morning."

"Wait a minute," I say. "Don't I have to interview with Miranda?"

"Miranda will do her interview alone today."

"What? Why? I really need to talk to her."

Ken starts flipping through some papers on his clipboard, like I'm the least important thing in the room. "I'm sure you'll find an opportunity to see her tomorrow."

But tomorrow isn't soon enough; I need to fix things now. "Can you at least tell me which room she's in?"

"I'm afraid I can't do that, Claire. She specifically requested not to see you."

I managed to keep it together in front of Will, but now I'm positive I'm going to cry. I close my eyes and take a deep, steadying breath, in for three counts and out for five, just

246

like my fifth-grade teacher taught me. Right now, I can't let myself think about how angry Miranda is. I can't think about how thoroughly I misread Will. I have a job to do, and that means I need to rise above my emotions and concentrate. For a little while longer, I need to focus on playing the game. There will be plenty of time to break down later, when all this is over.

I open my eyes and sit up straight. "Can I talk to you alone for a few minutes, then?" I ask Ken.

He looks at his watch. "Okay, but make it quick. We're on a tight schedule today. What's up?"

"I want you to be prepared for what I'm going to do tomorrow," I say. "I think you're going to like this, and I want to make sure you get all the footage you need."

Suddenly he looks more interested. "What are you planning to do, exactly?"

"I'm going to sabotage myself," I tell him. "And I'm going to take Samir down with me."

19

When I get back to my room, I hand-wash my Team Revenge T-shirt in the tiny bathroom sink and hang it over the shower rail to dry. Then I lie awake for eight hours, staring at the cracks in the ceiling and thinking about everything that's happened with Will and Miranda. Around midnight, I consider getting up, systematically knocking on every door in the hotel until I find my sister's room, and forcing her to let me explain myself. But that seems like a less-than-stellar plan, unless I want to get yelled at by a lot of angry Greek people. I'll just have to hope that my actions tomorrow speak loudly enough to show Miranda that I finally understand what she's been trying to tell me.

By the time my alarm goes off for my 3:15 a.m. departure with Samir, I haven't slept at all. I guess I'll have to get through today on coffee and adrenaline. My shirt is still a little damp, but I put it on anyway, hoping it'll give me strength.

Samir is waiting for me in the lobby, marking up a copy of *Backstage* magazine with a red pen. "Hey," I say.

He doesn't even look up. "I know you hate me," he says.

"I thought that was the whole reason you came on the show. So why did you pick me as your partner?"

"*I* don't hate you. Miranda hates you. And Miranda and I are fighting right now. I mean, no offense or anything, but I mostly picked you 'cause I thought it would piss her off. It seemed like a good way to show her that she and I aren't allies anymore."

For a minute I'm not sure he's going to buy it, but then he shrugs. "Whatever," he says. "Honestly, I don't really care if you *do* hate me, as long as you race well. It's not like we have to be friends. I just want to win."

"Yeah," I say. "Me too."

He gestures at my shirt. "So, is that supposed to be ironic or something, now that we're on the same side?"

"I still want revenge," I say. "I just have a different target today."

I spend the whole ride to the checkpoint taking deep, steadying breaths and promising myself that today I will be totally focused, totally in control. I won't let anything shake me or mess with my emotions. I won't even look at Will. I won't think about the fury in Miranda's eyes as she accused me of being selfish. Over and over, I tell myself that I'm strong and clever and that everything's going to turn out okay. If I think it enough times, maybe I'll actually start believing it.

We meet our new crew—Robby on camera, Kanesha on sound—and Robby gives me a secretive smile as he shakes my hand. The producers have probably told him all about my plans for today so he'll be sure to film the right things.

I smile back, and I must be showing more than I intended on my face, because Isis says, "Claire, you look ready to race this morning."

"Never been readier," I say. "Bring it on."

"Well, may the forces of love and luck be with you." She hands me our first envelope, and I rip it open and read the instructions out loud.

Fly to Glasgow, Scotland, then choose an Around the World car at the airport and drive yourselves to Glasgow Green. Once you arrive, find the world's largest terra-cotta fountain, where you will receive your next instructions.

All the way to the airport, Samir monologues about an idea he has for a new screenplay, which would star him as a mysterious, tortured model/spy/assassin who's living a triple life with three hot wives who are all played by the same actress. At first I try to listen, but as he delves into the "nuanced psychological aspects" of the story, I quickly discover that he just wants to hear himself talk and doesn't require actual input from me. When we finally arrive, we buy tickets for a British Airways flight leaving at seven in the morning. Martin, Zora, Will, and Janine are already at the gate, and when Will smiles at me, all the emotions I'm holding at bay threaten to flood back into my chest. I take a deep breath and turn away.

When Miranda shows up, I desperately want to run over and explain everything, but I can't very well do that without blowing my cover with Samir. I'm hoping she'll put the pieces together on her own when she sees me wearing my Team Revenge shirt, but she just shoots me a look full of anger and hurt from across the gate, and I know she doesn't get it. I tug twice on my right earlobe and once on my left, the sign we always used at family functions to mean *I need a break, meet me in the bathroom.* But after ten minutes of waiting by the automatic sinks, I'm forced to admit that she isn't coming. I guess Ken wasn't kidding when he said she didn't want to see me. I know I can knock Samir out of the race alone, but Miranda and I were supposed to do this together. It hurts to know that she thinks I've sided with the enemy when I'm really just trying to get rid of him for good.

When we get on the plane, I put my earbuds in so Samir won't try to talk to me again. Somehow, I totally forgot about the motivational playlist Natalie made me before I left for the race, and I listen to it on repeat for most of the trip, even the techno-ballad by Refried Death that I know she included just to annoy me. The songs make me feel like my best friend is cheering me on from a distance, like I still have an ally somewhere in the world, and by the time we arrive in Glasgow around two in the afternoon, I'm feeling pumped up and ready.

Samir and I make our way through passport control, then out to the parking garage, where we spot a row of *Around the World* cars. I slide into the driver's seat before he can get there, then spend several minutes meticulously adjusting the mirrors. When I can tell he's gotten good and antsy, I finally say, "Oh no. Is this car a manual? I don't know how to drive stick. Do you?"

Samir heaves an exasperated sigh. "Oh my God, Claire, are you serious? How did you not notice that the second you sat down? Look at the freaking gear shift!" Miranda and Steve pull out in front of us and zoom off, and Samir punches the back of the seat. "Crap, they're already ahead of us! Get in the back! How did you do so well on the last leg of the race when you don't pay attention?"

I shrug and switch places with him as slowly as I can. "Sorry, I'm really spacey today. I didn't sleep very well."

"Well, pull it together. Do you think you can manage to navigate, or am I going to have to do that, too?"

"No problem," I say, unfurling the map. "I'm great with directions." The moment we get to the highway, I call out a wrong turn.

We're one of the last couples to arrive at Glasgow Green. As Samir sprints toward the terra-cotta fountain, I lag behind, making exaggerated panting sounds. "I can't keep up with you," I complain. "Your legs are, like, twice as long as mine, and my pack is way too big for me. It makes it really hard to run."

"God, just give it to me," he snaps. Samir's not a big guy, and it delights me to see him struggle to run with both our packs. It's pretty cool outside for July, but by the time we locate the kilt-clad local who has our next instructions, his forehead is dripping with sweat.

I take a look at the world's largest terra-cotta fountain, but I can't figure out what's special about it. I mean, it's ornate and everything, but when it comes down to it, it's just a big, orangey-red fountain. Who even keeps track of the sizes of various terra-cotta fountains? Probably the same people who try to get in the *Guinness World Records* books for stuff like skateboarding while holding a goat for the longest distance. I tear open our envelope.

It's time for Cupid's Questions, the game that tests how much you know about your date! You've had hours in the air to bond, and if you've hit it off and gotten close, you deserve a reward! Enter one of our pink tents, where your Cupid will ask you a series of questions. You will both write down your answers, and if they match, you will earn a point. Rack up ten points to receive your next instructions!

This should be pretty easy to drag out—Samir and I haven't talked at all since we were paired up, so he hasn't learned a thing about me. I head toward the row of small pink tents across the field, but Samir grabs my arm. "Memorize this, okay? I was born in Santa Barbara, but we moved to Hartford when I was two. My mom's name is Shalini and my dad's is Dev, and they're computer programmers, and I have two older sisters and one older brother, and all of them are doctors. I'm allergic to cats and peaches, and my favorite color is red, and my favorite film is Fellini's *8½*, and I wanted to be an astronaut when I was little, but now—"

I hold up my hand to stop him. "Samir, I'm not going to remember any of this. You can't cram hours of bonding time into two minutes."

"Well, it's better than nothing, isn't it? Tell me about yourself really quickly."

"We're wasting time. Let's just go in there and do the best we can, okay?"

"The best we can isn't going to cut it if we don't know anything about each other, Claire! God, it's like you *want* us to lose!"

I try not to smile. "I'm sure they won't ask us anything that hard."

"What's your favorite food? What's your favorite band?"

It would look suspicious if I refused to tell him, so I'll just have to hope they don't ask those questions. "My favorite food is coffee ice cream, and my favorite band is Rhetorical Impasse, okay? Now come on!" I push into a tent before he can stop me.

Our "Cupid," a blond woman in her twenties, is wearing feathered wings and a white polyester robe that ends midthigh. She's also carrying a quiver of plastic arrows, which snags on the fabric of the tent every time she moves and makes her scowl in a very uncherubic way. Samir and I sit down in a matching pair of red vinyl armchairs, and our Cupid hands us red dry-erase pens and mini whiteboards with little hearts around the borders. This is almost as cheesy as the Love Shack. Robby positions himself across from us with his camera, next to Cupid.

"Question one," she says with a thick Scottish accent that makes me want to laugh. "How many siblings does Claire have?"

Crap—Samir obviously knows the answer to *this* question. When our Cupid dings a little bell after fifteen seconds, we both hold up our boards. Mine says, "One." Samir's says,

"One sister: Miranda Henderson." He's clearly angling for extra credit. What a suck-up.

"Correct!" our Cupid says. "One point. Question two: what is Samir's hometown?" I write "Santa Barbara," assuming he'll write "Hartford." He does, and we miss the point. Samir glares at me.

I do my best to get all the answers wrong—I even write that Samir has a cat named Peaches—but I'm not able to slow down the process that much. Dating Miranda for a year has given Samir a surprisingly large cache of information about me. He knows what year I was born, the name of my high school, and the name of the bookstore my dad owns. Somehow, he even knows that otters are my favorite animal. The only question he gets wrong, in fact, is my favorite color. I had always assumed Miranda never even thought about me while she was at Middlebury, but it seems like she actually talked about me a fair amount. I wish I'd known that sooner and that I hadn't found out like this.

It only takes Samir fifteen minutes to earn us our next pink envelope. We have to wait a few minutes before opening it—Robby has to refilm our Cupid asking all her questions from the front—and in that time, we see several other teams dash off to the next challenge, including Will and Janine. I wonder if they played the Question Game on the plane or if they slept snuggled together. I wonder if he's making her feel like she's the only girl in the world who matters. Does she know this is all a game to him, or is she falling for his act, just like I did?

Finally, Robby lets us open our envelope.

Shortly before her wedding day, it is traditional for a Scottish woman and her friends to perform a ritual called "blackening the bride." The bride dresses all in white, and her friends take turns throwing anything they want at her, such as molasses, tar, feathers, manure, and rotten eggs. Walk north to the middle of the field marked with an Around the World flag, where the female team member must change into the white clothes provided. Then the male team member must completely blacken her from the neck down using only his hands and the available sticky substances. The female team member may not assist him. You will receive your next instructions when no white fabric is visible!

I know I need to stop thinking about Will, but for the briefest of moments, I consider what this challenge would've been like with him as my partner. I gladly would have suffered through tar and rotten eggs if it meant he'd have to touch every tingling, eager inch of my body. But that's just the thing—he'd *have* to, and that's not the same as wanting to. Touching me would be another task to complete, and any other body would do just as well. I'm sure he'll be very happy with Janine's.

"Ew," Samir says as he stares at the instructions. "I have to touch manure and tar with my bare hands?" I can't believe he's complaining about his hands when I'm going to be coated from neck to toe, but I swallow my annoyance. I can't let him start to doubt that I'm on his side.

There are makeshift dressing rooms set up along the edge of the field, and I take my time swapping out my clothes for a white T-shirt and white scrub pants that are several inches too long. My bra is bright green and my underwear is black, and both show right through the fabric, but after the pool challenge in Java, I'm past caring about that. When I make my way out onto the field, I see that Martin and Steve are almost done blackening Zora and Miranda. Will and Janine are only about half done, and she squeals like a three-year-old as he dips his hands into a bucket and lovingly rubs something sticky onto her flat stomach.

I find a spot as far from them as possible, and Samir joins me, lugging two heavy buckets of brown goo. "I'm pretty sure this one is chocolate syrup and this one is pudding," he says. "I wasn't sure which would be easier to spread. Are you ready?"

"I'm as ready as a person can be to have her sister's ex paint her with pudding," I say. "Do what you have to do."

It's kind of funny to see Samir grimace as he cups his hands and scoops up some chocolate syrup, trying not to drip on his perfectly creased jeans. But it becomes less amusing very quickly when he tips the cold syrup down my back and drops of it crawl inside my collar like curious insects. I hold my arms out to my sides, close my eyes, and wait for it to be over. To distract myself, I think about being back home on the couch with Natalie, watching *Speed Breed* and eating banana muffins and regaling her with stories about all the absurd things I've done on this show. I just need to get through today, and then it'll all be over. But it's hard to think anything but *ew, ew, ew* when someone you hate is massaging chocolate pudding onto your butt.

Samir is a meticulous worker, and Tawny and Troy have arrived by the time he covers my last patch of ankle. He calls another kilt-clad guy over to check his work, and I spin around slowly, causing my chocolate-covered clothing to stick to my skin in new and horrible ways. Half my hair has come loose from my ponytail and is plastered to my neck, and I can't lower my arms without making horrible squishing noises with my armpits.

"Jolly good," proclaims our inspector. Do people actually *say* that in the UK, or is he just doing it for the benefit of the cameras? He hands me a tiny towel, barely larger than my mom's dish towels, and sends me back to the dressing room to change.

I can't figure out a way to pull the gooey shirt over my head without smearing chocolate pudding all over my face and hair, so I find my nail clippers, hack through the collar, and rip the T-shirt all the way down the front like The Hulk. I rub as much of the pudding off my arms as possible, but the towel is saturated in seconds, so I resort to lying down on the ground and wiping my arms on the grass. I can barely stand to put my normal clothes back on over my sticky skin, but I can't very well do the rest of this leg of the race topless, even if that might win me some sort of special award from Isis.

Samir is waiting with our next pink envelope when I come out, literally tapping his foot with impatience. "What took you so long?"

I hold out my arms, which are still streaked with pudding. "Um, this?"

"God, Claire, now is not the time for preening. We're in a race, not a beauty contest. I thought you wanted to beat your sister."

"I do," I say, pleased that he still believes that's my goal.

"Well, so far you suck at it. She's been gone almost ten minutes. If you really want to get ahead, you have to make some sacrifices, okay?"

I bite back all the retorts that spring to mind and give him my best penitent smile. "Sorry, I'll try to go faster."

"You better." He rips open the envelope and reads aloud:

Make your way to the Chimney Sweep, a famous Glasgow pub. Chimney sweeps are thought to bring good luck at weddings in the UK, and they are sometimes hired to kiss the bride. In the back room of the pub, you will find several replica chimneys much like the ones real chimney sweeps face daily. Both team members must enter a chimney together and search for the loose brick on the inside of the walls, behind which lie your next instructions.

I hope none of the other teams are claustrophobic, or this challenge is really going to slow them down, and it'll be impossible to stay at the back of the pack. I mean, it's not like I'm a huge fan of tiny spaces, but at least I'm not going to have a panic attack or anything.

Wait a minute. A panic attack.

I picture the way Will acted that first day on the plane, sweating and shaking and hyperventilating, and I'm struck with a brilliant idea. I must be grinning unintentionally, because Samir says, "God, why do you look so creepily *happy*? Is squeezing yourself inside a filthy, sooty chimney your freakish idea of *fun*?"

I just smile at him. "The soot won't bother me," I say. "I don't mind playing dirty at all."

20

The pub isn't one of the landmarks listed on our map, but there are tons of people strolling around Glasgow Green, and Samir and I ask random strangers where it is until we find someone who knows. Everyone stares at my sticky arms like they're afraid I have some horrible skin disease, but it doesn't even bother me. When I think about how nervous I was asking Taufik for help in the Indonesian marketplace, I can't figure out why I was so scared. It's weird how things that once seemed like a huge deal just fade into the background when there are bigger concerns to worry about.

I navigate us through Glasgow, hoping Samir has a bad sense of direction and won't notice we're taking a very circuitous route to the pub. When we finally arrive, Martin and Zora are on their way out, covered in soot and clutching their next envelope. Samir curses. "We're *so* behind! If you'd just listened to the stuff I told you before we went in that idiotic Cupid tent—"

"It'll be fine, Samir," I say, cutting him off. "We'll search quickly, okay? There can't be that many bricks inside a chimney. We can still catch up. We're not even in last place." He pushes in front of me and shoves the door open, and I give the camera a little wink as soon as his back is turned.

To my dismay, there's a bagpiper inside the pub—that sound has always reminded me of dying cattle. But aside from that, it's a gorgeous space, paneled in carved dark wood that looks like it's been polished smooth by hundreds of years of rubbing hands. At first I'm surprised by the number of people drinking this early in the afternoon, but they all raise their glasses to us in unison and shout *"Sláinte!"* when we walk in, so most of them are probably hired extras. I pause to give the drinkers a little salute before Samir practically drags me into the back.

There are four replica chimneys in the room. Through the openings where fireplaces would normally go, I can make out four pairs of feet, including my sister's red sneakers and Will's blue ones. As we pass Miranda's chimney, I hear a muffled voice say, "Reach behind my head . . . no, wait, ow, not there!" From Will and Janine's, I only hear high-pitched giggling, which makes my stomach squirm. A producer points us toward the chimney across from my sister's, and Samir crouches down by the opening.

"How are we even supposed to do this?" he asks. "There's barely room for one person in here."

"I guess we just have to squeeze. Should we go in front-to-front or back-to-back?"

Samir frowns as he eyes my pudding-smeared arms. "Back-to-back. I don't want your skin touching me."

I'm pretty sure that isn't going to work, but in the interest of killing more time, I say, "Great, let's go."

Samir goes in first, and then I do an awkward hop-scoot-crawl into the bottom of the chimney and worm myself upright. Once I'm standing, our bodies take up the whole space, and there isn't any room to raise our arms and search. The back room of the pub is pretty dark to begin with, and now that we're enclosed by sooty black walls, it's impossible to see anything at all. Samir sneezes, and his head cracks into mine. The tiny enclosure is already starting to heat up from our breath and the warmth of our bodies, and I can tell it'll be stifling soon. Until this moment, I hadn't even noticed that Samir was wearing cologne, but now the smell is so overpowering it makes me want to gag. How could Miranda have wanted to get close to this guy on *purpose*?

"Okay, this clearly isn't working," Samir says. "We need to turn around."

There's no room to maneuver, so I crouch down while Samir repositions himself, then skid my back up the sooty wall until I'm vertical again. Standing front-to-front is even worse; I can feel Samir's hot breath on my forehead, and when he reaches out to search the soot-covered bricks behind me, his chest presses against my boobs. I forbid myself to think about what Will and Janine are doing inside their chimney.

"Be methodical," Samir orders, like he has a PhD in chimney searching. "I only want to do this once."

"Trust me, you're not alone," I mutter.

I make a show of searching for about two minutes before I start breathing harder and faster, channeling Will on the plane. Then I start swaying a little and stumble into Samir like I'm growing unsteady on my feet. "Watch it," he snaps.

"This space is really, really small," I say, making my voice tremble.

"Thank you, Captain Obvious."

"No, I mean, *really* small. And hot. Are you hot? I feel super warm."

"Not really," he says.

I breathe faster. "Samir, I feel weird. I need to get out of here. I need air."

He sighs impatiently. "You can have all the air you want once we find the brick."

"No, I need it *now*. I can't breathe. I feel like the walls are closing in." I stagger, crashing into Samir's chest and knocking him back against the wall. "Oh my God oh my God oh my God . . . ," I chant in a high-pitched, hysterical voice.

"Claire, chill out! Just take a deep breath, okay? You're fine. We need to do this."

"I can't, I can't do this. I need to get out of here." I deserve an Oscar for this performance. Before Samir can protest, I duck down and crawl out of the opening, panting so hard I really am starting to get dizzy. I curl up on the floor with my head between my knees, cursing the insidious bagpipe music that's trying to eat my brain from the inside.

Right away, a producer appears beside me. "Are you hurt?" She puts a gentle hand on my back, even though I'm covered in pudding and sweat and dirt. She's the first person who's been nice to me in twenty-four hours, and even though my panic attack is totally fake, for a second I feel like I'm going to cry for real. *Stay on task,* I remind myself.

"No," I gasp. "I just don't do well with small spaces."

"Just breathe. You're going to be fine." She reaches out and taps Samir's ankle, and he squats down so he can hear her. "You have to stop searching until your partner is ready to rejoin you," she says.

He rolls his eyes. "Claire, hurry up. Are you almost ready?"

I put my hand to my forehead like I'm a fragile flower and take a surreptitious glance around the room. Miranda and Steve are gone, but Will and Janine are still in their chimney, and Tawny and Troy haven't even arrived. I need to draw this out longer. I take several infuriatingly slow breaths and say, "Okay, I can try again," in a weak voice.

The second I'm back inside the chimney, I start making small whimpering sounds that harmonize with the obnoxious bagpipes. "I hate this, I hate this, I hate this," I whine. "Where is that stupid brick?"

"Relax," Samir says with about as much sympathy as a drill instructor. "Close your eyes and pretend you're somewhere else."

"But I can *feel* how close together we are. You keep bumping into me. Oh God, I'm getting dizzy again." I flail my arms around and "accidentally" whack him in the face.

"Knock it off!" he shouts. "We don't have time for this. We're already way behind!"

"I can't help it! I'm claustrophobic! It's not like I'm *choosing* to be scared!"

"God, fine. Just . . . stand still, okay? You don't have to do anything, but you *have* to stay in here, or I'm not allowed to search."

"I'll try," I say. "But I can't promise anything."

I leave the chimney twice more to "get some air" before Samir finally finds the loose brick, which turns out to be near the bottom, behind my right knee. As we crawl out into the room, I scan the other chimneys for shoes and find that Will and Janine are gone and Tawny and Troy have finally arrived.

Samir rips open the instructions for our last challenge— our final challenge of the race, if everything goes as planned.

Drive yourselves to Sweetheart Abbey in Dumfries. This famous abbey was founded in 1275 by a lord's daughter in honor of her dead husband. When she died, his embalmed heart was buried in a small casket beside her. You must search the thirty-acre grounds of the abbey, where hundreds of small caskets have been scattered. Only one of them contains your next instructions.

Samir groans and rubs his eyes, leaving behind smudges of soot that make him look like a raccoon. "Oh my God, this could take forever."

"Maybe we'll get lucky and find it right away," I say.

He glares at me. "*Everything* takes forever with you. I have no idea how you've lasted this long in the race. I can't wait to switch partners."

I shoot the camera another secretive smile as I follow Samir out of the pub.

The ride to Dumfries is largely silent. Samir drives, and since we're supposed to stay on one road almost the entire way, there's hardly any navigating to be done. The silence leaves me too much time to think, and as I watch the Crayola-green farmland, low stone walls, and hills of scrubby trees rush by outside the window, my brain churns itself into a froth. What if I can't ensure that Samir and I come in last, and I've spent the entire day looking like an incompetent fool for nothing? What if I succeed, but Miranda's not even grateful? Have I caused so much damage that my grand gesture won't be enough to repair things between us?

We drive past a few small towns and through the city of Dumfries, then down a bunch of narrow, twisting village streets where all the doors are painted different bright colors. Finally, we spot Sweetheart Abbey looming ahead. Only the outside shell of the building is still intact, all crumbling brick towers and arches. The floor, where there must once have been an altar and pews, is a carpet of neatly trimmed grass. Martin and Zora are pulling out of the parking lot as we pull in, zipping toward the Cupid's Nest. When we get out of the car, I see Miranda and Steve searching a distant field. In the other direction, Will and Janine are tromping through some high grass. He's laughing uproariously at something she's said, and he seems to be holding her hand. My heart skips a couple beats before it starts limping onward again

"We should split up so we can search faster," Samir says.

"Nope," Robby says before I have time to object. "The camera has to be able to see both of you at all times." I've never heard him speak before, and he sounds eerily similar to Kermit the Frog. I almost burst out laughing, but I manage to turn it into a coughing fit just in time.

Samir heaves a soul-deep sigh. "*Fine.* Let's go around to the other side of the building and start there."

The far side of the abbey has huge arched windows that gape open to the overcast sky like wide, sightless eyes. Moss grows along the windowsills and covers the top of the wall that encloses a small graveyard. The stones are weathered by hundreds of years of rain and wind, and I run my fingers over the shallow inscriptions. Most of them are so old that I can barely make out the words. Scattered here and there are small wooden boxes that look brand-new—I guess these are the "caskets" we're supposed to be searching. I was picturing something much bigger, like those hexagonal coffins cartoon vampires live in. I crack open the lid of one, but it's empty. So are the second and third boxes I try.

Shockingly, the fourth contains a stack of pink envelopes.

It figures I'd finally get lucky *now,* when it's the last thing I want. If Samir and I find the envelopes this early, it'll put us in second place, and I can't let that happen, or I'll never be able to make things right with Miranda. I close the lid of the box very quietly, hoping against hope that Samir hasn't seen the flash of pink inside. But he's checking the caskets a few rows away and not paying me the slightest bit of attention. Robby, on the other hand, has his camera pointed right at me. I shoot him a questioning look, wondering if he got what just happened on film. He gives me a thumbs-up behind Samir's back.

"I've searched this whole side, and there's nothing here," I call to Samir. "They probably wouldn't put the envelopes this close to the main building anyway, would they? Let's head farther out." I start tromping toward one of the large empty fields nobody's searching, and I'm relieved when Samir follows me, totally oblivious.

"Remember where you've already looked," he tells me, like I'm five years old and learning to play one of those memory games. "Work smarter, not harder, okay?" For someone with an IQ of 146, he's falling pretty thoroughly for my ruse. But I just nod like he's spouting sage wisdom, not clichés you might find on posters in a guidance counselor's office.

A car door slams in the parking area, followed by the sound of Tawny's barking laughter. Good—now I just need everyone to find the envelopes in the graveyard before Samir does. Sabotaging myself is surprisingly difficult. You'd think it would be easy to lose.

Unfortunately, Samir is a little savvier than I'd hoped, and he keeps a close eye on the other teams while we search. I manage to distract him by pretending to twist my ankle when I see Miranda and Steve walking toward their car from the back of the abbey, but when he sees Will and Janine heading to the parking lot ten minutes later, he realizes we're searching the wrong side of the grounds. He's getting more and more frustrated, and I'm pretty sure he's not going to fall for my tricks much longer. Just as I'm wondering if I'll have to resort to more desperate measures, like filling our car with biodiesel or feigning food poisoning, I see Tawny and Troy heading for the graveyard.

"Let's search the front of the abbey again," I say, grabbing

Samir's arm and leading him in the opposite direction. "Maybe they put the envelopes somewhere so obvious we wouldn't even think to look there."

Samir rants and mutters as we check and double-check all the empty boxes in front of the abbey, followed by the ones inside the walls. And then Tawny lets out a whoop from the graveyard, advertising her exact location and the fact that she's found the envelopes, and my heart sinks. Doesn't she know you're supposed to be *sneaky* during challenges like this?

"It's over there!" Samir screams, pointing toward the back of the abbey just as Tawny and Troy rush past us on the way to their car. "We *looked* over there! How did we miss it?"

"Crap! I don't know!" I try my best to sound as panicked as he does.

Tawny and Troy's engine starts up, and Samir runs toward the graveyard with Robby at his heels. "Hurry!" he shouts over his shoulder at me, and I do. I have to keep myself between him and that envelope for as long as I can.

But it's no use. Samir dashes up and down the rows of graves like a sugar-high toddler, throwing boxes open, and he finds the last envelope in less than a minute. "It's right here!" he shrieks, waving it in my face. "*You* were searching this side of the graveyard. Why didn't you see it? Are you blind or something? God, you *suck*! We could have been done an hour ago!" He sprints toward the car, not even checking to see if I'm following.

"I'm so sorry," I pant as I run after him. "But at least we have it now, right?"

"It's *too late* now, Claire!"

I pray he's right, but Tawny and Troy hardly have any lead at all. "Maybe it's not. Just stop for a second and open the instructions! We have no idea where we're supposed to go!"

Samir tears the envelope open so forcefully the instructions rip down the middle. He reads the two pieces and then thrusts them at me in disgust.

Make your way to the front entrance of Drumlanrig Castle in Dumfries, the Cupid's Nest for this leg of the race. Hurry—one team's race around the world ends here!

Samir flings himself into the driver's seat and starts the car before Kanesha and I have even shut our doors. "You've cost me half a million dollars, you bitch," he fumes. "I hope you're proud of yourself."

I am, I want to tell him, but I need to save that for the finish line. Instead I say, "It's not over yet. Just drive, okay? Maybe someone will get stalled on the way to Dumfries." For a second, I'm afraid he's going to turn around and slap me. But instead he just peels out of the parking lot so fast our wheels spin and a literal cloud of dust flies up behind us.

Half the roads we have to take to Dumfries are barely wide enough for two cars to pass each other, but Samir barrels down them at such a breakneck pace that Kanesha and I slam into each other every time he turns. I hold my breath basically the whole way, praying no one else's car really *does* break down on the side of the road—at this rate, we actually might catch up to Tawny and Troy. Though if Samir keeps driving like this, it won't even matter if my plan succeeds, because we'll all die in a fiery crash before we make it to the castle. "God, Samir, slow down," I say. "Even if we're in last place, I'd really like to make it there alive."

Samir slams on the brakes so hard the car skids. My head snaps forward and then back as my seatbelt engages, and Robby's camera nearly flies through the windshield. "You don't have to stop entirely," I say, rubbing my whiplashed neck.

But Samir isn't paying any attention to me—he's staring out the front window, both hands on his head like he's about to tear out his hair in chunks. *"Are you freaking kidding me?"* he sputters.

Because the road is completely full of sheep, big and fluffy and huggable, like an animated movie come to life. There are about twenty of them milling around on the asphalt like they don't have a care in the world, and it's such a perfect, absurd roadblock that I burst into hysterical laughter.

"What is *wrong* with you?" Samir screams. "There is nothing funny about this!" His face is the color of a strawberry, and there's a vein throbbing on his left temple. He blasts the horn, but the sheep don't even bother to look up, which makes me laugh even harder. After all the difficult things we've been forced to do, my sister's ex is about to have an aneurism over farm animals.

"I'm sorry," I gasp, "but *everything* about this is funny."

Samir rolls down his window. "Move it, assholes! Do you want to be roadkill? 'Cause I will run you over! Don't test me!" He inches the car forward in what I guess is supposed to be a threatening gesture. A couple of sheep deign to glance up at him for a minute, but they just gaze at the car sleepily, then go back to what they were doing. A couple of them start nibbling on the grass at the side of the road.

Samir opens the car door and strides out into the flock, waving his arms like a deranged windmill and screaming obscenities, and Robby scurries out after him to document his nervous breakdown. Even when Samir plants both his hands on one of the sheep's butts and tries to push it off the road by force, it refuses to move. I'm laughing so hard now I can hardly breathe, and Kanesha is starting to giggle, too. Miranda's going to die when this episode airs.

Just when I think things can't get any funnier, one of the biggest sheep turns around and stares straight at Samir, then lowers its head and starts running right at him. Samir's eyes bug out, and he shrieks like a kindergarten girl with a bee up her dress as he bolts for the car. He dives through the open door headfirst, sprawling across both front seats in an incredibly undignified way. "That psycho sheep is trying to kill me!" he pants.

Samir's skinny ankles are still hanging out the door when the sheep stampedes right past him and heads for the fence at the other side of the road. When it reaches a post, it starts rubbing its head against the wood as gleefully as Will was rubbing Janine's stomach this morning. It makes a happy bleating noise, and tears of laughter start streaming down my face. I so hope Robby managed to get Samir's flying leap on camera. I can picture it being played over and over in slow motion, underscored with faux-heroic music. For once, I won't be the one who's portrayed as ridiculous.

"Oh my God," I gasp. "You were terrified of that sheep. You thought it was going to eat you. That was, hands down, the funniest thing I've ever seen in my life."

Samir has struggled back into a sitting position, but his face is now several layers of red, embarrassment on top of frustration on top of fury. "For the love of God, get off your lazy ass and help me, Claire! We're about to get eliminated because of a bunch of *sheep.* How do we get them to *move*?"

It takes five more minutes for the sheep to make their own slow, meandering way off the road. Samir spends most of that time leaning on the horn and shouting threats that involve the word "mutton," and Robby keeps the camera right in his face the whole time. A line of cars starts backing up behind us, and they add their horns to the mix, which doesn't seem to bother the sheep at all but makes Samir even angrier. By the time our wooly friends decide to amble back into their pasture, Samir has almost no voice left.

When we peel into the nearly empty parking lot of Drumlanrig Castle thirty minutes later, four other *Around the World* cars are waiting to meet us. There's no need to run at this point—we're obviously in last place—but Samir does, so I do, too, just to make things easier for Robby. Together we sprint through the gate, across the wide oval lawn, and toward the double staircase at the front of the castle, where Isis is standing. The enormous, brick-red building looms behind her, its chimneys and dome-topped turrets shining a soft gold in the light of the evening sun. I'm glad my elimination point is a beautiful one. With my head held high, I step into the spotlights that surround our host and her archway of flags.

"Welcome to the Cupid's Nest, Samir and Claire," Isis says. "You're in last place. Your race around the world has come to an end."

21

Samir lets out an unearthly howl as he hurls his pack onto the ground and kicks it. "This is all your fault!" he screams at me, flecks of spit flying from his mouth. "I *hate* you and your stupid panic attacks and your terrible directions and your total inability to retain basic information! I could have *won* this if it weren't for you! I swear to God, you could not have been a worse partner if you'd *wanted* to lose!"

The other teams were resting along the edges of the lawn when we arrived, out of sight of the cameras, but Samir's making such a scene that everyone creeps closer for a better look. I wait until I'm sure Miranda's within earshot, and then I turn back to Samir.

"I *did* want to lose, you idiot," I say. "You think I'm really as incompetent as I seemed today? I thought you were a theater major. Can't you tell when someone is acting?"

I'm pretty sure the vein in Samir's temple is going to explode and spray me with blood at any moment. "You *sabotaged* us on *purpose*? What the hell, Claire? If you couldn't handle the race, you could've just quit! You didn't have to throw away *my* chance at a million dollars. Don't you ever think about anyone but yourself?"

The way his words echo Miranda's is a little disturbing, but this time, I know I'm in the right. "Actually, I do," I say. I point to the Team Revenge logo on my filthy T-shirt. "Do you see what this says, Samir? It's not a joke. You can't treat people the way you treated Miranda and expect to get away with it."

His eyes bug out. "What happened between Miranda and me is none of your freaking business!"

"When you love someone, her happiness *is* your business. You messed with me when you messed with her. That's what loyalty means. But I guess you wouldn't know anything about that." I glance over at Miranda to make sure she's listening, and she is. "After what you did to my sister, she shouldn't have to look at your smug face for one more second. It's time for you to go home."

When I look around the lawn, I see shocked expressions on every face. Will is staring at me, but my eyes skate right over him and land on Miranda. My sister's lips are slightly parted, and her forehead is furrowed like she's trying to reset her brain. And for the first time since I was in middle school, I feel like she's actually seeing me. I'm exhausted and smelly and covered in soot and dirt and dried pudding, but I have never felt so powerful as I do right now. Even with all these eyes on me, I'm not the least bit stiff or embarrassed. I'm not even blushing. I want everyone to look at me, the girl who's wily and smart, the girl who stands up for the people she loves, the girl who nearly fell apart but rebounded stronger than ever.

Isis looks a little baffled, but she recovers quickly. "Samir, do you have anything to say for yourself?" she asks.

"If you're taking suggestions, you might consider apologizing to Miranda," I say.

I don't think I've ever seen anyone look as pissed as Samir does right now. "Screw all of you," he snaps. He turns on his heel and stalks off, leaving his pack behind. A producer tries to intercept him as he storms toward the parking lot, but he brushes right past her. "I don't have to listen to you anymore," I hear him say. "What're you gonna do, eliminate me?"

Isis squints past the floodlights that surround us. "Where's Miranda? Could you come over here, please?"

Miranda steps out of the shadows, but when she gets close enough to touch me, she holds back like she's not sure she's welcome. There's a lot we need to work through, but at this moment, all I want to do is hug her. I reach out my arms, and she throws herself into them. We're both sticky and filthy, but neither of us cares, and we cling to each other.

"You got yourself eliminated for me?" she whispers in my ear. I nod against her shoulder, and she pulls me closer. "Claire, I can't even . . . I just . . . *Thank you.*"

Isis clears her throat and we pull apart, but Miranda keeps a tight hold on my hand. "What would you like to say to your sister, Miranda?" our host asks.

Miranda turns and looks at me. "You are *the best ever.* You know you're basically my hero, right?"

"Miranda, can you talk to the camera, please?" Isis reminds her.

"Sorry." My sister looks into the lens. "What Claire did today is *totally crazy*. I can't believe she got herself knocked out of the race for me. And did you see how she fooled Samir? He had *no idea* what was going on. I mean, the guy's an asshole, but he's not dumb. Claire's just . . . God, she's so incredibly smart, and what she did was so selfless. I'm so lucky to have her as my sister. *And* my friend."

Her words make me feel weightless, like I could lift off the ground and fly joyous laps around the castle in the summer twilight. "Claire, what would you like to say to Miranda?" Isis asks.

Most of the things I want to say will have to wait until we're alone, so I settle for "Miranda's such an amazing person, and she deserves to be surrounded by people who treat her right. I hope she never has to deal with anyone as crappy as Samir ever again." I squeeze her hand. "I also hope she wins the race."

One of the producers appears by Isis's side. He's wearing an Angels cap, and I realize it's Chuck, the same guy who was in charge at the starting line. It feels like years have passed since we last saw him. "Let's hold off on the Proposal Ceremony," he says. "I want to get these two into an exit interview right away."

"No problem," Isis answers. "I'll be ready when you are." Someone materializes behind her with a cushioned chair, a magazine, and a glass of water, and the moment she sits, a makeup artist starts touching up her lipstick. I realize for the first time how easy it would be to seem perfect if you had no responsibility for the way you presented yourself.

Chuck pulls a radio off his belt and mumbles something about lighting equipment, and some crew guys spring into action and start setting up a makeshift studio on the steps of the castle. "Hang tight for a couple minutes," Chuck says before he herds the rest of the racers off in the other direction and leaves me alone with Miranda.

My sister tugs my hand, and we move out of the glare of the lights and into the soft golden glow of the sunset. For a minute, neither of us says anything, and I can hear birds calling good night to each other across the castle grounds. When Miranda finally speaks, her voice is quiet. "Hey, I shouldn't have said all those awful things to you yesterday. I'm really sorry. When the producers said you were refusing to see me, I thought you were never going to talk to me again."

My mouth drops open. "What? I never said I didn't want to see you! I begged them to tell me what room you were in, but they said you didn't want to see me!"

Miranda laughs bitterly and buries her face in her hands. "Oh my God, are you serious? This show *sucks.* I can't wait to go home and get away from all these people. Do you think they'd let me leave with you?"

"No, you can't leave! You have to keep going! You could actually win this."

Miranda shrugs. "What's the point, now that you got rid of Samir?"

"Just do it for yourself. Imagine what you could do with all that money. You could hole up in the woods for a decade and write fifteen Great American Novels. Or take another trip around the world where you'd actually get to stop and look at stuff. Or buy, like, two hundred ponies."

"These are all valid points." She pretends to flag down Isis. "Hey, which way to the Love Shack?" We both laugh, and for a second, things feel almost normal between us, but then Miranda's smile falters. "Seriously, though, this isn't how things were supposed to go. I don't want to do this without you."

"You were already doing it without me. I was busy ditching you for some guy I barely knew."

"It happens," Miranda says. "Don't beat yourself up about it. It's not like I've never ditched someone for a boy. It's obvious how much you like him."

Her comment startles me, but then I realize we haven't really talked in two days. I shake my head, and the emotions I've been holding at bay all come crashing back at once. "Not anymore," I say.

"What happened, Clairie?" my sister asks, and the fact that she's using my nickname again makes a renegade tear slip down my cheek. She reaches out to rub my back—*circle, circle, pat pat pat*—and I spill the whole story of what happened between Will and me. When I'm finished, I wait for the inevitable lecture about how I shouldn't have gotten attached to him, how I should have remembered that all of this is a game. But my sister just wraps me tightly in her arms. "I'm so sorry, babe. I know exactly what that's like."

"I can't even tell you how ridiculous I feel right now. I mean, I watched him lie to other people, and for some reason, I still thought I was different."

"You *are* different," she says.

"Team Revenge!" Chuck shouts. "We're ready for you."

"One second," Miranda calls. She lets go of me and digs through her pack until she finds her matching red T-shirt. It's creased and wrinkled, and it still smells like the Javanese fish market, but she pulls it on over her tank top anyway. Then she turns to me and smiles. "You ready?"

I wipe my eyes and slip my arm around my sister's waist, and together we make our way across the lush lawn and into the glare of the network's floodlights. When we're seated, Chuck says, "Claire, can you tell me a little bit about why you decided to sabotage yourself and Samir today?"

It's the last time I'll be in the spotlight, and I'm prepared to make the most of it, to get everything out in the open. "Part of what I did today was about revenge," I begin. "But I did it for other reasons, too—"

Chuck holds up a hand to stop me. "Sorry, hang on. We're having a little trouble with the camera. Can you guys start over?"

Miranda looks at me, a question in her eyes, and I smile at her.

"Yeah," I say. "I think we can do that."

Epilogue

It's a Sunday night in October, and for the sixth week in a row, my house is full of friends, relatives, and neighbors who are here to watch *Around the World in Eighty Dates*. Miranda and I sit side by side in the center of the couch, the best seats in the house—I'm still considered a guest of honor, even though my final episode aired a couple of weeks ago. We haven't seen Miranda get eliminated yet, but I know tonight's episode is her last, based on when she showed up at the Portuguese beach hotel where they kept the eliminated contestants until filming was over. (In keeping with the cheesy tone of the show, everyone referred to it as Heartbreak Hotel.) Next week is the finale, when we'll all appear one last time to cheer for Martin and Zora as they cross the finish line and are presented with a million dollars. Tawny and Steve, who came in second, each won a trip for two to Tahiti.

Natalie sits on my other side, her neon-green boots propped on the coffee table and the yellow crocheted pillow hugged tightly to her stomach. My other best friends, Chris and Abby, are sprawled on the floor at our feet, having a heated debate about whether they'd prefer to see Blake or Troy do a striptease. A couple of Miranda's college friends are up from New York City for the weekend, and they're taking her back down with them tomorrow to hunt for apartments in Brooklyn. Since I have Columbus Day off from school, Miranda has asked me to come with them to help her pick one out.

At one minute to eight, my sister stands up and taps her wineglass with a spoon, and everyone quiets. "I'd like to dedicate this episode to Claire," she says. "You all saw how she stood up to Samir for me, and this is my way of saying thank you."

Everyone applauds, and I take a surprised, confused little bow. "I'm flattered, but what does this episode have to do with me?" I ask. Miranda hasn't told me anything about what happened on the show after I left, claiming she didn't want to spoil any surprises.

She smiles cryptically. "You'll see."

The credits sequence starts, and everyone cheers and settles down in their seats. Chris and Natalie sing along to the superdramatic opening music, adding their own little harmonies and flourishes. When the pink heart-map logo pops up, flanked by animated Cupids, they both shout out the tagline: *Where in the world will you find* your *soul mate?*

Miranda's laptop dings to indicate a new Skype call, and Steve's face pops up on the screen. He's watched every episode with us remotely from his dorm room at the University of Minnesota. "Sorry I'm late," he says. "One of the dryers in the basement caught on fire again."

"Seriously, Steve, how many times do I have to warn you to check your pockets for explosives before you do laundry?" Miranda says.

He grins at her. "I have to keep things interesting around here somehow. It'd be a lot easier if you'd just come visit already."

Miranda's friends start *ooooh*ing and making smooching noises, and she blushes bright red, but she's smiling. Though she keeps claiming there's nothing going on between them, I've caught her on the phone with Steve late at night more times than I can count. Miranda's been skipping from boyfriend to boyfriend without a pause since she was about fourteen, and I'm glad she's finally taking some time for herself. But I do hope the two of them will get together eventually. I suspect Steve is one of the few guys who might actually deserve her.

Episode six opens with the Proposal Ceremony from last week, when Janine and Troy were eliminated in Sweden. After a brief reshuffling of partners, Miranda is left to race with Will Divine. Natalie boos loudly and throws a Cheez-It at the screen, and one of our cats bounds off my dad's lap to chase it.

It's been two months now, and though I don't exactly miss Will, seeing him onscreen every week still makes my stomach twist. I never spoke to him again after our last interview, but watching the show has cleared up a lot of things for me. By this point in the season, I've seen Will "reluctantly open up" to every single one of his partners, and his stories have been different each time, specifically tailored to the girl. He was only afraid of flying when he was with me, and it's clear to me now that he faked his panic attack in the air so I'd see him as vulnerable and reveal my own insecurities. With Philadelphia, he fabricated a girlfriend who had recently broken his heart. With Janine, he talked about his fear of failing his beloved dying grandmother. He told every one of us how beautiful and kick-ass and brave we were, and each of us looked equally flushed and flattered, convinced that we were special.

As disgusting as his strategy was, it was effective—the more of us he charmed, the earlier he was chosen in each Proposal Ceremony, giving him a bigger lead. Up on Acrocorinth, after my mortifying confession that I wanted Will to be my boyfriend, he wished that none of the girls in the race would realize that he didn't really care about us. All he ever wanted was that shiny, elusive million dollars.

In front of my friends and my family, I pretend to regret having anything to do with Will. But the fact remains that without his encouragement, genuine or not, I never would've grown into the person I became on the race. Nothing he said to me was real, but the switches he flipped inside me were. It's because of him that I pretended to be the bravest, boldest, best version of myself, and somewhere along the way, I slipped inside that girl's skin and made myself at home.

Of course, that doesn't mean I want to watch him hit on my sister. "I'm so sorry you had to race with him," I say now.

"I would've picked you if I could!" Steve calls from the laptop.

"I know, honey," Miranda says, patting the computer screen. "But then you wouldn't have gotten a trip to Tahiti."

Steve considers that. "Yeah. I made the right choice."

"Now, if you were to take *me* to Tahiti to make it up to me, I wouldn't complain. . . ."

"Shh," Natalie says. "Flirt later. I can't hear Isis."

Off to the side, my parents have already started whispering a never-ending stream of questions to our neighbor—they're the sort of people who listen to opera simulcasts and carry public radio tote bags, so reality TV baffles them. Weirdly, they've gotten kind of into the race, though they're still not too pleased that their daughters were on a show with a dating component. I've told them over and over that I never had to do anything too inappropriate, and I'm pretty sure they believe me. But watching them watch me lick honey off Will Divine's neck still ranks among the top five awkward moments of my life, just below the time my dad tried to give me the Sex Talk when I was *sixteen*.

On the screen, the teams are instructed to fly to Nairobi, Kenya. Will and Miranda book a flight through London, and the other two teams go through Frankfurt, which should get them there at the same time. But Will and Miranda arrive at Heathrow in the middle of a thunderstorm, and their connecting flight is delayed six hours. By the time they finally arrive in Africa, I can tell that no matter what they do, the game is over for them.

In the outdoor market where their first challenge is taking place, Screen Miranda reads an instruction card aloud.

"In Kenya, some men dress in women's clothing for a month after their weddings to get a sense of what it feels like to be their wives. In homage to this, the male member of your team must complete this entire leg of the race dressed in women's clothing his female teammate chooses at the market. Have fun dressing your date!"

When Tawny and Zora dressed their men earlier in the episode, they chose long, loose, comfortable dresses that allowed Steve and Martin to move freely. But Miranda has other ideas. The shot cuts to her talking directly to the camera, and she says, "I knew we were way too far behind to stay in the game. And you all saw how my sister went out with a bang, right? I knew I had to live up to her amazing example."

"Oh my God, are you really about to do what I think you're about to do?" asks Natalie. "Because if you are, you'll be my hero forever."

The next thirty seconds are a montage of my sister dressing Will Divine. First comes the short red skirt, so close-fitting he can barely separate his thighs. Then comes the purple bra with cups pointy enough to satisfy 1980s Madonna and some sort of pink tunic. Then come the heavy beaded necklaces and the strappy gold sandals with stiletto heels—I don't know what those were even doing in a Kenyan market. Will's hairy toes poke out the front by at least an inch, and he can barely balance without clinging to Miranda. Last of all, my sister plucks off his stupid gray hat and replaces it with a pink headscarf, which the laughing merchant gleefully ties for him. As he totters off to do the next challenge, there's a shot of his lucky hat lying abandoned in the dust.

By this time, Natalie and I are laughing so hard we're crying. When Nat insists on rewinding the sequence and watching it twice more, nobody objects. After what Will put me through, there's nothing more delightful than watching him stagger around like a drunk sorority girl, looking exactly as ridiculous as he made me feel. For the next twenty minutes, we watch him try to herd cattle and learn a traditional Bantu dance in his insane outfit. As I watch him curse and trip over his own blistered feet, that last breath of sadness over what happened between us flies out with my laughter and dissipates into the air.

When Will finally stumbles into the Cupid's Nest with my sister hours after the other teams, perfectly composed Isis takes one look at him and lets out a legitimate guffaw. When she manages to rearrange her face into a sympathetic expression, she says, "Welcome to the Cupid's Nest, Will and Miranda. You're in last place. Your race around the world has come to an end."

We all knew that was coming, but everyone in our living room boos and shouts in protest. Natalie throws more Cheez-Its, one of which hits Chris in the face. "It's okay," Miranda calls out. "I'm still glad I did it."

As if on cue, Isis asks, "Miranda, what has this race taught you?"

"I learned to be flexible enough to change my expectations," my sister answers, and I feel like she's talking directly to me.

Isis nods at her sage words. "And, Will? What have you learned?"

Will pulls off a gold shoe and flings it furiously into the darkness. "I learned that being a girl *sucks*."

"It's not so bad," Miranda answers. "Nature made us stronger. It's the only way we could possibly deal with men." Isis holds up her hand and gives my sister a totally undignified high five.

As everyone in our living room breaks into applause and whistles, I scoot closer to Miranda on the couch and link my arm with hers. "Thanks, Mira," I say quietly.

"There once was a dumbass named Will . . . ," she says in response.

I grin. "He seemed oh-so-charming until . . ." .

"He proved he was evil . . ."

"And caused an upheaval . . ."

"So kicking his butt was a thrill."

On the screen, there's a closing shot of Will struggling into his pack and walking away, tottering unsteadily on one gold heel.

"Man, karma's a bitch, isn't it?" my sister says.

"Yeah," I say. "For real."

Closing Credits

Thank you, thank you, thank you to the following people, without whom this book and I would both be total disasters:

Wendy Loggia, my genius editor, who looks at a manuscript and so clearly sees what it could become. Thank you for never settling for anything less than my best work. You were so, so right about . . . well, everything.

My astonishingly awesome agent, Holly Root, who talks me down and builds me up and makes me laugh while she's doing it. Thanks for standing by me through all the years (and books) it took to get that dancing-sisters scene out into the world.

Everyone at Delacorte Press who has worked so hard to make my books beautiful and get them into readers' hands. Special thanks to my cover designer, Heather Daugherty; my copy editor, Stephanie Brommer; my publicist, Lydia Finn; and Krista Vitola.

My whip-smart beta readers, some of whom have read this book so many times they can recite it from memory: Lindsay Ribar, the gentlest note-giver in all the land; Corey

Ann Haydu, who points out which scenes I've forgotten to write; Nicole Lisa, who keeps me PC; Liz Whelan, my taskmaster; Jennifer Malone, who makes me smile with her green highlighter; Kristen Kittscher, my Brain Twin; and Elizabeth Little, without whom I wouldn't be writing YA at all. Thank you all for the impromptu brainstorming sessions, the last-minute reads, and the endless supply of perspective.

Brandy Colbert and Claire Legrand, who always answer my frantic texts and reassure me that my book is not, in fact, irreparably broken.

The many, many people who let me turn their offhand comments into reality-show concepts and band names, notably Adam Bowker, Liz Nett, Rae Carson, Rachel Hawkins, Steve Berns, Sean Kelso, Jerad Schomer, Jenna Scherer, Julia Reischel, and Lissa Harris. I'm lucky to have friends who say such fantastically weird stuff all the time.

Shannon McCarty, Jay Bienstock, Hilary Weisman Graham, and Clifton Early for answering my endless questions about the logistics of reality television.

The Lucky 13s, a supportive and lovely group of writers. I'm so honored to share shelf space with you.

My nonwriter friends, for reaching into my deep, dark revisions cave and pulling me back out into the sunlight at regular intervals. Sometimes it's really nice to complain about my first-pass pages and have someone say, "I don't know what that means. Want to get some pizza?"

Erica Cherry, the best sister and friend a girl could have. May we never fight while throwing pomegranates at each other (or while throwing anything else, for that matter). I would gladly circumnavigate the globe for you.

And my mom, Susan Cherry, who reads every draft, listens to me rant and rave, and never stops believing I can do it. I love you, for real.

*Don't miss Alison Cherry's
next novel!*

A summer away from the city is the beginning of everything
for Brooklyn Shepard....

Thoughtful, funny, and steeped in the wild drama of
growing up, LOOK BOTH WAYS is the story of a girl hoping
to find a place to belong ... only to learn that neither talent
nor love is as straightforward as she thinks.